A man stood beside the door.

Tall and lean, he was thoroughly soaked from the rain.

As she watched, he paced to the porch steps. He turned back, and she saw his face more clearly. A bruise marred his jaw.

Who was he? If she'd met him before, she'd have remembered. In spite of his bruises, he had the kind of face a woman would notice. Eyes as gray as the stormy skies, a firm, sensuous mouth above a square jaw, and the hint of a cleft in his chin.

"I've had an accident." He drew in a sharp breath, put a hand against the house as if he needed support.

What should she do? Send the stranger back into the storm?

Something was telling her not to. Instead Christy opened the door.

Dear Reader,

Love is in the air, but the days will certainly be sweeter if you snuggle up with this month's Silhouette Intimate Moments offerings (and a heart-shaped box of decadent chocolates) and let yourself go on the ride of your life! First up, veteran Carla Cassidy dazzles us with *Protecting the Princess*, part of her new miniseries WILD WEST BODYGUARDS. Here, a rugged cowboy rescues a princess and whisks her off to his ranch. What a way to go…!

RITA® Award-winning author Catherine Mann sets our imaginations on fire when she throws together two unlikely lovers in *Explosive Alliance*, the latest book in her popular WINGMEN WARRIORS miniseries. In *Stolen Memory*, the fourth book in her TROUBLE IN EDEN miniseries, stellar storyteller Virginia Kantra tells the tale of a beautiful police officer who sets out to uncover the cause of a powerful man's amnesia. But this supersleuth never expects to fall in love! The second book in her LAST CHANCE HEROES miniseries, *Truly, Madly, Dangerously* by Linda Winstead Jones, plunges us into the lives of a feisty P.I. and protective deputy sheriff who find romance while solving a grisly murder.

Lorna Michaels will touch readers with *Stranger in Her Arms*, in which a caring heroine tends to a rain-battered stranger who shows up on her doorstep. And *Warrior Without a Cause* by Nancy Gideon features a special agent who takes charge when a stalking victim needs his help…and his love.

You won't want to miss this array of roller-coaster reads from Intimate Moments—the line that delivers a charge and a satisfying finish you're sure to savor.

Happy Valentine's Day!

Patience Smith
Associate Senior Editor

Please address questions and book requests to:
Silhouette Reader Service
U.S.: 3010 Walden Ave., P.O. Box 1325, Buffalo, NY 14269
Canadian: P.O. Box 609, Fort Erie, Ont. L2A 5X3

Stranger in Her Arms

LORNA MICHAELS

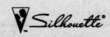

INTIMATE MOMENTS™

Published by Silhouette Books

America's Publisher of Contemporary Romance

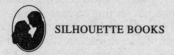

SILHOUETTE BOOKS

ISBN 0-373-27419-X

STRANGER IN HER ARMS

Visit Silhouette Books at www.eHarlequin.com

Printed in U.S.A.

Books by Lorna Michaels

Silhouette Intimate Moments

The Truth About Elyssa #1124
Stranger in Her Arms #1349

LORNA MICHAELS

When she was four years old, Lorna Michaels decided she would become a writer. But it wasn't until she read her first romance that she found her niche. Since then she's been a winner of numerous writing contests, a double Romance Writer's of America Golden Heart finalist and a nominee for *Romantic Times* magazine's Love and Laughter Award. A self-confessed romantic, she loves to spend her evenings writing happily-ever-after stories. During the day she's a speech pathologist with a busy private practice. Though she leads a double life, both her careers focus on communication. As a speech pathologist, she works with children who have communication disorders. In her writing, she deals with men and women who overcome barriers to communication as they forge lasting relationships.

Besides working and writing, Lorna enjoys reading everything from cereal boxes to Greek tragedy, interacting with the two cats who own her, watching basketball games and traveling with her husband. In 2002 she realized her dream of visiting Antarctica. Nothing thrills her more than hearing from readers. You can e-mail her at lmichaels@zyzy.com.

To Barbara Sher,
who taught me to dream.
And in memory of Rita Gallagher,
who taught me how to make my dreams come true.

Chapter 1

Christy Matthews loved storms—the noise, the roiling sky, the hint of danger. And what better place to enjoy one than on San Sebastian Island in her parents' vacation cottage, with a rerun of *Raiders of the Lost Ark* on the tube? She'd left the back blinds open so she could see the oleanders tossing wildly in the yard, the lightning zigzagging overhead.

The weather report said the rain was likely to continue all night and into tomorrow. Christy smiled and inhaled the aroma of warm popcorn. It was a buttered-popcorn kind of evening, with weather that encouraged her to put the fat content of butter out of her mind.

She grabbed a handful of popcorn as Indiana Jones battled furiously with a pit full of hissing snakes. This was her favorite part.

The telephone rang. "Nuts," she muttered as she picked up the receiver. "Hello."

"Hi, Toad."

"Steve." Her older brother had become overprotective since Christy's divorce. And when Steve used the nickname he'd bestowed on her when she was five, Christy knew she was in for a long and heavy dose of brotherly concern. Too bad she'd settled for the classic movie channel instead of renting a video. With a last longing look at Indy, she pressed the mute button on the remote.

"How's the weather?"

"Wet but not too bad." An earsplitting crash of thunder, surely loud enough for her brother to hear, belied her words. "Um, thunder always sounds louder at the beach."

"Maybe you should leave."

"No way. This isn't a hurricane, for heaven's sake. It's a tropical depression."

Never the greatest listener, her brother said, "Karen and I will drive down and pick you up. You can spend your vacation with us."

"No, Steve. I appreciate the offer, but I need some time alone."

"Christy—"

"No, listen. In the year since Keith left, I haven't had a minute to sit down and think about the future. Now that I have the time, I need to make some decisions. Do I stay in Houston, or leave, sell the house, put it up for lease—all that stuff."

"You can make decisions here," he insisted.

"I have to do this on my own. I *am* on my own now." For sure. Her husband—*ex*-husband, she reminded herself—was on his honeymoon with Christy's replacement even as she spoke.

"Besides," she continued, "I want to relax. I'm going to spend two weeks reading steamy novels, roaming the beach and watching old movies." Her eyes strayed to the TV. Indy galloped through the desert on a white horse, then swung into the cab of a truck as it careened along at breakneck speed.

"I worry about you staying in the house alone."

Christy rolled her eyes. One trait she was working hard to cultivate was independence. She wouldn't let anyone, including her well-intentioned brother, make decisions for her ever again.

"Are the Bakers next door?"

She was tempted to lie, but if she said they were in residence, Steve would probably call to ask them to keep an eye on her. Then he'd find out the truth. "They left this morning."

"Anyone else around?"

"Warner and Ellie Thompson."

"They're way at the other end of the road. And you think you're fine? In an isolated house with your nearest neighbor a mile away? You're being naive."

A bubble of anger formed in her chest. "It's *half* a mile, and I'm not naive. Not about anything. Not after Keith."

"I heard on the news there's a serial killer loose in Houston."

So the news about the Night Stalker had gone statewide. If he wasn't caught soon, there'd be national coverage, as well, she supposed. "Houston's over an hour away. I'm safer here than in the Medical Center," Christy said. Every one of the Night Stalker's victims had worked somewhere in the huge complex of hospitals where she was employed. "Besides," she added, "I have protection."

"What?" he said in that scornful big-brother tone she'd hated when she was a kid. "Did you bring a hypodermic syringe from the hospital?"

"Nope, my own 38 special."

"You…you have a gun?"

"And I know how to use it. I took one of those courses you need to get a gun permit." She and several fellow nurses had decided that was essential, when two women who worked in their very same hospital turned up dead within a week, victims of the maniac who'd been prowling the city since spring.

"Good God, Toad." Steve's voice sounded choked. "Be careful with the damn thing."

Christy laughed. "You want me to be safe, but you worry that I have a gun. Make up your mind, brother dear." She reached for the popcorn. Steve's concern for her safety was misguided. Nothing was likely to happen to her in an isolated corner of a lazy family vacation spot. And if some small difficulty did arise, no problem. She could take care of herself.

Not far away, a man lay on the beach. He heard the rumble of thunder and stirred. Another sound, deeper and more constant, roared in his ears. A flash of lightning penetrated his closed lids; raindrops splattered against his bare forearms. His clothes were damp and uncomfortable. Must've left the window open, he thought. But why had he gone to bed with his clothes on? With an effort, he forced his eyes open.

He wasn't in bed, wasn't even in a room. He was…outside, sprawled on his stomach on a wet, sandy beach. And the tide was coming in. Salt water swept over his feet and up to his knees, then receded. A sand dune shielded him from the wind, but he was unprotected from the rain and the rapidly encroaching tide.

How in hell had he gotten here?

He tried to get up, but a wave of pain made him clutch his head and freeze. His vision blurred. Must've hit my head, he thought fuzzily. But how?

He had no time to think. He had to get up and away from the angry surf. Another flash of lightning and a roll of thunder told him all hell was about to break loose.

On hands and knees he scrambled around the sand dune, then tried to stand, but dizziness and nausea forced him down again. He touched his head, and his hand came away wet. Rain, he thought, then glanced at his fingers. *Blood!*

Had he had an accident? Been mugged? He couldn't remember.

He ignored his throbbing head and struggled to his feet. He'd think about his head later, get himself to a hospital if necessary. First he had to figure out what was going on. Panting with exertion, he clambered up a low bank and away from the beach. Cold rain pelted him, and he shivered as he surveyed a deserted road and flat marshland on the other side of it.

Where was he? And how had he gotten here? His mind was too fuzzy to dredge up the answers.

He peered through the rapidly advancing darkness. He saw no one. If he'd been beaten, whoever had done it was long gone.

He scanned the area again and noticed a cluster of small cottages some distance from the beach. A light shone in the house on the end. A light meant people who could tell him where he was. Ignoring the rain, he crossed the road, walking carefully to avoid another attack of lightheadedness, then, with head bent, started up the narrow lane that led to the houses. Rain chilled his neck, drenched his clothing, but he kept going. He'd ask to use the phone and call…

Who?

He groped for a name, a phone number, but nothing came to mind. Surely he should be able to remember his…

Wife? Office? Home? The only phone number he could recall was 911.

Despite the deluge, he stopped and shut his eyes. In a minute, something would come to him: the color of his car, what he'd eaten for lunch, his shoe size. Rain coursed down his cheeks as he waited, but his mind whirled in confusion, his head throbbed with pain.

Opening his eyes, he forced himself to think, to concentrate. Facts flashed through his head: the capital of Minnesota, the number of symphonies composed by Beethoven, the square root of 144. His brain seemed to be a treasure trove of trivia. Totally useless information.

"My name is…" he muttered but couldn't complete the sentence. He recited the alphabet, hoping he'd recognize the first letter of his name. But he couldn't. He didn't know who to call, where he'd come from, or where he'd been going.

He didn't know who he was.

His jeans' pockets were empty. Quickly, he searched the pockets of the denim shirt he wore. No wallet. No driver's license. Not a clue to his identity. Nothing.

Fear clutched at him, and though he couldn't recall anything about himself, he was certain he was a man who seldom knew fear. Clenching his fists, he started off again, walking faster. Obviously, he'd suffered a blow to the head. Loss of memory was natural under the circumstances. Soon everything would come back to him.

Mud sucked at his shoes, slowed his pace, but doggedly, he kept going. Not much farther. Before him, the light gleamed like a beacon. Fixing his eyes on it, he plowed ahead.

Christy reached for the last handful of popcorn. She should go to bed, but she was too lazy to get out of the chair. Maybe she'd sleep here in the—

The doorbell rang.

She smothered a gasp and jumped up, scattering kernels on the floor. Who in the world would be out in this weather? Putting a hand to her heart, she pattered across the living room. The bell rang again. Whoever her visitor was, he didn't have much patience. "All right," she called. "I'm coming."

She flipped on the porch light and peered out through the living-room window. A man stood beside the door. Tall and lean, he was disheveled and thoroughly soaked from the rain. In the glow of the light, she could make out his features well enough to tell that she didn't know him. She didn't open her door to strangers, storm or no storm.

As she watched, he paced to the porch steps. He turned

back and she saw his face more clearly now. A bruise marred his jaw and one eye was turning a grisly purple. Had he been in a fight?

Who was he? If she'd met him here before, she'd have remembered him. In spite of his bruises, he had the kind of face a woman would notice. Eyes as gray as the stormy skies, a firm, sensuous mouth above a square jaw, and the hint of a cleft in his chin.

He punched the doorbell again. Reaching up to be sure the dead bolt was fastened, she called, "Yes?"

"Sorry to bother you," he said, "but I need to use the phone."

She wasn't about to fall for that ploy. He might be dangerously handsome, but on the other hand, he could be just plain dangerous. "Give me the number, and I'll call for you."

"I don't know the number. I've had an accident, and I…" He grimaced, and she heard him draw in a sharp breath. He put a hand against the house as if he needed support.

Christy squinted through the rain, trying to see his car, but couldn't. He must have walked from the beach road.

A car drove past and slowed, its headlights glimmering through the rainy darkness. Perhaps, Christy thought hopefully, the car belonged to a friend of this man, someone who would help him. But it drove on.

Nervously, she chewed on her lip. What should she do? Send the stranger back into the storm? *Cruel.* Let him in? *Foolish.*

The gun.

"Just a minute," she called and darted into the bedroom. She pulled her revolver out of the dresser drawer and returned to the door. Thanks to her course, she knew how to use the gun and if the guy tried any funny stuff, she would. More confident now, she turned the dead bolt. The man straightened, waited.

Christy opened the door.

He came inside. The wind howled banshee-like through the oleanders behind him. Rain followed him in, needle-sharp drops pelting Christy's face.

He took a step, then halted, staring at the barrel of the gun. Slowly, he raised his arms. "I won't hurt you."

"No, you won't." She gestured for him to walk ahead of her. "The phone's that way, in the living room."

"Thanks. I'll make a call and then..." He staggered forward. "...and then...I'll be...on...my..."

He fell heavily against the side of a chair, dislodging a lamp from the table beside it. The lamp crashed to the floor and broke, but Christy hardly noticed. Her eyes were on the man. He'd landed on his stomach, and she could see an ugly wound on the back of his head. His hair was matted with blood, he lay spread-eagled on her living-room floor, and he didn't move.

Chapter 2

"Oh, my God." Christy set down the gun, knelt on the floor and leaned over the unconscious man. "Wake up!" she said. No answer. "Can you hear me?" she called louder, but he didn't rouse.

Grunting with the effort, she managed to turn the man onto his side. His face was pasty white, his skin cold. Christy searched for the pulse at his throat and drew a breath of relief when she found it. She pried open his lids and checked his pupils. They were symmetrical, not dilated. *Good.*

Unbuttoning his shirt, she searched for other injuries. His chest was smooth; she had no trouble seeing a line of bruises that probably meant cracked ribs. No wonder he was heavy. His leanness was deceptive. He wasn't as tall as she'd thought, but he was six feet of solid muscle.

She went to her room, dragged the quilt off her bed and covered him. He smelled of the sea and, with his bronzed skin and stubbled cheeks, he reminded Christy of the buccaneers who once roamed the Gulf of Mexico. She watched him for a moment, but when he still didn't move or make a sound, she hurried into the kitchen to dial 911.

No dial tone. Only static.

The phone lines must be down because of the storm. She dashed into the bedroom for her cell phone, grabbed it out of the charger and dialed. A busy signal.

She tried again. Again. Each time she got the same result.

She shoved the cell phone in her pocket. She'd just have to drive him to the hospital herself. Provided he woke up and could walk. She was strong, but no way could she drag a six-foot-tall, unconscious, dead-weight man outside and lift him into her car. Maybe, despite the weather, one of her neighbors had come to the island and could help. She opened the door and went out on the porch. No lights shone in any of the windows. Disappointed, she went back inside.

Halfway down the block, obscured by the darkness, a black sedan was parked. The driver stared at the house, then pounded his fist against the steering wheel in rage and frustration. Today had been one piece of damn rotten luck after another.

He reviewed the evening in his mind. His plan had been so simple. Take the sonofabitch out with one quick, powerful blow to the head, drag him onto the beach, leave him there and let the tide take care of him. And in case it didn't sweep him out to sea, empty his pockets so he'd be hard to identify.

First stroke of bad luck: he'd had to do the job quickly. A patrol car stopped on the other side of the highway, the cop warning him a storm was coming in. What'd the deputy think, he was blind? He could see the rain coming down as well as anyone.

He'd driven away without checking to be sure the bastard

was dead, then he disposed of the wallet further down the beach. He didn't want the deputy to stop by again and find him with a body, so he'd gone into town for a hamburger and a beer. Later, he went back to check on his prey and, more freakin' bad luck: the sonofabitch was gone.

A cold dread took hold. Had someone rescued him?

He'd sped away from the beach, looking from right to left in the gray darkness. Then he'd seen the bastard on the porch of a house at the end of a block of small cottages. How the hell had he made it that far? Was he some kind of superhero?

A woman stood in the doorway. And dammit to hell, the worst luck of all: she opened the door and he went inside. Dumb broad. Didn't she know better than to let a stranger into her house?

Now he ran over his options. Best thing would be to break in and finish what he'd started, get rid of the woman, too. He was about to get out of the car when he noticed a black and white around the corner. It didn't turn onto the street he was parked on, but if it was patrolling the neighborhood, it'd be back soon. Okay, he'd go with plan B. And he'd be quick.

Inside the house, Christy turned back to her unwelcome visitor. He hadn't moved. "Don't do this to me," she muttered…and then she heard him moan.

Thank heavens. She bent over him, put her hand on his forehead. "Can you hear me?" she asked.

Cool hand on his brow. Scent of flowers. A soft voice. "Can you hear me?" the voice called. He tried to answer, to form the word *yes,* but could only manage another moan.

"Good. You're waking up," the voice said. Such a sweet voice, the kind that belonged to an angel.

Angel? Good Lord, had he died?

"Can you open your eyes?" the angel-voice asked.

He wanted to see the owner of the voice, so he tried. With

a monumental effort, he managed to force his eyes open—
and saw, not an angel, but a woman bending over him, her
green eyes filled with concern. He blinked, then recognized
her. He'd rung her doorbell, he remembered, and she'd let him
in. So how had he ended up on the floor? "Wh-what happened?" he rasped.

"You came in to use the phone and passed out."

"Passed out," he repeated. "But why…?"

"You had a wreck."

Had he told her that? "No," he muttered. "Have to call—"

"The phone's out of order. The storm…"

As if to underscore her words, thunder rattled the windows.
And then he heard the sound of hail. He felt every hailstone
that pounded the roof as if it were slamming against his head.
He struggled to think. "How about…a cell?"

"I tried a minute ago but the line was busy." She pulled a
phone out of her pocket and dialed. "Still busy. We'll have to
try again later."

He didn't want to wait until later. He needed to get out of
here now and go…somewhere. He pushed against the floor,
seeking leverage.

"Don't get up." She put her hand on his shoulder with surprising firmness. "I don't want you fainting on me again."

"I need to—"

"You don't need to do anything right now but lie still," the
woman said, then with a half smile, added, "Trust me, I'm a
nurse."

"Okay." He would have trusted that voice and that smile
no matter what. She sat silently beside him and he kept his
eyes on her. Her face began to blur, and the floor seemed to
tilt. *No, dammit,* he wasn't going to pass out again. Using all
his willpower, he forced himself to stay alert, to concentrate
on her eyes until the dizziness passed.

She reached for his wrist and took his pulse. "Better now," she murmured, then leaned over him, an anxious look on her face. "We need to get you to a doctor. No use waiting. My car's in the garage out back. I'll bring it around so you won't have to walk so far." She jiggled the gun at him. "Don't move."

"Okay." He had no intention of moving. He shut his eyes and waited, hovering on the edge of sleep until the slam of the door roused him.

He opened his eyes and looked up. She stood in the doorway, her face taut with frustration. "The car," she said in a voice midway between tears and anger. "It won't start."

"Flooded?" he asked.

"No." She turned to stare at the rain pelting against the back windows.

"Then what's wrong?"

"I don't know." She spun around and glared at him. "I'm a nurse, not a mechanic. The motor makes a sound but it doesn't catch."

Their eyes met, and he knew they were both thinking the same thing: they were alone here, isolated, with no way to get out.

Swallowing a groan, he raised himself up on an elbow. "I'll get out of your way," he said. "I can walk to the hospital. How far—"

"Too far," she said flatly. "You wouldn't make it to the end of the street in your condition." Then her eyes brightened. "What about your car? Is it driveable after the wreck?"

"Car," he echoed stupidly. "Wreck. I don't remember a wreck."

"You said you had an accident."

He may have said so, but that didn't mean a damn thing. Frustrated, he clenched his fist and felt a sharp pain in his chest. He made his hand relax. "I don't remember what happened to the car," he said. "I'm not sure I even had one. I don't remember anything."

"Not…anything?"

"Nothing. Not a car, not where I was going. Hell, I don't even know my own name." He hadn't meant to blurt that out, hadn't meant to say anything about that at all. But dammit, here he was in soaking-wet clothes, his chest and his head hurt like hell, and he didn't have the brain power to figure out who he was or the willpower to keep the words from coming out.

"You have a head injury, probably a concussion. You'll remember soon." She sounded as if she were trying to convince herself.

That's what he'd told himself as he crossed the field. He remembered *that* all right. He remembered waking up and walking over here, but other than that, zero. He hesitated, then asked, "Where…are we?" He felt stupid asking, but he had to know.

"San Sebastian Island…Texas coast, near Galveston."

The name sounded familiar. Did he live here? Or had he come on vacation? He shook his head, wishing he could shake a thought loose. "Well, um… I, uh, guess you know *your* name?"

A tight smile crossed her lips. "Christy. Christy Matthews. My—my husband will be home any time," she continued, but she spoke without conviction. She was lying, he could tell. There was no husband coming home.

Under the circumstances, she had to be scared. "Look," he said, wanting to reassure her, "I don't remember much about myself, but I'm not dangerous."

Christy Matthews raised a brow. "You're in no shape to be dangerous," she agreed, but she kept her gun pointed at his chest.

She sighed, then said, "Since no one seems to be going anywhere, let's get you to some place more comfortable. I'll give you a hand."

He was tempted to wave her away. He didn't enjoy being treated like an invalid. He had a little bump on the head, that's all. But something made him reach for her.

Damn, getting up was harder than he'd expected. All the blood seemed to rush out of his head, and the room took a sharp turn to the side.

"Easy," she murmured and slipped an arm around his waist. His body brushed against her breast, and she jolted and leaned away from him. But she was close enough for him to notice her scent again. Something light and flowery. Roses, maybe. He also noticed she grasped the gun firmly in her free hand.

"Are you okay?" she asked.

He gritted his teeth. "Fine."

He wasn't fine. His legs were as shaky as a newborn colt's, and beads of cold sweat popped out on his face. Even walking as far as the couch wore him out. When they bypassed it and Christy led him into a hallway that appeared endless, he wondered if she'd decided to torture him to pay him back for his unwanted visit.

"I have an extra bed," she said.

"I don't want to put you to any trouble," he muttered, "I can bunk on your couch for a while." Or on the floor, since he was about to fall flat on his face.

Christy shook her head and urged him forward. "The bed. You're hurt, and you need it." She opened the door to a bedroom and steered him toward the double bed. They stopped beside it, and she pulled off the spread.

As soon as the sheets came into view, he sat.

"Whoa," Christy said. "Let's get you out of those wet things."

He was dead certain she wasn't the first woman who'd asked him to take off his clothes, but this was probably the only time he'd felt uncomfortable with the idea.

Correctly reading him, Christy smiled fully this time. "I'm a nurse, remember?"

"Yeah," he muttered. But this wasn't a hospital.

She set the gun down on the nightstand. *Inexperienced with weapons,* he noted. If he'd been so inclined, he could easily have grabbed it.

She turned to him again and pressed him firmly back against the pillows. Hand on the snap of his jeans, she paused and said, "I'll lend you a pair of my husband's pajamas." He heard a tremor in her voice and was doubly sure that, pajamas or not, Christy Matthews's husband would not be coming home tonight.

To distract himself from the feel of her hand at his waist, he tried to concentrate on the sound of the storm—the rain pounding against the windows, the wind rattling the panes. But the distraction didn't work. Regardless of his physical *or* mental condition, his reflexes—*and* his hormones—were in working order. His body reacted quite normally to soft female hands undressing him. He pushed the hands away. "I'll take care of it," he said gruffly.

She let him deal with the snap but insisted on helping him peel off the jeans, and he got rock-hard as her fingers brushed his thighs. For a second, before she assumed a professionally distant air, he saw the light of awareness in her eyes and the tinge of pink in her cheeks, and he knew she hadn't missed the bulge beneath his briefs.

She tugged the jeans lower, then her hands stilled. He followed her gaze down to his thigh. An old scar puckered the skin.

"That's a bullet wound," she said. She seemed surprised but not repulsed. He guessed, with her medical background, she'd seen a lot of those.

Well, apparently he wasn't a doctor because the sight of the wound shook him up a bit. "Is that what it is?"

"Yes." She gave him a level look. "Where'd you get it?"

How in hell did she expect him to know? He searched his mind, hoping her question would elicit an answer. It didn't. "I don't know. I told you, I can't remember anything," he said, hearing the frustration in his voice. He stared at his thigh. "Maybe the scar's from something else."

"No," she said. "I've been a nurse long enough to know a bullet wound when I see one." She took a step back. "Who are you?" she whispered.

"Dammit," he growled, clenching his hands, "*I don't know. I—*" Pain seared his chest and he lost his breath, lost all awareness of what he wanted to say. Spots danced in front of his eyes. He couldn't see Christy, couldn't see anything but the damned specks, then he felt a cool cloth on his forehead, and her face swam back into view.

She bent over him, her fingers resting lightly on the pulse at his throat. "I'm sorry," she murmured. "That was a dumb question."

He tried to say something.

"Hush, take it easy," she warned. "Your ribs are bruised, you've hit your head, and whoever you are, we need to get you taken care of." She pulled his jeans the rest of the way off, and this time he had no problem controlling his arousal. He doubted if Hollywood's sexiest love goddess could have awakened his libido at that moment.

When the jeans were off, Christy said, "We need to wash some of that sand off. I'll give you a sponge bath."

In other circumstances, he might have welcomed a sponge bath by this woman with the soft hands and springtime scent. Not just now. He hurt like hell, but he didn't relish being coddled. Besides, the thought occurred to him that if he looked in the mirror, he might remember who he was. "I'll handle it," he told her firmly. "Where's your bathroom?"

She pointed toward the hall, and he sat up and eased off

the bed. Immediately, she was at his side, grasping his arm to steady him. God, her scent was intoxicating. Honeysuckle? Violets? Whatever, it woke his hormones again.

Unwilling to deal with his body's inevitable reaction to her nearness, he held up a hand to ward her off. Clenching his jaw, he staggered out of the bedroom.

She followed along behind him and when he reached the bathroom, said, "Call if you need me."

He managed a nod, then went into the small room, papered with a leafy design and smelling of a garden. He flipped on the light, shut the door and approached the mirror slowly, his heart beating heavily in his chest. Outside, rain drummed against the window. He stood still for a moment, listening to the storm and wondering. When he looked in the mirror, who would he see?

He stepped closer to the sink, took a breath, and lifted his eyes. Would he recognize himself?

He didn't.

He must have looked in mirrors thousands of times, but tonight the man who stared back at him was as unfamiliar as a stranger he might pass on the street.

How could you see your own face and not know yourself? Dizzy with despair, he grasped the sink to keep from falling. "Who are you, damn you?" he snarled. He shut his eyes and concentrated, searching his mind.

No use. All he came up with was a blank.

Chapter 3

While the man was in the bathroom, Christy got the first aid kit her father kept for emergencies. Then she found a pair of his old pajamas, went into the hall, and knocked on the bathroom door. The stranger opened it a crack, stretched out a hand, and took the pajamas.

The sight of his bare arm, roped with muscle and bronzed from the sun, unsettled her. She felt as flustered as she had when she'd helped him undress. She, who'd been a nurse for nine years, who'd seen hundreds of naked men—*totally* naked men. None of them had raised her pulse one beat. Why did *he*?

Because she was alone and vulnerable, she decided as she went back into the bedroom to wait for him. Darn, she shouldn't have mentioned a husband. How would she explain when her spouse didn't show up? Maybe the stranger would forget what she'd said.

But she had more pressing matters to consider. Like how badly he was injured and how long she was going to keep him under her roof. She felt a twinge of fear as she thought of her brother's warning. Was this man dangerous? If he was, she had no one to protect her. She had to take care of herself. A shiver went up her spine, and she picked up the gun she'd laid on the nightstand, wondering if she'd really have the guts to use it.

After a few minutes the man shuffled into the room. Clearly, every step was painful.

He looked less disreputable now that he'd cleaned up. In fact, he looked pretty good. Although the pajama pants came barely to his ankles and the sleeves were well above his wrists, the material stretched across broad shoulders, hugged a muscular frame, and made Christy uncomfortably aware again of the stranger's masculinity.

He glanced at the weapon in her hand. His lips thinned but he said nothing, only lay down on the bed and waited.

"You have a nasty wound," she said. "I'm going to clean it. You'll have to lie on your side." He turned, and she added, "I'll try not to hurt you too much." She opened a bottle of hydrogen peroxide and dribbled liquid into the wound. The peroxide fizzed, and she heard the man catch his breath.

"Try harder," he muttered. "What are you cleaning it with? Battery acid?"

"Peroxide. You'll feel worse if you get an infection." She unscrewed the cap from a tube of antibiotic ointment and spread a liberal amount on the wound, then reached for a bandage and the adhesive tape.

Carefully, she pulled the edges of the gash together and taped them. The man's breath hissed out, but he kept silent. "There. All done."

"Are you sure you're a nurse and not that crazy woman from *Misery?*" he muttered.

She chuckled. "Lie on your back now and unbutton the pajama top."

"You didn't answer my question."

She laughed. "I'm a nurse. Cross my heart." She bent over him and gently probed the bruises on his chest. His flesh had warmed. Her hand brushed a flat male nipple and immediately it puckered. The pulse at his throat beat strongly. She glanced up, and his gaze caught hers.

She cleared her throat, forced a professional tone. "You've got some bad bruises, but I don't think your ribs are broken. You should get a tetanus shot at the emergency room, but—" She glanced at the window and shrugged. Rain beat steadily against the pane. "—we're not going anywhere tonight."

"Don't worry about it. My shots are up to date."

She started and frowned at him. "I thought you said you couldn't remember anything. How do you know that?"

"I don't have a clue. It just came to me." He squeezed his eyes shut and sighed. "That's all. I don't remember anything else."

She stared at him dubiously, then shrugged. Injured or not, he was too big and imposing to risk arguing with him over what he could or couldn't recall. "I'm going to put your clothes in the washer."

She picked up his discarded clothing, took the gun and left the room. She didn't feel comfortable leaving the man alone, but she decided she could chance it for a little while. He was pretty weak from the blow to his head. As long as she didn't provoke him, she doubted he'd do any damage. Still she turned and looked over her shoulder as she started down the hall, then glanced pointedly at the gun in her hand.

In the utility room, she turned the washer on hot and poured in detergent. She tossed in his jeans, then paused with his long-sleeved blue shirt in hand. Maybe the pockets contained a clue to their owner's identity. She wondered if he'd thought to check them.

The pockets were empty. She retrieved his jeans and checked their pockets next. Nothing. Why would a man wander around without a driver's license, a wallet or any kind of identification?

Unless he'd been robbed. That would explain the empty pockets and the blow to the head.

Or had he gotten rid of the identification himself? Was he a fugitive, using her house as a convenient place to hide out? Feigning amnesia, playing her for a fool?

Slow down, Christy, she ordered herself. Why should she jump to that conclusion? Fueled by the storm, her imagination was working overtime. The stranger was probably a nice, normal guy, an attractive man she'd want to know better if she met him at a party. On the other hand, she thought, as her brother's warning voice played in her mind, nice, normal guys didn't walk around without any sort of ID. And didn't have scars from bullet holes on their thighs.

Forgetting her resolve not to antagonize him, she marched back down the hall and faced the man in the bed. "What are you up to, mister?"

He gazed up at her blankly.

"You don't have a wallet," she snapped. "You don't have a driver's license."

He stared at her, then shrugged. "You think you're telling me something I don't know? I already noticed that."

"The point is you've gotten rid of every means of identification. Why? Are you running from something? Dammit, you've invaded my home. Quit this 'I-don't-remember' business and tell me the truth."

He struggled up on one elbow, his face a mask of fury and frustration. Even barely able to move, he looked dangerous, and again Christy realized what a formidable man he was. "Lady, I would if I could. I don't know any more about myself than you do." He swung his legs over the side of the bed. "If you want me out, give me my clothes and I'll be on my way."

That was what she wanted, wasn't it? For him to vanish as abruptly as he'd appeared. Whatever he was dealing with wasn't her problem. Only a fool would keep him under her roof.

And yet—

She saw him wince with pain as he stood. She glanced outside at the unrelenting blackness, at the rain that pounded against the window. She'd been trained as a healer. Caring for the sick was ingrained in her. How could she toss an injured man out into the storm?

"Go to sleep," she sighed. "You can leave in the morning."

"You sure about that?"

"Yes. Get back in bed." Maybe she *was* a fool, but she couldn't order him to go.

She shut the blinds, turned the ceiling light off and a night light on, and sat in the rocking chair beside the bed.

"What are you doing?" he asked. "Aren't you going to bed?"

"I've pulled night shifts before." She kicked off her shoes and settled back. "I'm going to be right here all night. And don't forget, mister, that I'm the one holding the gun."

Bandaged head resting on the soft pillow in Christy's guest room, the stranger fell asleep immediately. His dreams were hazy, disjointed. The roar of a motor, the crack of a rifle shot. Shouts, curses, gasps, a muffled sob and the stench of blood. He woke with his heart pounding, sweat pouring down his back.

He heard another roar, but this time of thunder, and he remembered the storm, remembered Christy, and opened his eyes. She sat beside the bed, her eyes on him, the gun pointed squarely at his chest.

The crash of thunder echoed in his head. He felt as if someone was pounding it from the inside with a massive hammer. He groaned and wiped his face with the pajama sleeve.

She leaned forward. "Want a drink?"

"Yeah, something strong enough to put me out of my misery."

"Alcohol would be the worst thing for you," she said, rising. "I'll bring you a couple of aspirins with some water and an ice pack for your head."

She brought him a glass and he drank thirstily, then lay against the pillows. She put the cold pack on his head and he sank back into sleep.

Other dreams came, vivid and disturbing. At intervals he woke, always to find Christy beside the bed. Once she brought a cool cloth and wiped his face. Her voice was soothing, her hands gentle. "Go back to sleep," she murmured. Hoping his dreams would help him remember, he did.

Once he found himself in a long, dark hallway. Shadows glided ahead of him, tantalizing him, and he quickened his pace, but each time he reached them, the phantoms he chased eluded him. A wall of doors appeared, and he opened them, only to find empty rooms. He heard voices, but they were garbled and he couldn't make out the words.

Near dawn he woke. His head ached, his ribs hurt, and his mouth felt as if it was stuffed with cotton. The glass he'd drunk from during the night was empty.

He was about to get up to refill the glass when he heard a sigh. *Christy,* he thought. And turned to see her, eyes shut, gun still in her hand but pointed downward, aimed straight at her toes.

Forgetting his thirst, he lay back and studied her. She wasn't beautiful, but she *was* girl-next-door pretty. Wavy auburn hair, smooth skin, a figure that was neither fashion-model gaunt nor screen-goddess voluptuous but just right. Sweetly curved hips, perky breasts that would fit a man's hands to perfection. He felt a tightening in his lower body again and, with an effort, changed the direction of his thoughts.

She was in her late-twenties, he thought, and she had the appeal that came with maturity. She seemed to know who she was and to be comfortable with the knowledge.

In the gray light, he could see how tired she was. He didn't know how she'd passed the previous day, but she'd spent the night alternately caring for him and holding a gun on him. Couldn't have been easy.

He let her sleep for a while, but the position of the gun made him edgy. A reflexive movement could cause her to squeeze the trigger. Talk about shooting yourself in the foot.

Deciding he'd better let her wake slowly, he cleared his throat.

Her eyes popped open and she straightened, aiming the gun again. Voice raspy with sleep, she asked, "Do you need another drink?" He nodded, and she picked up the glass and backed out of the room, keeping her eyes—and the gun—on him. In a minute, she returned with the water. "How are you feeling?"

"Okay," he lied. He drank, set the glass on the nightstand, and carefully swung his legs over the side of the bed. "I'll be out of your way as soon as I'm dressed."

"Where will you go?"

Good question. He didn't have a clue where to go. "I'll figure something out," he said with more certainty than he felt.

"You should see a doctor."

"You've done a pretty good job of putting me back together."

"Nevertheless. There's a hospital in town, only a few miles from here." She gestured vaguely. "I'd drive you to town if I could," she added.

"No problem. If you'll point me toward the road, I'll walk or hitch a ride."

She nodded, went to the window and pulled up the blinds. "Oh, my God."

He got off the bed, crossed the room and looked over her shoulder. "Damn," he muttered, staring at the scene before him. He could forget his plan of walking into town. Water, high enough so that only the top of the mailbox showed above it, filled the front yard and lapped at the porch steps. A lawn chair and several broken tree limbs floated toward the drive.

He glanced up at the leaden sky. Rain still fell in sheets and he doubted it would stop any time soon. A few more hours and water would be at the door.

As a crash of thunder resounded, his eyes met Christy's. He wasn't surprised to see nerves, wouldn't have faulted her if she'd given in to them. She didn't. "You'll have to stay, at least for now," she said, her voice steady.

"Looks like it. As long as I'm going to be here a while, I can help you out. Unless you like your furniture decorated with water marks, we need to start moving it and getting things off the floor."

"Thanks, but you should take it easy."

The way his head felt, he'd have to. "I'll do what I can."

She nodded. "I'll get your clothes out of the dryer. And then I'm going to fill the tub. If we need water, we'll have it."

When she returned with his clothes, he went into the bathroom to dress. He peered into the mirror again but a stranger still stared back. No time to dwell on his problems now. Dealing with the flood took precedence. He dressed quickly and followed the sound of the television and the odor of frying bacon down the hallway.

In the living room, he halted. Out the back window he saw the gray of the Gulf and above it an ominous, pewter-colored sky. Waves thundered in, one after another, slamming across what had once been a beach. Water frothed at the edge of

Christy's yard, threatening to swallow it up, too. "Do we need an ark?" he called to Christy.

He left the window and went into the kitchen where she stood at the stove, scrambling eggs. She'd tucked the gun in her waistband. "You know," she said, "I've always enjoyed storms, but this one is a little more than I bargained for." Without looking up, she continued. "Pour yourself a glass of juice and have a seat." She gestured toward the television. "The news isn't good."

Sipping his juice, he listened.

"Hal McCormick is standing by in the small town of Lerner, across the bay from San Sebastian Island."

Christy took the pan of eggs off the burner and went to stand in front of the set.

"Hal, how does it look out there?" the anchor asked.

"Wet, Ray. And no let-up in sight." The camera swung back for a wide-angle view. Abandoned cars were parked haphazardly by the seawall. Wind whipped the trees along the road. Three teenagers lugging a rubber raft waved and mugged for the camera. "What was labeled a tropical depression yesterday has been upgraded to a tropical storm and given the name Coral. Winds are not yet at hurricane force, but with Coral stalled over the Gulf of Mexico, nearly eight inches of rain have fallen here, leaving cars stranded, homes flooded, and power lines down. And the forecast is more of the same."

"At least we have electricity," Christy murmured. She returned to the stove, spooned eggs onto plates, added bacon and bagels, then joined him at the table. She reached for the gun, set it beside her plate, and watched as he lifted a forkful of food to his mouth. "Eggs okay?"

He nodded, glanced pointedly at the revolver. "I'd enjoy them more without the artillery." He smiled at her. "I like the sound of snap, crackle, and pop, but from cereal, not from bullets."

"You'll have to put up with it."

He shrugged, and they ate without further conversation.

The news broadcast continued. "San Sebastian, across the bay, is cut off from the mainland. Access to the causeway bridge was washed out early this morning."

The implications of that were clear. "We're trapped," he murmured.

"Maybe we do need an ark." Christy tried to smile but failed miserably.

Before he could answer, another voice blared from the TV. "We interrupt the weathercast for this bulletin, just received from the San Sebastian Island Police Department. A thirty-four-year-old woman, Martha McLane, was reported missing last night."

Christy's head jerked up.

"Mrs. McLane, who was vacationing on the island with her husband and two children, left their room at the Gulf View Motel around 5:00 p.m. to walk to a nearby supermarket and did not return." The picture of a woman with dark, wavy hair appeared on the screen. "Witnesses who were in the Kroger parking lot reported seeing a woman meeting Mrs. McLane's description getting into a dark-blue Toyota Corolla driven by a dark-haired white male, wearing jeans. Witnesses were uncertain about the color of his shirt, but it may have been blue."

"Dark hair," Christy muttered. "Jeans…blue shirt." She turned from the TV set. Her eyes stared into his. It didn't take a mind reader to figure out what she was thinking.

He laid down his fork. It clattered against his plate. Christy reached for the gun. "Was it you?"

"I don't know."

The news reporter continued, "San Sebastian police are concerned that the serial killer who has been terrorizing Houston has broadened his territory even further. They are working with an artist on a sketch of the driver of the car Mrs. McLane was seen entering."

Both he and Christy swivelled to face the screen. He held his breath. Would he see a likeness of himself?

"As soon as the sketch is available we will interrupt regularly scheduled programming to broadcast it."

Christy sighed, then turned to him again. In her eyes, he could see the question: was he the kidnapper? "Look, if it was me, I wouldn't be the one beaten up," he said reasonably.

"I don't know about that. Maybe she grabbed the steering wheel, made you go off the road."

He stared down at his plate, frustration churning in his gut. Without looking up, he shook his head. "I...don't...know."

"Maybe you don't, or maybe you're faking. Whichever, it doesn't matter." She grasped the gun with both hands. "Until you can tell me different and *make me believe you,* I'll have to figure you might be him."

"I understand how you feel—" he began.

"No, you don't. You haven't got a clue how I feel." Her cheeks were flushed, her eyes flashing. She glanced out the window, then quickly returned her gaze to his. "You wouldn't be able to get far in the flood, so I won't send you out. And I tried my cell phone again. All I get is a busy signal, so I can't call the sheriff's department. You'll have to stay here and help me." She leaned forward. "But if you try anything—anything at all, I won't think twice. I'll shoot you, understand?"

"Yes."

He couldn't blame her. She'd never seen him before last night. He had no identification. He'd come to her door with some cock-and-bull story about losing his memory. What was she to think? Hell, *he* didn't know what to think.

He wanted to reassure her, wipe the fear off her face. He shut his eyes and strained to remember. But his memory extended only as far back as waking last night. He recalled no blue Corolla, no pretty dark-haired woman. There was nothing. Only an endless black void.

He opened his eyes and stared at his half-eaten breakfast. The thought of finishing it, of putting even a morsel of food into his mouth, sickened him. He pushed his plate away and started to get up.

An earsplitting crash sounded.

For a moment he thought Christy had shot him and wondered why he felt no pain. Then he realized he'd heard thunder.

The television screen was black. The kitchen light was out, the hum of the air conditioner stilled.

"The power," Christy groaned, then slammed her fork down on her plate. "Dammit to hell. What next?"

Chapter 4

After a moment he saw Christy pull herself together. She squared her shoulders. "There's nothing we can do but get to work," she said. "These dishes need washing."

"Dishes?" he asked, surprised she'd waste time in the kitchen with the water lapping at the porch steps.

"The water's not up to the door yet. We have time, and I like things neat." She gestured with the gun. "You do them. I'll watch."

She wasn't going to turn her back on him, and in spite of the quandary they were in, that amused him. He hid a smile as he headed for the sink.

Christy impressed him. Some people would cry over the situation and some would curse louder and longer than she had moments ago. She was playing the hand she'd been dealt.

He'd have to do the same.

Keeping busy—that would get him through this. At least he felt better this morning. The pounding in his head had given way to a dull ache, and now that he'd eaten part of a meal, his strength had begun to return.

Christy watched him and aimed the revolver at his back. If her family had any idea what she'd done—opening her door to a stranger, maybe a kidnapper—they'd have her committed. At least, with the gun in her hand, she felt more in control. Still, she watched the dark-haired man's every move as he scrubbed and rinsed the dishes.

Then she saw the bread knife.

On the counter, inches from his hand. She'd left it there after she'd sliced the bagels.

Silly to be afraid, she told herself. After all, *she* had the gun.

But would she use it? She'd told him last night she would, but in her heart, she wasn't sure.

What if he grabbed the knife and refused to give it up? *Big man with knife versus small woman with gun.* She was afraid he'd have the edge.

Maybe he hadn't noticed the knife yet. Should she casually walk over and get it? But then she'd be beside him and he could snatch her gun.

Uncertain, she watched him put a plate in the dish drainer, wash another. Then he reached for the knife.

She was on her feet, her finger trembling on the trigger when he dunked the knife in the soapy water. He ran the sponge over it and dropped it into the rinse water.

Legs like jelly, she sank back down on the chair. He'd had his chance with the knife, and he didn't take it. Now she could get through the morning with a little less stress.

The man turned and their eyes met. His were a deep, smokey gray. The eyes of a criminal? No, she didn't see evil there. The stranger's gaze conveyed sincerity, even compassion.

As a hospital nurse, she was used to seeing people in the

worst of circumstances, in situations where they were stripped down to their essential selves. What could be worse than losing your memory? Yet he was handling his predicament better than most.

Unmoving, he continued to hold her gaze while outside the storm raged and Christy's heart pounded. Which did she fear most—him or the storm?

The storm, she thought. The man wouldn't hurt her, she assured herself. They were in this together. For now, she'd have to trust him. She tucked the gun back in the waistband of her jeans. "Let's get started on the living room," she said.

Insisting he walk in front of her, she followed him into the living room.

Hands on hips, he surveyed the room. "We'll need to sandbag the doors first. Got any old blankets or pillows we can use?"

Christy frowned. He'd put himself in charge. Just like Keith. Give her ex a problem, anything from a broken teapot to a patient with head trauma, and he was certain he knew what to do. Better than anyone. Stop being ridiculous, she told herself. Just because she'd had an overbearing husband didn't mean she had to reject the advice of every male she met. Her helper was probably right. And injuries or not, he'd be better able to handle the heavy work than she. "I'll see," she murmured and went to get some blankets.

They barricaded the front door with a faded old beach blanket, then did the same with the back, using a cartoon character blanket that had once belonged to her brother Steve.

Then they got to work, dragging furniture around until they could roll up the dhurrie that covered the living-room floor and set it on the sofa. They put small items—a lamp, a magazine rack, an umbrella stand—on tables.

As they worked, Christy kept her eyes on the man, watching for any tricky moves. Her trust only went so far.

Periodically she stopped to dial 911 on her cell, always with the same result: a busy signal.

She was concerned about the stranger's strength. A sheen of sweat covered his face, but he seemed to be holding up all right. "Are you okay?" she asked.

"Yeah."

She frowned. "What should I call you?"

She saw him stiffen, then he turned. "Aren't unidentified males called John Doe? How about J.D. for short?" His voice was flat. Not a shred of emotion showed in his eyes. The man had iron control.

Christy nodded. "J.D. All right."

Not sure how he felt about giving himself a "name," he turned away, mouthing the initials silently, wondering if he'd chosen his own. He went down the alphabet as he had last night. *J* slowed him down a bit, and he muttered, "Joe. Jack. Jerry." None of the names felt right.

What else? He tried a few sentence beginnings: "I live in…" "My social security number is…" "Hell," he muttered under his breath. "My social security number is zero zero zero."

Obsessing over his identity wasn't going to help him remember. He let his thoughts wander, and they came to rest on the woman working beside him. The voice of an angel, he thought. But she had a revolver tucked in the waistband of her jeans. Sweetness and spunk; the combination was immensely appealing. She was the kind of woman he'd enjoy sharing a burger and a beer with…or chateaubriand and champagne. If the weather were calm and she were his, he'd like to stroll along the beach with her under the summer sun. Or on a starlit night, with a soft Gulf breeze ruffling the hair that would drift like moon shadows to her shoulders.

A romantic image. Was he a romantic man? He pondered that for a moment and decided that no, he was more practical than poetic; yet something about Christy stirred him, called forth pretty words.

She bent to pick up a magazine that had dropped off a pile and gave him an enticing view of her backside. Nicely rounded. His hands itched to touch, to mold.

If she were his, on a day like this, they'd finish in here and he'd take her back to the bedroom and make love to her while the thunder growled and the storm battered the windows.

If she were his…

But she wasn't, and the thought jerked him back to reality. She'd mentioned a husband last night. But the spouse was clearly an invention she'd come up with to protect herself from a stranger who might get ideas about a lone woman.

Well, he'd gotten them.

He'd like to…

A sudden question halted him midthought. What if *he* was married and thinking this way? Damn, this was a helluva mess.

He glanced at her to find her with the cell phone at her ear again, punching in 911. While he'd been imagining romantic scenes, *she'd* been doing her best to try to get rid of him.

She caught him staring. "What?" she asked.

Had he said something out loud? "Nothing," he muttered. He pointed to the crowded bookshelves. "You don't want these books ruined. We'll move the ones from the lower shelves." He pulled out a well-worn copy of *The Secret Garden.* "Looks like you've read this more than once."

She nodded. "It was my favorite book when I was growing up. I read it every summer we were here, at least five years in a row."

"You came here when you were a kid?" he asked.

"Yes, this is my parents' beach house."

He glanced around the living room. Big windows that could be opened to catch the Gulf breeze, shut now to keep

out the rain. Comfortable furniture but not fancy. A fireplace.
One that was actually used. A log lay in the basket beside it.
On the mantel was a picture of a man holding up a huge fish.
Christy's father, he guessed. He scanned more of the book ti-
tles. "You have a brother."

She nodded.

"Older than you."

She cocked her head and stared at him. "Yes, but how do
you know that?"

He gestured to the dog-eared volumes. "His books are on
a higher shelf."

He read more titles. *The Hardy Boys, Huckleberry Finn,*
and *Tom Sawyer.* Funny, he knew the contents of all those
books but couldn't remember reading them. Dammit, why?
Rubbing his hand over his temple in frustration, he turned
away from the shelves.

"Let's take a break," Christy said. "I'll fix us some lunch."

"Okay." He led the way into the kitchen without her asking. He already knew the drill; she didn't want him behind
her.

"I'll make some cheese sandwiches," she said.

Christy dawdled over her sandwich. J.D. was certain she
did that to give him time to rest. He liked that, appreciated
that she didn't make a big deal out of it. He guessed she knew
that would embarrass him.

She'd gone out of her way to help him, even though she
still didn't trust him. She kept plenty of space between them
so he couldn't snatch her gun, and except for that one delicious view she'd given him of her derriere, she never turned
her back on him.

He wondered about her, this woman who was so strong.
Not just physically, but emotionally, too. "Did you always
want to be a nurse?" he asked.

She shrugged. "A nurse or an archaeologist."

"And you settled on nursing."

"I decided I wanted to be in health care."

"Why not a doctor?" he asked, but she only shrugged.

He tried to picture her at work, wearing scrubs, her hair pulled back from her face. "What hospital do you work at?" he asked.

"You ask too many questions."

"Sorry," he said, "I didn't mean to pry." He pushed his sandwich away. "I can't do much but ask questions. I can't tell you about me."

She shrugged. "That's okay. I don't go for the 'strangers on a plane' routine." She got up abruptly, punched 911 on her cell phone and backed away from the table.

At the kitchen door she stopped. "I'm getting through," she said excitedly, and hurried out of the room.

J.D. sighed. Now she could call the paramedics or the police. Or both. Wouldn't do much good though, he decided, looking out the window. No one would be able to get here. The roads were filled with water. The Gulf of Mexico was right at their doorstep.

Christy counted the rings as she stepped into the front hallway. After nine of them, a woman's harried voice answered. "Emergency."

Thank God. "This is Christy Matthews, 136 Gulf Bank Road. I have a man at my house who was in an accident last night—"

"Is his condition critical?" the woman interrupted.

"No, but—"

"We're only picking up in life-and-death situations."

"What about the police? I don't know who the man is. I—I think he might be, um, dangerous."

"You said he's been there since last night? Has he threatened you?"

"Um, no—"

"Well then, you'll have to sit tight. Police cars can't get through and they only have one helicopter. Call back later. Or tomorrow."

"I—" Before she could plead her case, the line went dead.

Well, what did she expect? This was like triage in an over-crowded emergency room. Priority went to the worst cases. But darn, the woman hadn't even given her a chance to say the man had lost his memory and to ask if there was a missing person report. She dialed emergency again and this time got the familiar busy signal.

She dropped the phone back into her pocket. Somewhere, someone must be worried sick about J.D. Some woman, probably...

She shuffled back to the kitchen.

J.D. looked up.

"I got through. They'll get here as soon as they can," she said, deciding on a half-truth to make him think the paramedics or even the cops were on their way. He nodded but she saw he didn't believe her. Why should he? Only his memory was gone; the rest of his brain seemed to be functioning just fine.

Didn't matter anyway. With the rain still coming down in torrents, she'd just as soon have him here. She needed his help. She needed company, too. Having him here was better than facing the storm alone.

She didn't like his asking questions though. It was safer not to give him any personal information.

A thought flashed into her mind. Last night she'd told him her husband was on his way. The water wasn't high enough then to prevent his coming. Wouldn't J.D. be wondering why he had never shown? *So, Christy, why not?* Okay, he worked in Houston and had planned to join her last night. He'd said he would be late and by the time he got started, he couldn't get through. Sounded plausible. "My husband—"

"You're not married."

Stunned at the matter-of-fact statement, she stepped back. "How…what gives you that idea?"

"You don't wear a wedding ring."

"I—I was at the beach yesterday. I didn't want to take a chance on losing it."

He glanced at her ring finger. "Then you've left it off all summer."

She followed the direction of his gaze. The skin of her fourth finger was evenly tanned.

"You haven't tried to call him," he pointed out.

He was infuriatingly logical. And, of course, he was right.

"Besides," he added, "when I said that just now, about you not being married, you started to say, 'How did you know?'"

"Okay, you're right." Deflated, she dropped into the chair across from him.

Eyes narrowed, he continued to study her. "You've *been* married though."

Annoyed now, she frowned at him. "And what brings you to that conclusion?"

"Your choice of vacation spots. You picked your parents' beach house. Doesn't seem like a singles haunt."

"Maybe I don't like to travel."

He shook his head. "The girl who once thought of becoming an archaeologist? I don't think so."

Christy felt a chill run down her spine. She didn't like this man guessing so much about her. "What are you, some kind of mind reader?" she asked irritably.

"Just a good observer." He studied her intently. "So why are you here?"

"I told you, you ask too many questions."

"Then I'll stick with answers. I believe you're here to think things through, get away from nosy questions." He flashed an engaging grin. "Like mine." When she didn't answer, he rose. "I'll go back to work."

Christy watched him leave. He'd disturbed her, intrigued her, and darned if that sexy grin hadn't kindled a spark. *Dumb, Christy.* Dumb for her to feel it and it would be even dumber for her to let him see it. She'd have to be careful.

Feeling edgy, she rose abruptly, went to the breakfast-room window and stared out at the waterlogged landscape. The front yard looked like a lake. With a pang, she noticed that her parents' beloved oleanders were awash in salt water. She remembered her mother planting them the summer they'd bought the beach house. "We'll enjoy them when we're old and gray," her dad had said, touching her mother's hand. They loved this house so much. Now she wondered if any of the bushes would survive the flood.

And whether the house itself would survive. Certainly not without damage. She'd heard shingles fly off the roof, seen a crumbled board floating toward the street. Sighing, she turned away from the window and joined J.D. in the living room.

Damn, the house was stifling. J.D. mopped his brow with his sleeve as they dragged more furniture around, putting rolled-up towels under the larger pieces, pots from the kitchen under the smaller ones. "Mind if I take my shirt off?"

"Go ahead," she said, but he saw she was uncomfortable. She didn't meet his eyes. He couldn't worry about that though. The heat and humidity were wearing him down. He shrugged off his shirt and laid it in the corner of the room.

He needed to rest for a few minutes, so he leaned against the wall. "Can I ask you something?" When she shot him a forbidding look, he added, "Nothing personal."

She stiffened but nodded.

He pointed to the fireplace. "Ever use that?"

Apparently relieved at the innocuous question, she smiled. "Yeah, a lot. It was one of the features that convinced my parents to buy this particular house. I remember Steve asking why we needed a fireplace in a summer home and Dad saying we could come down in winter, too."

"Did you?"

"Almost every year at Christmas." She smiled. God, she had a sweet smile. "Even if it wasn't cold—and usually it wasn't—Dad would build a fire and we'd sit around drinking eggnog and singing carols."

"I wish I could tell you how I spent Christmas growing up…or even last year," he said.

"We should try some word associations," she suggested. "Maybe that'll help you remember something."

"Can't hurt," he said. "Go."

"Summer," she said.

"Hot."

"Island."

"Beach," J.D. answered.

"You woke up there, didn't you?" Christy said. "Let's go with that. Beach."

"Tide."

"Why tide?" she asked. "I would have said sand or shells."

"It was coming in when I came to." Thinking of that made his head ache.

"Okay, let's try wreck."

"Crash."

"Did you?" she asked quickly.

He rubbed his head. "I don't know."

"Just say what comes into your mind."

"Bang."

"Not good," she said. "Try again."

"Hell, I don't know. Bam." He rubbed his head. "Forget it. This isn't working."

"You're right. Let's take a break."

J.D. nodded, rotated his shoulders. "Mind if I borrow a book?"

"Go ahead." As he glanced over the shelves, she came up behind him and touched his shoulder. "Sorry I upset you."

Gentle. Her touch was so gentle, her hand so soft. It took every ounce of self-control not to turn, pull her into his arms and bury himself in that sweet, feminine embrace.

"'S okay," he muttered and forced a smile. He pulled a volume off the shelf and headed for the kitchen.

Christy watched him go, then glanced at the hand that she'd laid on his shoulder. Her skin felt flushed, not just her hand but all over. Surely it was a natural reaction. Man, woman, locked up here together…alone. Natural for sexual tension to manifest itself. But would she feel the same if she were marooned with Dr. Ramsey, head of orthopedics, or Barry Walters, the physical therapist who saw patients on her floor? The answer was no.

She needed to think of something else. Where had she left the book she'd started yesterday afternoon? That seemed so long ago she could hardly remember.

She found it on top of a pile on the couch, picked it up, then put it back. She didn't want to read a thriller. Why did people call them that anyway? She was in the midst of her own personal adventure; she didn't need a fictional one. She scanned book titles and grabbed one of her dad's books, a biography of Robert E. Lee she'd never read.

Since all the living-room chairs were propped on towels, she took the book into the kitchen. J.D. had chosen another of her father's old books, an international adventure with agents, double agents and high-tech gadgetry, written by a relatively unknown writer trying to emulate Tom Clancy.

Christy sat across the table from J.D., opened her book, and glanced at him. Here she was, spending the day with a man she hadn't known twenty-four hours ago. She'd housed him, fed him, tended to him…and now she was providing him with reading material.

Unable to get interested in her reading, she watched him. His head was bent over the book. Despite the black eye and the bruise along his jaw, he was a handsome man. A man she acknowledged she'd have been attracted to in a different situation. No, she was a woman who tried to be honest with herself. Judging from her reaction to barely touching him, she admitted that even in these circumstances she was strongly attracted. There was strength in his features and an animal magnetism about him that could draw a woman's eye…and fuel her dreams.

Abruptly, she turned her chair sideways so that she faced away from him and tried to read. But she couldn't concentrate. She had to force herself to keep still.

Thump!

She gasped at the unexpected sound. Heart racing, she fumbled for the gun as she looked up. J.D. had tossed his book on the table, that was all. "Wh-what?"

"Asinine story. Makes no sense. The author knows nothing about international intrigue."

"And you do? Is that your line of work—espionage?"

He blinked as if he'd just awakened from a deep sleep. "I can't say." He got up and paced to the window and stood staring out into the gloom.

Christy watched him, noticing the rigid set of his shoulders, the hands clenched at his sides. He wasn't faking his amnesia. He was confused, out of control, and like the majority of men she knew, what he needed most of all was control.

He unfolded his hands, spread them on the windowpane and leaned close to the glass. He reminded her of a caged animal, straining against the limits of his enclosure.

He turned and met her eyes. Quickly, she looked down at

the book and pretended she was absorbed. But she knew he was watching her, felt his eyes bore into her like twin lasers.

Finally she couldn't stand him staring any longer. She shut her book and stood. "It's almost dinner time. I have some tuna in the pantry. I can't do much with it. We'll have to take it like it is. And I'd better light some candles. It's getting dark."

She placed the candles on saucers and set them on the table and prepared their meager meal. "Thanks," he said. "Tuna by candlelight."

Not what you'd expect of a candlelight dinner, Christy thought. Tasteless tuna on paper plates in a steamy kitchen. And yet, in the near-dark, with the candles flickering, and the light playing across J.D.'s skin and adding bronze highlights to his hair, she felt her heartbeat quicken.

Christy couldn't keep her eyes off his smooth chest, the muscles that rippled in his arms. She'd seen his body—more of it, actually—last night, but this was different. Then he'd been a patient; now he was a man.

Disturbed by the powerful figure before her, confused by her response to him, Christy forced her gaze down to her plate. Her hand trembled as she picked up her fork. She knew why. There was always an attraction in danger—the challenge of seeing how close you could venture to the fire without getting burned. J.D. was danger personified.

They ate in silence. The only sound was an occasional growl of thunder and the incessant rain. And then it slacked off.

"It's stopping." Christy jumped up and ran to the window. The force of the rain had lessened, but even in the dark she could see that the sky was still leaden. Water lapped threateningly at the porch. No one was going to rescue them tonight.

She got out more candles, set them in saucers and lit them. The flames cast shadows that fluttered against the walls and disappeared like ghosts.

J.D. rose. He yawned and stretched, and, to Christy, his figure, silhouetted on the wall behind him, looked large, menacing. The man who'd intrigued her minutes ago now seemed threatening.

"You should get some rest," she told him. Her voice sounded thin.

He nodded and picked up one of the makeshift candleholders. "You should, too."

He was right. She couldn't stay awake to watch him for another eight hours.

What should she do?

She wished she could lock him in the front bedroom, but the bedroom doors had no locks. Carrying her own candle, she followed him down the hall and into his room. "I want to check your wound," she told him.

He gave her a little-boy frown. "Aw, geez, Mom, do you have to?"

"Yes, I do. Sit."

He sat on the edge of the bed and clenched his fists while she dabbed more peroxide around the wound. "Nurse Ratched," he muttered.

"I heard that."

"Sorry."

"You remember the book or, later, the movie," she said hopefully.

"Sure. *One Flew Over the...um, Robin's Nest.*"

"Cuckoo," she corrected.

"You talkin' to me?" he asked.

"Nope, and that's another movie."

He looked up. "*Taxi Driver.* Also about a nut case," he said and gave her one of his dazzling smiles.

She backed quickly away. "Good night. Call me if you need anything."

She hurried down the hall to her bathroom. She needed a long, cool shower, but she settled for a short one, then went to the bedroom. She shut the door, stared at it, then got a chair and shoved it against the door and under the knob. It wouldn't keep him out if he really wanted in, but at least it would slow him down, give her time to get her weapon. Lord, how could she have predicted when the doorbell rang last night that she would spend tonight barricaded in her room?

She lay down and shut her eyes, but couldn't sleep. The room was stifling. She cracked the window open, then shut it when rain blew in.

A floorboard creaked somewhere in the house. She held her breath. Was it him? Was he coming this way? She sat up, reached for her revolver and waited. Nothing happened and she ordered herself to calm down. They'd been alone all day and isolated. Why should she be any more afraid of him at night?

Who was he?

Unable to answer that question, she asked another. What did she know about him? What had she learned in the day they'd been together?

He was strong. In spite of his injury and what had to be considerable pain, he'd worked all day without a word of complaint. He'd been helpful and—and kind. He'd backed off immediately when she'd let him know his questions and his uncannily accurate observations made her uncomfortable. No matter who— or what—he was, there was something about him, something that drew her. Maybe it was his combination of strength and compassion; maybe it was because he was a mystery, even to himself. Although she believed people control their own destiny, she had a strange feeling that Fate had sent him to her door. Finally she fell asleep, seeing his face in her dreams.

Down the hall, J.D. lay awake, staring at the ceiling. Through clenched teeth, he whispered, "Who am I?"

Was someone searching for him? Agonizing over his disappearance? Maybe not.

For a while at least, Christy had thought he might be a criminal. Could she be right? He wanted to say no, but he remembered the bullet wound in his thigh, the blow to his head last night—evidence of violence, even though he didn't think he was a violent person.

Maybe he didn't remember what happened because he didn't want to. He had no clue.

The only thing he was sure about was Christy. When she'd bent over him, he'd wanted to touch her, to draw in her scent, to see if her skin was as soft as it looked. He'd had to clench his fists to keep from reaching for her.

He shut his eyes, pictured her face and fell asleep.

His dreams were as disjointed as they had been last night and frightening. Empty rooms that weren't really empty. Faces in the shadows. Someone stalked him, grabbed him by the throat. He twisted, groaned, trying to get away.

Christy woke abruptly. She sat up in bed, hugging the sheet around her. What was that noise?

A man's voice.

Had someone broken in? Or was it J.D.? Was he all right?

Reaching for the gun, she held it in front of her as she'd been taught, then made her way down the hall. The noise came from his room: a moan, then a half scream.

With a trembling hand, she opened the door.

The sheets tangled around him, he tossed and turned on the bed, muttering unintelligible words.

She moved closer. The sheets were damp, his skin soaked with perspiration. She put her hand on his brow. "Shh, it's all right," she murmured…

From under the sheet, his hand whipped out. He grabbed her arm and jerked her forward with surprising strength.

Christy screamed as she toppled to the bed.

Chapter 5

"No!" Christy choked, struggling against J.D.'s superior strength. "No." The gun dropped out of her hand and crashed to the floor.

All her earlier fears about him now stared her in the face.

He had her by the shoulders. She tried to kick, but her legs were tangled in the sheet, tried to twist away, but he held her fast. He forced her onto her back and she lay powerless, helpless to get away.

Terrified, fighting for breath, Christy stared up at him.

He loomed over her, nostrils flaring, his lips peeled back in a grimace. His eyes were…shut.

Asleep. He had to be asleep.

Forcing air into her lungs, Christy cried, "Stop, J.D. Let me go."

He made a growling sound in his throat. And then his eyes opened.

"Wh—?" He stared at her as if he'd never seen her before.

Then recognition dawned. "Christy?" he muttered. "What's... going on?"

"You—you were having a nightmare."

His grip loosened. "What happened? How did you...? How did I...?"

She sat up and struggled to control her shaky voice. "I—I stumbled into your bad dream. I came in to see what was wrong and—and you grabbed me."

He stared down at the hand that had seized her. "Ah, Christy, I—I—"

She saw the shock on his face, heard the revulsion in his voice, and her fear faded. "You were asleep. You didn't know what you were doing." But still, she rubbed the arm he'd jerked.

He sat up, wide awake now, his tone sharp. "Did I hurt you?"

She dropped her gaze. "Not much."

"Let me see." He took her arm, carefully this time as if afraid he might break it. "You *are* hurt. Bruised." His voice filled with self-loathing, he let go of her. "Damn, what kind of man am I?"

"Don't," she said softly. "You didn't mean to hurt me. I'm sure of that." And she was...now.

Without thinking, she bent toward him and gently touched his cheek. "Relax," she murmured to him. "Go back to sleep."

He raised his eyes to hers. "Christy," he breathed as she stroked the rough stubble on his face. "Christy..."

He leaned closer; his mouth was inches from hers. Her lips parted.

He put his hands on her shoulders. He was going to kiss her. She wanted this—the warmth of his breath, the taste of his mouth. Her eyes closed.

Gently, he pushed her away. "No."

Her eyes flew open. Humiliated, she straightened as her ex-husband's mocking voice sounded in her ear: *I don't want you.* Neither did J.D.

This man was a stranger. His rejection shouldn't sting the way Keith's had. But it did.

She wanted to run away, hide her embarrassment and her hurt. Turning her back on J.D., she struggled to her feet.

J.D. caught her hand. "Christy, wait."

"No, I…you…need to get back to sleep." But he held her in place.

"Look at me," he said, giving her arm a gentle tug, and slowly, unwillingly, she turned.

He urged her back down on the bed. When she perched stiffly on the edge, he dropped her hand and caressed her cheek, his fingertips soft on her heated skin. "I don't know…who I am…or what my situation is." He glanced at his left hand.

Christy's eyes followed his. "There's no ring," she murmured.

"It doesn't matter," he said, his voice filled with regret. "There could be someone. I…don't know, and until I do, I can't do this to you. It wouldn't be fair to either of us."

"You're right, of course," she said. "I don't know what I was thinking."

"I do. And just for the record, I was thinking the same thing."

If he could fight this attraction, so could she. She cleared her throat. "I, um, should go."

"Yeah, you should."

She got up, bent and picked up the gun. "Good night," she whispered.

In her room, she sat on the edge of the bed and touched her still-warm cheek. She'd told J.D. she hadn't known what she was thinking. Trouble was, she hadn't been thinking at all. She'd been feeling. Wanting.

She'd been alone for nearly a year. Was that the reason? No, she'd had her chances to be with a man. Friends had urged her to start dating so she'd given in and gone out a few times. But she hadn't enjoyed the dating scene, the rush to take someone to bed. Acquaintances—really nonacquaintances—of a few hours were ready to hit the sheets. Not Christy.

But tonight had been different. If J.D. hadn't said no, she'd be in his bed right now. She covered her face with her hands.

He was a man with integrity, she thought. He'd saved them both from embarrassment, maybe even heartache.

She thought of the gentleness in his tone when he'd let her go, the sincerity in his eyes.

How different he was from Keith. J.D. didn't know if he was involved, yet still he wouldn't take a chance of hurting someone. Keith had no compunctions about betraying the wife he saw every day.

Christy glanced at the revolver she'd set on the nightstand and shook her head. Another embarrassment.

All her pride in her ability to defend herself had been in vain. Even with a gun in her hand, J.D. had easily overpowered her. In his sleep.

With a snort of disgust, she opened the drawer and shoved the gun inside, all the way to the back.

When Christy woke the next morning, she hurried to the window and opened the blinds. The rain had stopped, but the sky still looked ominous, and though the water was beginning to recede, the road was still flooded.

She dressed slowly. She dreaded coming face to face with J.D. after last night. After she'd practically jumped into bed with him. Well, she couldn't avoid him. They were, after all, the only two people in their tiny, isolated world. She'd just have to pretend last night had never happened and hope he had the good manners not to mention it.

He didn't say a word. He greeted her in the kitchen and

handed her a glass of too-warm orange juice. "Sorry, the kitchen is still closed," he said.

"Did you try the phone?"

"Still down."

She took out her cell. Low battery, the screen said. And of course, she had no way to charge it. Damn, if something could go wrong, it would. She wanted to fling the phone onto the table. Instead she put it carefully into her pocket.

Now they could do nothing but wait.

She glanced across the table at J.D. as she nibbled on half-stale, untoasted bread.

He looked up from his breakfast and met her eyes. Goosebumps erupted on her arms, a blush warmed her cheeks, and all her plans to keep silent about what had happened between them evaporated. "Um, about last night—"

"I don't recall a thing. I have amnesia, remember?" That quick, charming grin spread across his lips.

"I guess I don't remember either, then," Christy said. But she knew she wouldn't forget, not even when J.D. was out of her life. She'd still wonder how his lips would have tasted, still regret not finding out.

They finished their breakfast. "Do you want to put the furniture back?" J.D. asked.

"I don't think so. It may rain again."

"Didn't you say your car wouldn't start?" he asked. "Want me to take a look?"

Even with amnesia, the guy figured his auto mechanics gene was still functioning. Typical male. "Doesn't matter if it works or not," she said. "My Toyota's so low to the ground it would drown in a few inches of water."

"We could—"

The doorbell rang and Christy jumped up.

Was this a delayed response to her 911 call?

But when she opened the door, she found Warner Thompson, the retired banker who lived down the street, his ruddy face wreathed in a smile. "Glad to see you survived the storm, young lady. Have any problems?"

Her heart began to pound. Here at last was her chance to tell someone about J.D.

Christy hesitated as Warner waited for her answer. Say you have a problem, say a stranger invaded your house, ask Warner for help. Do it.

Yesterday she would have, without hesitation. But the words didn't come. She and J.D. had reached a turning point last night. Everything was different now. She shook her head.

Behind her, she heard footsteps. J.D. strolled into the living room, carrying a glass in one hand and a dishcloth in the other. Warner's eyes widened.

What did her neighbor see? A delightful domestic scene. He was probably mentally congratulating Christy on replacing Keith with such an attractive man.

"Hello there," Warner said and put out a hand. "Warner Thompson."

J.D. shook it. "J. D. Russell."

Christy's gaze leaped to J.D.'s. Had he remembered? Was that his real name? But J.D.'s smile was bland and his eyes focused on Warner.

"I'm going to try and drive my SUV into town," Warner said. "You two want to ride along?"

Christy nodded. "That would be great. J.D. had a little accident yesterday. I'd like Dr. Mayes to take a look at it."

"Come on then."

As they drove to town through streets filled with debris and still knee-deep in water, Warner unabashedly quizzed J.D. about himself.

"Where are you from, son?"

Christy cringed. Warner had always reminded her of a

jovial Santa Claus, but today she wished he weren't so outgoing and interested in others.

J.D., however, fielded the question with ease. "Houston."

"Nice place for you young folks, but too chaotic for Ellie and me. We like the quiet life here. Haven't been back to Houston but a couple of times since we retired here three years ago, and that was for doctor's appointments. Under protest." He glanced at J.D. "What kind of work do you do?"

"Consulting. Human relations."

"Teach those CEOs to be more compassionate, eh?"

J.D. smiled. "Something like that."

Christy's eyes widened at his glib answers. Either J.D. was an accomplished liar who'd been feeding her a line about having amnesia these past two days, or he'd regained his memory. She tried to send him a what's-going-on? message with her eyes, but he avoided her gaze and continued the conversation.

"How'd you two meet?" Warner asked as he turned onto San Sebastian's main street.

"At a party," Christy said.

"At the gym," J.D. replied at the same time.

Christy's cheeks heated as she met Warner's startled gaze. "Which?" he asked.

"Party," Christy repeated, then forced a chuckle. "We'd seen each other at the gym, but we didn't really meet until that party. Remember, hon?" She turned and patted J.D.'s hand. "J.D. has such a bad memory for, um, details like that."

"Terrible memory," he agreed, and added, "Really all I remember of that evening is Christy. She bowled me over. You could say I fell at her feet."

"Yeah, you could," Christy muttered. She let out a breath of relief when Warner pulled the SUV into a parking space.

"Well, here you are," Warner said. "I need to pick up a few

things for Ellie. Why don't you two meet me at the hardware store around the corner in, say, three hours?"

"Fine." Christy could hardly wait to escape from his curious gaze. She tugged J.D. across the street toward the small medical building where Dr. Mayes practiced. She stopped in front of the door. "You remembered everyth—"

"Nothing."

"But you gave Warner your name."

J.D. shook his head. "When you went to answer the door, I figured I'd be meeting someone. I saw a notepad from Russell's Pharmacy on the counter, so I used the name. The rest—I had to say something."

"Maybe some of it was true."

"Don't know, except for falling at your feet."

"Yeah," Christy muttered. "You did do that." If he hadn't, she'd have had him out of her house in minutes, and then she'd have missed:

A. The adventure of her life.
B. A lot of grief.
C. Both of the above.

Didn't matter. Here she was, and here *he* was. "Let's go see if the doctor's in," she said.

They found Dr. Tom Mayes's waiting room filled with patients and his receptionist's chair empty. They rang the bell and waited at the window. After a few minutes, the doctor bustled out of an examining room, followed by a young woman with a whimpering toddler. "You just give him a couple of baby aspirin every few hours, Amanda, and he'll be fine."

He spotted Christy at the desk and his face lit up. "Christy Matthews," he said, raising his arms. "The Lord has sent me an angel." He peered around her and called, "Come on in, Mr.

Truman," and a large man heaved himself up out of a chair and shuffled through the door.

"What brings you in, Christy?" Dr. Mayes asked as he motioned Truman toward the examining room.

"My, uh, friend has a head wound. I'd like you to take a look at it."

The doctor thrust a clipboard toward J.D. "Take a seat and fill this out. You're about number one thousand in line." He turned to Christy. "My nurse couldn't get out of her subdivision this morning. As long as you're here, would you mind playing Florence Nightingale until your friend here is finished?"

"I'd be glad to." She glanced at J.D. "Will you be okay by yourself?" she asked softly.

J.D. scowled at her. Did she think he was incompetent? Was this how people with head injuries were treated? "I can manage," he said through gritted teeth.

"I know you can. Sorry," she said. Dr. Mayes opened the door and she went inside.

J.D. sat down and stared at the clipboard in his hand. Health History. *Yeah.* He turned it over, picked up a copy of *Time* and riffled through it, hoping to find something familiar. No luck. He put the magazine down and listened to other patients chattering about Tropical Storm Coral. Each person seemed to be trying to one-up everyone else with survivor stories. He bet his story could top them all.

A good hour later the doctor called, "J. D. Russell."

He glanced around the waiting room, wondering who—

Then he saw Christy in the doorway, beckoning to him. *J. D. Russell. Me.* He got up.

Dr. Mayes was in the examining room, drying his hands. He motioned to the examining table, tossed the paper towel in the waste can and took the clipboard from J.D. "Got a problem with your he—" He glanced at the clipboard in his hand. "You haven't filled this out."

"I can't," J.D. said grimly. "I don't remember any of it."

Dr. Mayes regarded him thoughtfully. "So this head wound—"

"Is more than a cut," J.D. said. "I woke up on the beach last night and couldn't remember anything." He forced himself to speak without emotion. "I still can't."

Dr. Mayes nodded. "Any other injuries?"

"His ribs," Christy said.

"Take off your shirt. Lie down and let's take a look, then we'll talk. Okay with you if Christy gives me a hand?"

"Sure. I've already had a sample of her nursing skills." J.D. lay back and shut his eyes while the doctor probed the head wound. It didn't hurt as much today and he couldn't resist saying, "You're a lot gentler than Ms. Nightingale here."

Christy huffed. "You're already starting to heal. That's why it doesn't hurt as much."

"Your nurse has done a fine job on you," Dr. Mayes said, "but we'll put in a few stitches for insurance."

After the stitching was done and the doctor had apologized for his inability to X-ray J.D. without electricity, he checked J.D.'s chest and pronounced the ribs bruised but probably not broken. He looked intently at J.D. "You said you don't remember anything about what happened?"

"I don't remember anything about anything." J.D. heard the despair in his voice and, with an effort, lightened his tone. "No name, no rank, no serial number. Nothing. I think the medical term is amnesia."

"Yes."

"What's the prognosis?" He felt as if he were waiting for a judge to pronounce a sentence on him.

"The majority of amnesiacs recover their memories in time," Dr. Mayes said.

"But some don't?"

The doctor nodded. "The ones who don't are usually in

a lot worse shape than you are. All you can do is be patient."

"I can remember some things," J.D. said. "General information, like what to do in a storm or names of movies. Why can't I remember anything about myself?"

Dr. Mayes spread his hands. "The mind is a curious thing. After head trauma, a patient may remember just the sort of information you mentioned, but when it comes to himself, he's like a brand-new puppy. No history."

"Isn't there anything J.D. can do to help matters along?" Christy asked.

"Yes," Dr. Mayes said, "but the advice isn't easy to follow. Try to relax and let your mind open."

"Okay," J.D. said. He felt hopeless.

"Forcing things won't work." Dr. Mayes put his hand on J.D.'s shoulder. "Good luck."

J.D. tried to read the message behind the words. Did the doctor mean good luck was likely or good luck living with no past?

He didn't trust himself to speak as he and Christy walked out of the office. She looked pretty miserable herself.

J.D. wondered if he was in "the majority." Or was he doomed to go on like this for the rest of his life? What did a man do when he was suddenly a blank slate?

He glanced at Christy again, remembering the softness of her skin, the sweetness of her parted lips. He wanted her in his arms again. Didn't he have a right to print on that slate whatever he chose?

Before he could answer that, he had things to take care of. Then he could wrestle with his future. He noticed a sign down the street and headed in that direction. "Come on," he said to Christy. "We need to make a stop at the San Sebastian Sheriff's Department."

As J.D. and Christy trudged down the street, a shaft of sunlight broke through the clouds. An omen? Christy wondered. Perhaps the sheriff would have information that would clear up all her questions about J.D. Maybe he'd have a missing persons report that would enable J.D. to reclaim his former life.

And then she'd never see him again.

Selfish of her to be thinking like that, she told herself. She should be happy for him if that happened. Of course she would be.

They pushed open the door and left the humidity of the sidewalk for the hot, stale air of a windowless, un-air-conditioned office. Christy swiped her hair back from her already sweaty face.

An aging deputy looked up as they approached the desk and quickly stubbed out a cigarette. "Can I he'p you?" he asked.

"Any reports of missing persons come in recently?" J.D. asked.

The man shoved his glasses up on his nose. "Somebody lost?"

Christy watched as J.D.'s fingers clenched. "Me," he said grimly. "I had an accident—"

"What kind of accident?" The deputy eyed J.D. curiously. "If you caused any property damage, I gotta make out a report."

"No, nothing like that. I got hit on the head and suffered a…slight memory loss. I thought someone might be looking for me."

"No, sir. Cain't he'p you out with that. Phones been down so cain't nothin' come in."

"Once they're up again, I'd appreciate your letting me know if you get anything." He turned to Christy, and she gave the deputy her phone number.

"How about cars?" J.D. continued. "Any abandoned ones towed in?"

"About a thousand," the man said. "You wanna check on yours, the lot's over on Third and Dune."

If J.D. couldn't identify himself, surely he couldn't recognize his car, Christy thought. On the other hand, maybe some vehicle would jog his memory. They could walk over to the lot later.

J.D. spread his hands on the desk. Christy studied them. They were strong, she knew. His fingers were long and lean, the nails clean and neatly clipped. They weren't the hands of a workman. They belonged to a man who used his mind more than his muscles. Of course, that left a lot of possibilities open. Doctor, lawyer, merchant—

A white-collar person could still be a kidnapper. Why didn't J.D. say anything about the missing woman? Christy could say something herself, but she wanted *him* to do it. That would remove the last little bit of doubt that nagged at her. *Ask,* she begged silently.

"Did you find that woman who was reported kidnapped the other day?" J.D. suddenly asked, as though he'd read her mind.

Christy breathed a sigh of thanks, then clenched her hands as she waited for the answer. Her intuition had to be right. J.D. couldn't be a criminal.

"Yeah," the deputy said, "lady turned up a couple hours ago. Got in the car with some fellow she knew. They were stuck on the road all night and the next day. Dropped her cell and it was too wet to use. Her husband came in right after sunup t'let us know."

Thank God. "I'm sure he was relieved," Christy said. No more than she was.

J.D. glanced at her, and she knew he read her mind.

Outside a couple of minutes later, he said, "Feel better?"

Christy fidgeted uncomfortably. "I didn't really think you were a kidnapper."

His laugh was bitter. "Sure you did."

"At first, yes, but not after I got to know you."

He quickened his step. "You don't know me. Hell, *I* don't know me."

"I do," Christy said, hurrying to keep up with him. "I've learned you're a decent, kind person."

He stopped abruptly. "Because of last night?"

Christy didn't meet his eyes. "Yes."

"What I did then was as much for me as for you," he said.

"Okay, but there were other things. You had the upper hand. You could have…taken advantage."

J.D. shook his head. "Maybe I didn't want to bite the hand that fed me."

"Stop it," Christy said angrily. Tears threatened to fill her eyes. "Stop tearing down everything you've done because—because you're upset."

"I am upset," J.D. said with a sigh, "but I shouldn't take it out on you. I owe you."

"No, you—"

"I do. This may sound crazy, given my circumstances, but I won't forget what you've done for me."

"You sound like you're thinking of leaving," Christy said, staring at him in disbelief. "That does sound crazy."

"Storm's over," he said. "I need to get out of your hair."

"And do what?"

"I'll figure it out."

"We gave *my* phone number to the deputy. How will he reach you?" Christy argued.

"I'll go back and check with him."

He started to walk away, but she caught his arm. "Stop, J.D. We both know you have nowhere to go."

He flinched. "Direct hit."

She saw his reaction and could have kicked herself. She was desperately afraid he would leave and just as desperate to prevent it.

Across the street was a small park. "Let's go over there where we can sit down and talk," she urged.

"Okay." He didn't sound thrilled with the idea but he followed her.

They slogged through the wet grass and sat on a damp stone bench. At their feet, dragonflies hovered over puddles.

"Where were you thinking of going?" Christy asked.

J.D. ran his fingers through his hair, winced when he skimmed his wound. "I have to stay in San Sebastian until I find out if someone's looking for me. I'll get work. People have storm damage."

"*I* have storm damage," Christy said. He didn't answer, and she went on. "You can help me with repairs. I can pay you—" He started to interrupt, but she hurried on. "And you'll have a place to stay." He hesitated, and she added, "Don't worry. I won't jump you."

J.D. laughed. "That's not much of an incentive, but thanks. I appreciate your offer."

"Let's stop at the grocery store. Then we can go to the hardware store and pick up some supplies."

"Sounds like a good plan."

They walked companionably down the street. Christy knew she was foolish to feel so lighthearted, but she couldn't help it.

At the grocery store they stopped, waited, then looked at each other and laughed. Of course the automatic doors didn't open. J.D. pushed. "Amazing," he said with a teasing grin. "You can work them by hand."

Inside, Christy asked, "What do you like that doesn't need cooking?"

"You don't cook much anyway," J.D. remarked.

He was right, but, "How do you know?" she asked.

"I saw what you had in your refrigerator."

The man noticed everything. Maybe his real name was Sherlock.

As they started down the produce aisle, Christy asked, "Do you think we'll run into someone here who knows you?"

"I'm hoping we will." She saw him look into the eyes of other shoppers. He was watching for a spark of recognition. "No one looks familiar," he said, "and no one knows me." He grabbed a can of juice off a shelf, dropped it in the basket. "I feel invisible."

Though she doubted a man as handsome as J.D. would ever walk through life unnoticed, she knew he didn't mean that. He meant he was still a stranger, to everyone. Her heart broke for him.

When they finished their shopping, the cart held peanut butter and jelly, a loaf of bread, more tuna, a can of Vienna sausages, several kinds of juice, and fruit. Christy eyed a bottle of wine on the last aisle, then changed her mind. She didn't need to loosen her inhibitions with wine. They were on the verge of disappearing on their own.

Since they were due to meet Warner in twenty minutes, they decided to postpone looking for J.D.'s car. At the hardware store they picked up boards, nails and shingles. They finished just as Warner drove up.

Back home, they walked around the house, surveying the damage. "About two days' worth of work," J.D. concluded, then said, "Let's take a look at your car."

Christy opened the garage. The water had receded, leaving a line on the wall about eight inches up. "Thank goodness the car wasn't flooded," Christy said. She leaned inside and popped the hood.

Before she'd straightened up again, J.D. slammed the hood down.

"Found the problem already?" she said. "What a mechanic."

"It's not a mechanical problem," he said, his face forbidding. "Someone cut the distributor wire."

Chapter 6

Shocked, Christy stared at him. "Cut the wire? But—but who would do such a thing? Kids playing a prank?"

He shook his head. "Someone," he said thoughtfully, "who saw me at your door and didn't want me to get away. He knew I didn't have a car, and he dismantled yours so you couldn't drive me to a hospital or the police station."

"Be-because he beat you—"

"More than that," J.D. said. "I think…because he tried to kill me and he wants another chance."

Christy shuddered. He *couldn't* be right. She didn't want him to be right, couldn't imagine J.D. dead. She shut her eyes, then opened them as a thought occurred to her. "If he wanted to—to do that, he could have broken a window and gotten into the house."

"Something stopped him," J.D. said. "Someone on the street…or a car going by."

"He could have waited."

"The street was flooding. He wouldn't have been able to drive away," J.D. said. He glanced at the wide road in front of Christy's house. "But the water's down now. He'll be back."

"J.D., you're scaring me," Christy said.

"That makes two of us. I'm scaring me, too."

"What should we do?" she asked. "Call the sheriff?"

"Yeah, we can try," J.D. said.

He turned, and suddenly he slammed his fist on the hood of the car. "Damn, I should never have knocked on your door."

"You needed help—"

He glared at her. "And *you* should never have let me in. Dammit lady, don't you know better than to open your door to a stranger?"

"Apparently not."

"And now you're in a helluva mess. *My* mess."

"Ours."

"For the moment," he said. "Until I can get you out of it, we're in this together." He glanced at the street. It was deserted and so was the field across from Christy's house.

She followed his gaze. At the moment the field looked like a pond, but usually it was an open expanse of low grass. She remembered the car driving down the street when she'd let J.D. in. Had the driver been the man he thought was after him? She pointed toward the field. "What do you think? Could he be watching us from there?"

"No place to hide there," J.D. said, "but easy enough to run through if someone wanted to get away fast. The water there now would slow him down, but it'll be gone tomorrow. I don't like it.

"The sheriff may be busy but he needs to know what's gone on," J.D. continued. "I doubt our buddy the deputy told him much about us. I'll walk down to Warner's and use his cell, call 911 and ask the dispatcher to let the sheriff know. Stay here, lock the door and don't open it to anyone but me."

"I'll go with you."

"Christy—"

"Please," she said. "I'll feel safer."

"Okay," he said, and they headed down the street, skirting puddles that were still ankle-deep. Pewter-gray clouds hid the sun, but the air was as hot and humid as a steam bath. With each step, their shoes squished into mud. Mosquitoes, newly hatched and ravenous, whined around them.

As they trudged along, Christy glanced nervously from side to side, imagining a car careening into them or a man leaning out the window of one of the beach houses and spraying them with a shotgun.

"Don't worry," J.D. told her. "Whoever he is, he isn't likely to do anything in broad daylight. He'll figure some of those houses *are* occupied and there'd be witnesses."

"I don't think any of the cottages are occupied right now," Christy said.

"*He* may think they are, so he'll stay out of the way," J.D. pointed out, and she felt relieved. Until he added, "You'd be better off looking for snakes. They come out after floods."

"Great," she muttered peering into the unmown grass along the side of the road, "that makes me feel so much safer."

The walk to the Thompsons' house seemed interminable, but they encountered no snakes, reptilian or human. She was relieved when they approached Warner's house. An airy, rambling structure, it was large enough to accommodate the Thompsons' children and their spouses and the growing brood of grandchildren. Big enough to house Christy, too, if she'd had the sense to come down here when the storm started. Then, she told herself, she wouldn't be in this mess.

The door opened. "Well, hello there," Ellie Thompson said. "Warner told me you were here with a…friend." Her eyes gleamed with delight. "Come on in. You can cheer up

Mr. Grumps. He can't keep up with his investments because of the storm."

She ushered them into the living room where Warner was camped out in a recliner, reading a week-old copy of the *Wall Street Journal.* "Company," she said.

"Hello again." Warner rose to shake J.D.'s hand. "Did I tell you our Dallas grandkids were supposed to come down this week? Of course, the storm changed their plans," he said. "We're lonely. Come cheer us up."

Christy sat beside Ellie on the couch, and J.D. asked if he could use the cell phone.

"It's in the kitchen," Ellie said and pointed. "Right through there."

When J.D. left, Ellie leaned toward Christy. "Warner told me you had a new boyfriend. Honey, he is hot."

"Hot?" Christy gaped at her neighbor. Had Ellie, well into senior citizenship, really referred to J.D. as hot? "Um…"

"You know, dear," Ellie said. "*Hot,* as in *cool.*"

Christy blinked.

"Or as in *sexy,*" Ellie explained.

Warner cleared his throat. "Woman learns all that trash talk on the World Wide Web."

Ellie shook a finger at her husband. "And you don't?"

"*I* follow the market."

Ellie smoothed her salt-and-pepper hair. "*I* keep up with popular culture."

Christy hoped their good-natured bickering would forestall any more comments about J.D. He came back into the room, caught Christy's eye and gave her the slightest of nods. "Thanks for the use of your phone." He sat down on the other side of Christy, and Ellie beamed at them.

What would her neighbors think if they knew the real situation here? Christy turned to J.D. "Were you, um, able to order what we needed?" she asked.

"Yeah, it's in stock," he said, smiling at her.

"Good. I hope by tomorrow phone service will be restored and I can call a garage to repair my car." she added.

"You don't have to wait, young lady," Warner said. "I've got Billy Coates's cell number. Best mechanic on San Sebastian."

"Thanks," Christy said and went into the kitchen.

Billy picked up on the second ring. "I can get by some time tomorrow," he said when he heard what she needed. "It'll give me a little break. Putting in a distributor wire will be a breeze compared to working on all these flooded transmissions."

Christy thanked him and returned to the living room where Warner was holding forth on the current state of the market. J.D. didn't say much, just nodded now and then. Christy sat anxiously, trying to keep her foot from tapping the floor, until they had a chance to leave.

As soon as they were outside, she asked, "What did the dispatcher say?"

"Same thing you did, that it was probably kids. But she said she'd let the sheriff know. She also told me they're concerned about thugs looting vacant homes that have had storm damage, so they'll be patrolling this area all night."

Christy stopped. "So we'll be safe?"

"Relatively."

"Relatively is better than not at all, I guess," she said doubtfully.

"Realistically, they can't be on this street at all times," J.D. explained. "But having them in the area should deter our guy."

"I suppose." She began walking again, then thought about his conversation with Warner and asked curiously, "Is the stock market one of the things you've forgotten?"

J.D. ran his hand through his hair. "In theory, I know how it works, but when you get to how specific companies are performing or the current Dow Jones average, I'm one of those brand-new puppies Dr. Mayes talked about."

"So you probably aren't a stockbroker."

"Or not a successful one."

They arrived at Christy's house, and he said, "There's plenty of daylight left, so I'm going to start replacing some of the shingles that blew off."

"All right, but promise me you'll come in if you start to feel tired or dizzy. I don't want you passing out and falling off the roof."

"I'll be careful."

Christy went inside and began straightening the living room, putting some of the lighter items they'd moved yesterday back in place. Every few minutes she stopped to look out the window. J.D. was alone out there, exposed, a perfect target for a sniper. The man who'd beaten him up could be holed up in one of those vacant cottages. Each time she headed for the window, she prayed she wouldn't see J.D. lying in a pool of blood.

In a pile of old mail she found a brochure from Aruba. She picked it up and studied it. Sugary white sand, palm trees, the turquoise waters of the Caribbean, and of course, smiling, sun-tanned couples toasting one another with tropical concoctions in tall glasses. She'd brought the brochure along when she and Keith were here last Labor Day, figuring they'd have time to plan their island vacation. Planning a trip was half the fun for Christy, but Keith hadn't been interested in joining her as she perused the names of hotels and restaurants. "The trip's your idea. You do the planning," he'd said. Hindsight told her he'd never intended to go. At least, not with her. He had another companion in mind.

Were Keith and Betsy in Aruba now, basking in the sun, frequenting the casinos, strolling through the shops? With a snort of disgust Christy tore the brochure in half and threw it into the wastebasket. She didn't miss Keith, hadn't in a long time. And she wouldn't waste another minute thinking about her ex-husband. Wherever he and Betsy were, they were two of a kind. They deserved each other.

She turned her thoughts to the man outside. There had to be a woman in his life, she mused. He was too "hot" not to attract female attention. He probably had a wife or a girlfriend, someone sleek and sophisticated. Blonde, she thought, running a hand through her tousled locks. Auburn highlights were *her* only claim to fame, hardly competition for an eye-catching blonde.

The sound of the door opening interrupted her thoughts. J.D. came in, tracking mud on the floor. "I'm finished for now. Mind if I clean up?" he asked, wiping his face on his sleeve. Christy nodded and he added, "Do you have a razor I can borrow?"

"Sorry, only an electric one." She rather liked the sight of his stubble-darkened cheeks. He looked even more like a pirate than when he'd rung her bell.

Christy decided she needed a sponge bath, too, and headed for the bathroom next to her bedroom. She would have liked a shower, but they should conserve water. When she finished her makeshift bath, she couldn't resist spraying on cologne. Not that she was trying to attract J.D.'s attention; she just wanted to feel fresh and feminine. She'd do this even if she were alone, she told herself.

In the kitchen she found J.D. studying the canned items they'd bought. They debated their dinner choices and decided on Vienna sausages. That, along with plain bread, constituted their evening meal. Again, they ate by candlelight.

After dinner, Christy rinsed the box of strawberries they'd bought at the grocery and put the fruit into a bowl. She carried it back to the table. "Want some?"

J.D. glanced up and nodded but said nothing. He'd found

a deck of cards she'd left on the serving cart by the table and was shuffling them with practiced ease.

"You handle the cards like a pro," she observed, sitting across from him. "Maybe you are."

He stared at his fingers as he continued deftly mixing the cards. "How should I know?" he said harshly. He looked up and the eyes that met hers were so bleak that Christy felt his pain as intensely as if it were her own. Then his expression changed. As if he'd drawn a curtain over them, he concealed his emotions behind a blank gaze. "Poker or gin?" His voice was even.

"Gin." She'd never play poker with a man who could disguise his feelings so easily.

He held out the cards. "Cut."

She cut the cards, watched him deal, pick up his hand, and scan it with slow deliberation. Each card he drew received the same careful scrutiny. Each discard was calculated. Every move was made with forethought.

"Gin." After drawing no more than half a dozen times, he laid down his hand. Here was a man who didn't intend to lose in a gin game. In anything?

He dealt again. While he was busy with the cards, she reached for the bowl, chose a strawberry, and bit into it. For a moment, she forgot the oppressive heat and her vandalized car and closed her eyes, savoring the fruit. Juice slid over her tongue, ran down her fingers. She finished the berry and licked one finger, then another. Sensing his gaze on her, she glanced up, straight into J.D.'s eyes.

Something simmered there, something dangerous. Her fingers stilled in midair, her gaze locked with his. Tension pulsed between them, waves and waves of it. The heat in the room intensified.

Seconds ticked by. Neither of them moved; neither spoke. Finally, with an effort, she forced herself to look away. "Shall we play another hand?"

"Yeah." He shuffled the cards and dealt. His gaze dropped to her breasts. "Discard." His voice was low, rough.

Her nipples tightened, pushing against her blouse. A flush spread across her cheeks, along her throat, and down to her breasts, where his gaze lingered. Her thoughts muddled, she put down a seven.

He picked it up and rearranged his cards. She watched his hands. Long, lean fingers, callused palms.

He discarded the nine of clubs, took a strawberry, bit it in half and chewed slowly while he studied his hand. Christy stared, fascinated by the movements of his mouth and throat. He glanced up and caught her watching him but said nothing, only smiled lazily in a way that caused heat to zing through her body.

He ate another berry. A drop of juice trickled down his chin. He wiped it with the back of his hand, then discarded.

She looked away, grabbed a card from the deck, and stared at her hand with no idea whether the new one fit. She dropped it on the discard pile.

They continued to play while awareness, as electric as the storm that had brought them together, crackled in the heated room.

Then they both reached for the strawberries at the same time. Their hands brushed. She jerked hers back, empty. "Excuse me."

"Sorry."

Christy discovered that her hand was trembling from that brief contact. Crazy! Silly to quiver like a frightened bird because of the merest brush of fingers. She'd touched his body the night before last, even undressed him. And they'd been far closer when she'd wakened him from his nightmare.

But this was different. This was…different.

Today they were involved in a game, not gin rummy, but a far more ancient male-female pastime: foreplay. And her body was responding. Her breasts strained against her blouse. Her skin grew warmer. Even her breathing was shallow.

Foreplay! The realization shook her to the core. Though they didn't touch or speak, they were engaged in a prelude to lovemaking as surely as if they were in bed together, she and this stranger. She had to put a stop to it.

"Would you like something to drink?" she asked hoarsely.

"Thanks," he said.

She filled two glasses with bottled water, all she had to offer, and squeezed some lemon into each. When she handed J.D. his, she was careful not to touch him. She drank her water, welcoming the liquid as it slid down her suddenly parched throat. She glanced at J.D., found him watching her and quickly looked away.

The candle beside her flickered. Soon it would burn down and they'd be cocooned in darkness. Without light and vision, her other senses would sharpen; she'd smell the bath soap he'd used, hear the cadence of his breathing, the mellow tone of his voice….

Abruptly she rose, hurried to the pantry and got another candle. She lit it, then one more and placed them on the table. "Better," she said.

J.D. didn't answer, and silence stretched between them. She had to break it. "Shall I—?"

"Did you—?" he began at the same time.

"Go ahead," Christy said.

"Did, um, you and your husband come here often?" he asked.

"Not much." Of all the topics J.D. could have come up, this was the best. Nothing would work better than thoughts of Keith to put a damper on her torrid imagination. "Keith was too busy. He's a doctor."

"Did you meet him at work?"

"No, in school," Christy said. "He was in medical school

and I was a nursing student. We'd run into each other occasionally and say hello. And then one day we were in the hospital cafeteria at the same time. He sat down next to me and we talked. After that we had lunch together every day."

His lips quirked. "You fell in love over hospital food?"

"Yeah, BLTs and soggy fish."

"So did you get married right away?"

Christy shook her head. "No, we dated for nearly two years before we got engaged."

"You took a long time."

Christy bit her lip. "Long enough so you'd think we knew everything about each other. Later I found out I didn't know him at all."

"Tell me about your marriage."

His voice was so gentle, his expression so compassionate that Christy couldn't hold back. The words tumbled out.

"We got married when Keith finished medical school. He got his first choice for a residency, Massachusetts General, and I took a job at the same hospital. Our lives were chaotic. One of us always had night duty when the other was on the day shift, but we handled it. At least I thought so. I knew he'd be finished in a couple of years, and then we'd have a more normal life, at least as normal as a doctor can expect."

"And did you?"

"No, Keith decided to do a two-year fellowship at Johns Hopkins. I'd wanted to start a family, but this was too good for him to pass up. So we went to Baltimore." She sighed. "I hardly remember those two years. They're just a blur."

She glanced at him in time to see the pain in his eyes. "Better than nothing," he murmured, then asked, "What happened then?"

"I felt like we were both running in place, never getting enough rest, never spending time together, never making love." She sighed bitterly. "I thought Keith was too tired then. In retrospect, I suppose he was 'otherwise engaged.'"

J.D. said nothing; his eyes spoke for him.

Christy went on, unable to stop. "He finished his fellowship. We moved to Houston. Now, I said, we could start our family. Keith wanted to wait until he'd established his practice, so we did."

"You always did what Keith wanted."

She stared at her hands. "Yes."

"Did you decide to leave him because of that?"

"No, he decided. Last year he finally agreed we should have a baby. We planned to take an island vacation—not San Sebastian, but someplace more romantic—Antigua or Aruba. I was thrilled."

"And?"

"And then he dropped his bombshell. One morning over breakfast, in the same tone he used to ask for more coffee, he told me he wanted a divorce. He'd met someone else." Christy swallowed a sob. "I don't know why I'm telling you this."

J.D. reached across the table and pressed her hand. "You need to talk. How did you feel?"

"Like the world had ended. I couldn't believe what he was saying. I'd always trusted him. I don't know how I could have been so blind. It was the old cliché. I was the only one surprised when Keith asked for a divorce." And she'd spent hours asking herself why it had happened. And what she'd done to cause it.

"Anyway, I gave him what he asked for, just like I gave him everything else. Now we're having our island vacations, but on different islands. I'm here, and Keith's in Aruba…with Betsy."

"Was she a friend of yours?"

"No, I never met her, thank goodness. She's rich, twice divorced, and predatory as a lioness. She wanted a trophy husband. Keith was more than happy to fill that role."

J.D. said gently, "Keith was a bastard. He didn't deserve you."

Christy laughed bitterly. "How do you know? You've only known me a couple of days. Maybe I'm a bitch."

His fingers tightened on hers, then he smiled. "Oh, no. Not a chance."

"Thanks. And thanks for listening. It helped."

J.D. continued to hold her hand, his fingers stroking softly. But Christy longed for more. For something forbidden. His arms around her, his body against hers. But he was shackled to a past he didn't remember. And how could she get involved? If she couldn't trust her own husband, how could she trust a stranger?

And yet, she suddenly realized, she did trust J.D. Knowing nothing about his past, she already had more faith in him than she had had in her husband.

Beside them, the candles flickered. Soon they'd go out.

Silence wrapped around them.

Christy forced herself to break it. "We'd better call it a night. We have a lot to do tomorrow." She was surprised to hear how normal her voice sounded. It didn't feel normal at all. She got up.

"Good night, then," J.D. said and left the room.

Exhausted from the riot of emotions she'd felt today, Christy remained at the table. For a moment, she closed her eyes and savored the peace of being alone. Then she heard the sound of a car driving down the street. Opening her eyes, she saw the glimmer of headlights. She jumped up and rushed to the window in time to see a police car cruising slowly by. Thank heavens.

She returned to the table, gathered up the paper plates and plastic dinnerware they'd used and tossed them in the trash.

They hadn't thought to buy cups. She brought their glasses to the sink and washed them. Her neatness gene wouldn't allow her to leave them overnight.

God, she was tired. She dried her hands and shuffled down the hall. She slowed as she came to J.D.'s room. The door was open and she glanced inside.

He stood at the window, forehead against the pane, staring out into the darkness. One hand grasped the windowsill; the other lay, palm open, against the glass. What was he thinking? What emotions did he feel? Desperation? Loneliness? What did he need?

He'd given her so much tonight. He'd listened to feelings she'd never confessed, even to her family. Listened with kindness and compassion. What could she give back?

Without another thought, she stepped across the threshold and went to his side.

Chapter 7

"J.D.," Christy murmured, "you need to rest."

His gaze fixed on the darkened street, he shook his head.

"Dr. Mayes said not to force the memories," she said gently. "Maybe you'll dream something—"

"I do dream," he said. "The memories start to come, but they fade away. I can't quite grasp them." His hand fisted.

Christy put her hand on his arm. His muscles were so tense. She knew he was hurting, and she longed to reassure him, to hold him, but that was a threshold she *couldn't* cross.

So she tried to let him know through her touch that she understood. As much as a person with a lifetime of memories could understand someone whose past had been erased in a heartbeat.

As if he read her thoughts, he spoke. "Do you have any idea what this is like? I know how a car works but not what kind of car I drive. I know how to replace the shingles on your house but not what kind of house I live in, or even if I have a house…" His voice trailed off.

"You'll remember," Christy said.

"How?" he asked harshly.

"Maybe tomorrow we should walk back to the place where you woke up and see if that helps. We might see something you left there."

"Anything I left was probably washed away."

"It can't hurt to try," she said. He shook his head but she went on. "You have nothing to lose."

He sighed. "Okay, we'll give it a shot."

She could tell he was humoring her, that he had no confidence her suggestion would work.

He said nothing more, and they stood together, watching the night. Only the sound of J.D.'s breathing broke the silence. After a time, he seemed to forget Christy, seemed lost in his own thoughts. No, just…lost.

She touched him again. "J.D., let me help you."

He pivoted to face her. "How?" His voice was rough, anguished. He caught her shoulders, pulled her closer. "The way we both want?"

"No! No, I can't." She stopped him with her hands on his chest. "*We* can't. You know that. You said so."

"Yeah." His hands fell to his sides and he turned away. "Sorry," he muttered. "Mistake."

"Me, too." She backed away, wishing she could say something to ease the tension between them, but not knowing what. "Get some sleep," she managed. That seemed inadequate, but it was the best she could do.

"Sure."

At the door she turned and saw that he'd walked over to sit on the bed. Maybe he would try to relax.

Their eyes met for a long moment, and then she went

down the hall to her room. Tonight she didn't bother to barricade the door. She had more to fear from herself than from J.D.

After a restless night, J.D. woke early and found the house quiet. He glanced at the clothes he'd tossed over the back of a chair and smiled wryly. Not much choice of attire. He shrugged into his too-familiar jeans, left his shirt unbuttoned, and tiptoed down the hall so he wouldn't wake Christy. She'd probably lain awake much of the night, just as he had. Damn, he hated having gotten her into this.

He looked out the living-room window, scanning the field across the street. It was empty, so he opened the front door and stepped outside. A brisk Gulf breeze made the air feel like fall instead of late summer. The water in Christy's front yard had drained off, but the grass was coated with a thick layer of mud. For the first time since he'd been here, the sky was clear.

The morning was beautiful, the kind of day that should make a man glad to be alive. He realized he hadn't thought how lucky he was until this moment. He could see and hear, walk and talk. Whatever had happened to him, he'd been given a precious gift, the gift of life. He took a deep breath of salt-tinged air and smiled.

A newspaper lay near the walk. Hallelujah! The paper's publisher must have an emergency generator. Hoping some article would jog his memory, he retrieved the paper. The *San Sebastian Breeze* was a small-town paper, but maybe a headline, a photo, even a letter to the editor would be the key that would open his past. Before he was back inside, he unrolled the paper and perused it eagerly.

Tropical Storm Coral and her aftermath consumed the entire front page. He found a story about the woman who'd been reported kidnapped but nothing about a man who'd disappeared. He guessed he didn't live on the island or *someone* would have called in a missing persons report on him. Surely someone had, he thought, but where? How did you find your home when you had no recollection of it?

He sat on the living-room couch and opened the paper. Inside he saw a few articles about local events: a firefighters' picnic, a meeting of the Rotary Club, the fiftieth anniversary of the hardware store he and Christy had visited yesterday.

Next, the sports page, dominated by scores of major league baseball games. He murmured the names of teams. Was he a fan? He studied the rosters but none of the players' names rang a bell.

Page four contained an editorial about proposed changes in the parking regulations on Main Street along with several letters to the editor. Nothing that spoke to him, in fact, nothing that even interested him.

He noticed an ad for fishing equipment. He glanced at it, wondering why it appealed to him. Was he a fisherman? Was that why he'd come to San Sebastian? Somehow, he didn't think so.

He saved the ad and put the rest of the paper aside. Then he went into the kitchen. He was leaning against the counter, sipping orange juice, when Christy wandered in, rubbing her eyes.

Her hair was appealingly tousled. Her feet were bare; so were her legs. This was the first time he'd seen her in shorts. He took a gulp of juice and wondered if she had any idea of the way her legs affected a man. Apparently not. But he felt pretty sure the evidence was becoming visible, so he quickly sat down at the table.

Christy yawned as she opened a can of pineapple juice.

"Did you sleep?" they both asked at the same time.

J.D. chuckled. "Tried."

"Me, too."

He was glad she refrained from asking if he remembered anything.

"Want to walk down to the beach after breakfast?" Christy asked.

He shrugged. "Might as well."

"We'll take the gun," she said and went to get it.

Then she insisted on straightening the kitchen before they left. J.D. would have settled for dumping the paper plates in the trash, but she had to wipe off the table and counters and rinse out the juice cans. "You must be a great nurse," J.D. said, watching her. "I bet you zap every germ in sight."

"I do." She laughed as she tossed the last paper towel in the trash. "I guess I picked up neatness from my mother. If my brother and I didn't keep our rooms straight, we got grounded. I remember almost missing a birthday party because of a dirty sock."

"Almost?" He opened the door.

"I convinced Mom I dropped it on the way to the hamper." When he raised a brow, she defended herself as she went outside. "There was just one sock on the floor so that made sense to her. Besides, it was the truth."

They strolled the few blocks to the beach as if this were an ordinary outing on a bright summer morning. But as they approached the spot J.D. pointed out, his mood became somber.

The sand was littered with seaweed and bits of driftwood that had washed in during the storm. Broken seashells lay like sad mementos of the surging tide. But other than that, the long expanse of beach seemed undisturbed.

J.D. stared at the Gulf. Two nights ago it had been a raging beast, close to swallowing him alive. Now the water was calm, broken only by whitecaps dancing over its surface.

He waited for a revelation, but nothing came. Neither the beach nor the road gave him the slightest hint about how he'd gotten here. Despair clutched at him. His mind was as empty as ever.

"We should search the area," Christy said.

She was right, but he had little hope of finding anything. They began looking, moving in concentric circles. J.D. bent every now and then to peer closely at the sand or to scoop up a handful and let it run through his fingers. It told him nothing. It was just sand.

Buried under a pile of sand, he found a beer can. It wasn't rusted, so he surmised it hadn't been there long. He picked it up, turned it around. Had he been drinking and driven off the road?

He shut his eyes and imagined himself at a bar. What would he ask for? He conjured up a bartender, had him ask, "What'll you have?" The first thing that came into J.D.'s mind was Scotch.

Okay, maybe he wasn't a beer drinker, or maybe his imagined scene didn't mean a thing. He hurled the can down the beach.

"Are you okay?" Christy said, frowning at him.

He'd almost forgotten she was here. "Fine," he said.

"Look, there's a piece of metal over by the rocks," she said, pointing. "Maybe it's from your car."

And if it was, would he recognize it? More to placate Christy than anything else, he started for the rocks. She tagged along beside him.

He picked up the mangled piece of chrome. Could be from a bumper. Any bumper. From *his?* No way to tell. Archaeologists constructed whole civilizations from shards of clay. That sure as hell wasn't his field because this metal object told him nothing. He tossed it, watched it hit the rock and bounce off into the sand.

"I guess this was a bad idea," Christy said. "There's nothing here."

"Yeah," J.D. mused, "which makes me think I'm right. I

didn't have a wreck. Someone drove me here or drove my car away."

"Could you have crashed somewhere else and walked here, then passed out?" Christy asked.

"Maybe, but that doesn't match with someone messing with your car."

"Couldn't that be a coincidence?"

He shook his head. "Fits too well with my scenario. Someone didn't want me getting help or reporting what happened to the police." He turned his back on the surf. "Let's check along the road. We have a better chance of finding something there."

"What?"

"Something I dropped, provided I recognize it." Which wasn't likely. He started up the rise, remembering how difficult the same walk had been the other night. At the side of the road, he began another slow survey.

Christy walked beside him. "There's a cigarette pack," she remarked, "but you don't smoke."

He glanced at her. "Oh?"

"No, if you did, you'd miss it too much by now. In fact, you'd be a raving maniac."

"You're right," J.D. agreed.

Christy grinned at him. "See, I'm picking up your skills." When he smiled back, she added, "I also know that earring over there isn't yours." She picked it up and held it up to his lobe. "No holes."

"Right again, Miss Marple," he said, then sobered. "How did I know to call you that?"

"Everybody knows Miss Marple. It's world knowledge, not personal information," Christy said.

J.D. refrained from kicking a rock in his path. "Yeah, I'm a walking encyclopedia. Britannica Man."

He turned slowly, taking one more look around. From

what could be seen now, no one passing by would guess the drama that had played out on the beach the other night. He supposed whoever had dumped him there had counted on that. "Let's go back," he said. "I'll get some work done on the house."

As they started along the road, the sound of a car behind them, coming fast, alerted J.D. He grabbed Christy's hand and pulled her away from the road. They stumbled down the hillock to the beach and waited. Her pulse thudded under his hand, his own echoed it.

The car drove past without slowing. He stared after it. Inside were a boy and girl, two teenagers out for a joyride. Nothing sinister after all.

As the car disappeared, something flashed in J.D.'s mind. Fear? Recognition? No, a sense of being confined. Dark all around him. His lungs crying for air. Then nothing. The spark of memory died.

"Are you all right?" Christy asked. "You're dead-white. Did you remember something?"

"Only a feeling. Claustrophobia."

"From the sound of a car?"

"Yeah, makes no sense," he said, then added, "Ready to go?" She nodded, and he took her hand to help her up the steep rise to the road. He didn't want to let go, and she didn't ask him to, so he kept her hand in his all the way home.

Christy busied herself inside while J.D. worked on the exterior of the house. She could hear him hammering. Such an everyday sound, she thought. She almost felt as if this cottage was becoming *theirs*. Not a good idea.

Midway through the morning Billy Coates showed up to repair her car. In the garage, he peered under the hood, then turned to her. "How'd this happen?" he asked in a puzzled voice.

"Beats me," Christy said. "I drove it the morning before the flood. Somebody must've gotten into the garage later that day."

"Did you report it?" he asked. She nodded, and he said, "Probably won't do any good."

Exactly what she thought.

Billy connected a new distributor wire in minutes, she paid him and he was on his way.

Christy went back inside, cleaned the spoiled food out of the fridge, and opened cans for lunch, then went back out to call J.D. He was up on the ladder, his shirt off, his bronzed skin shiny with sweat, his muscles bunching as he pounded a board into place. He was, she thought, a mouth-watering sight. He looked like an ad for tools. The kind of ad that would make a man want to grab a hammer and build. The kind of ad that would make a woman want to grab *him*.

She swallowed. "Lunch is ready."

"Coming." He backed down the ladder, wiped his hands on a rag and came toward her.

"We have tuna and iced tea. I found some cans in the pantry."

His eyes brightened as he came inside. "Iced tea? Is the electricity back on?"

She shook her head. "You'll have to imagine the ice."

J.D. chuckled as he scrubbed his hands with bottled water. When he sat at the table, he poked the tuna with his fork. "And this must be a thick, juicy steak." He tapped the empty spot on his plate. "Mmm, and these look like great baked potatoes."

"In our dreams," Christy said.

He took a bite. "Want to look over what I've done after lunch?"

"Sure," she said.

When they finished and Christy had left the kitchen spick-and-span, they went outside. They circled to the back of the house and J.D. explained what he'd done. "I've replaced most of the shingles that blew off, repaired some of the boards that came loose and cleaned up the branches in the yard." He led her around the front and pointed to one of the windows. "I've put the shutter back in place, but it's old, so it's deteriorated. Your folks may want to buy new sh—"

A loud crack drowned out his voice.

Christy turned, but J.D. slammed against her and knocked her to the ground. "What—" she gasped.

"Rifle. Stay down."

Another shot rang out, then another.

J.D. shielded her. She smelled mud and grass, felt the heavy weight of J.D.'s body over hers, and knew what terror was.

J.D. rolled off her and motioned to the side of the house. "Get behind the bushes. Go."

Panicked, she began to crawl. "Keep down," he whispered, and she flattened herself on the grass and moved snakelike toward the oleanders.

She glanced back and saw J.D. rising to an elbow. "What are you doing?" she whispered.

"Trying to distract him—"

"No!" She scrambled back toward him and grabbed his arm. "Don't sit up."

He shoved her hand away. "I have to—"

The sound of rock music made them both turn. A van filled with teenagers sloshed down the street.

"He won't shoot now," J.D. muttered. "Let's go." He grabbed her arm and they flew up the porch steps and into the house.

Christy collapsed on the couch. J.D. peered cautiously between the window blinds. "Can you see him?" she asked.

"Uh-uh."

With J.D. hidden behind the blinds and Christy sprawled

on the couch still gasping for breath, they waited. Nothing happened.

J.D. sat down beside her. Gently, he wiped mud off her cheek with his finger. "You okay?"

"For now," she said, but she wasn't. She was scared to death.

"Need anything?" he asked. "Water? An aspirin?"

Christy shook her head and swallowed tears that threatened to overflow. What she needed was human contact. She wanted J.D. to hold her, wanted it so much she ached, but she couldn't find the words to ask him.

She straightened, glanced at the closed blinds. "Will he come back?"

"Good chance."

She shivered, and he said, "No point in lying to you. Let's try the phone. Maybe the lines are repaired and we can get hold of the sheriff."

No such luck.

"What do we do?"

J.D. went to the door and turned the dead bolt. "Stay inside for now. Hope the phone is working by tonight."

"And if it isn't?"

"I'll keep watch."

Christy nodded, then got up and went to her room. She returned, carrying her gun. "You'll need this," she said and handed it to J.D.

Chapter 8

J.D. stared at Christy. He needed a weapon, but he hadn't expected the woman who'd stayed up all night with a gun pointed at him to suddenly put one in his hands. He felt a lump rise in his throat. "You're—you're giving me your gun?"

"You saved my life," she said softly. "You could have been shot."

Their eyes met. Messages passed between them, words he couldn't say, might never be able to say. Words like, *I'd do anything to keep you safe. Put myself in harm's way without a second thought.* He settled for, "You saved mine the other night."

"I guess we're even then." She gave him the sweetest smile.

"Yeah." He turned the shiny new revolver over in his hand. "Is it loaded?"

"Um, actually, no."

God, had he fallen for that old trick? "Were you pointing an *unloaded* revolver at me the other night?"

"Oh, no. It was loaded then. I, uh, took the bullets out after we came back from the beach."

He laughed and the tension in the room evaporated. "Guns usually work better with bullets."

She reddened all the way from her forehead down to her neck. "I'll, uh, get the—the ammunition." She scurried out of the room and returned in a moment with a pouch of ammunition. Quickly he put the bullets into the chamber.

Christy frowned as she watched him. "You do that like you've done it a thousand times."

He glanced down at his hands. "Maybe I'm an arms dealer. People like that get into trouble. It could explain why someone's after me."

Christy shook her head. "You said 'people like that.' I don't think you'd use those words if you were one of them."

"Maybe I'm not proud of my profession."

"Don't be ridiculous. You wouldn't make a living at something you weren't proud of."

He smiled at her. "You have a lot of faith in me."

"If I didn't, I wouldn't have given you the gun."

He laid the revolver on the table beside the couch. "Why'd you buy it? You're clearly not comfortable with it."

"For safety. Sometimes I work late, and the Medical Center in Houston is a big place. I have to walk a long way to get to my car."

He eyed her thoughtfully. "I asked you once where you worked and you wouldn't tell me."

She looked surprised. "I guess things are different now."

"Yeah," he agreed, then asked, "The other day, would you have shot me?"

Christy stared down at her hands. After a moment, she raised her eyes. "I don't know."

He gave her a hard look. "Don't threaten someone with a gun if you're not sure you'll use it."

"I—"

"If you hesitate for even an instant, whoever you're aiming at will disarm you in seconds."

"*You* didn't."

"I must be one of the good guys, then. I could have."

Christy shuddered. "J.D., you're giving me the creeps."

"I mean to." When he saw her hand tremble, he said, "After this is over, I'll take you out to a firing range and teach you about guns."

"I already took a course," she protested.

"Yeah, but you need to gain confidence."

"And you can help me do that?"

"Sure."

She grinned. "Then it's a date."

God, what in hell had caused him to make that offer? He needed to get out of her life, not prolong their…association, or whatever they had. Not that coaching her in gun safety was a date, but it suggested they'd continue to see one another.

She seemed to sense his discomfort and said gravely, "I won't hold you to it."

"Don't," he said. "I don't know what kind of complications I have in my life."

"And you don't want to add more complications."

"I didn't mean— Ah, hell," he said. "I don't know what I meant."

She smiled, but her eyes were serious. "I'm sort of flattered that you consider me a complication. But don't worry. I don't consider a lesson in self-esteem for carriers of concealed weapons a lifelong commitment."

"Good," he said soberly, "because I need to take things one day at a time."

"Me, too," Christy said. "Now, since we're stuck inside, why don't we finish putting the rest of the things in the living room back in place?"

"Good plan." It would keep their minds off whatever danger lurked outside.

That night J.D. sat in the darkened living room. Holding the gun, he waited. He was certain whoever had shot at them wouldn't give up. He'd come again, and this time he'd come closer.

One thing J.D. was pretty sure about: the culprit didn't know J.D. was armed. He'd cleaned out J.D.'s pockets the other night so if J.D.'d had a gun, the man had disposed of it. And he had no reason to assume Christy owned one.

So J.D. figured he was one-up on the bad guy.

He walked into the kitchen and peered out the back door. As he'd done each time he made the rounds of the house, he checked the lock. He went from room to room, checking the windows, looking out. He skipped Christy's room. Although she'd protested, he'd insisted she get some sleep. And she'd had enough of a scare this afternoon without his awakening her in the middle of the night. He surveyed the backyard from the bathroom window next to her room, and he was satisfied all was well. For now anyway.

As he passed Christy's door on his way back to the living room, he slowed, allowed himself a quick glance inside. She was curled up on one side of the double bed. Her cheek rested on one hand. Because of the heat, she wasn't covered. Thank God it was plenty dark so he couldn't see what she wore, or didn't.

Being a gentleman was tough when you were alone in a house with a woman you desired, but he guessed he was a gentleman because he'd kept his distance. So far. To be sure that didn't change, he tiptoed on down the hall.

Back in the living room, he cracked the window a couple of inches, bent down and listened. In the distance he heard the steady sound of the Gulf. A vehicle turned onto the street, kept going. He stood and moved the blinds apart just enough to watch the car's taillights disappear into the moonless night.

He closed the window, sat on the couch and wiped sweat from his brow. After the hot, sunny day the house was stifling. And pitch-black.

Darkness surrounded him, pressed against him. He took a breath, but his lungs didn't seem to fill. Another breath and still he couldn't get enough air. Funny, when he walked around, he didn't have this sensation of suffocating. As soon as he sat down, he felt as if someone had put a hood over his head and was slowly, systematically draining the oxygen from his body.

He gasped, stood and stumbled against the coffee table as he lurched across the room. He opened the window, wider this time, and dragged in a breath of still, humid air. After a few minutes, he shut the window, then pulled a chair next to it and sat.

Here, he felt somewhat better, but the anxiety he'd experienced at the beach this morning still lurked on the edges of his mind. His buddy out there must have locked him up someplace. Where? More importantly, why?

Would he and his nemesis meet face to face? He hoped so. Then he'd know.

The minutes ticked by, turned into hours, and still no one came. J.D. made his rounds and returned to the living room once again. Alert to every passing sound, he waited.

Waiting was tough when you had no memories to keep you company. He felt as if he were suspended in some eerie third dimension. Once in a while, a thought flitted by, achingly close, but he could no more capture it than he could a moonbeam.

His eyelids drooped, his head dropped forward, and he

jolted. Straightening, he forced himself to remain vigilant, but he'd had so little sleep these past nights. Eventually, his eyes closed, and this time he didn't wake up.

And then, a rattling sound.

The front door. Instantly alert, he was on his feet, gun at the ready.

The doorknob twisted slowly, slowly. J.D. edged toward the door.

Suddenly Christy appeared from the hall. She pointed to the door. "I heard something," she whispered.

J.D. put his finger to his lips. He motioned her to go back. A stubborn glint in her eye, she shook her head. J.D. scowled. "Then get behind me," he mouthed, and she did, standing still as a statue.

He inched toward the door, aware of Christy following close behind. Then he heard a sound. Was that a footstep? The knob jiggled but this time it didn't turn.

Cautiously, J.D. reached up and unlocked the dead bolt. Then quietly, holding his breath, he turned the doorknob.

Now! He yanked the door open.

And found himself looking into the soulful brown eyes of a German shepherd. "For Pete's sake," J.D. muttered. "A goddamn dog."

"A dog," Christy echoed and began to laugh. She laughed until she collapsed on the couch.

Hysterical or on the verge of it, J.D. thought. "Hush," he ordered. "The dog didn't rattle the door the first time. He followed someone here."

The animal had turned to face the bushes, ears pointed forward, tail aloft. It growled deep in its throat.

J.D. leaned around the door and fired a shot over the shrubbery, then another.

A tall, broad-shouldered figure burst out of the bushes, tore across the yard and into the field with the dog barking at his heels.

"Did you hit him?" Christy whispered.

"No, he's gone," J.D. muttered, "and dammit, I didn't get a look at his face." He slammed the door, locked it and turned to Christy.

She'd gotten up and now she stood in the middle of the room, her eyes wide. She'd quit laughing. Instead, she was white as chalk and trembling.

J.D. set the revolver on the coffee table and stepped toward her. "It's over," he said. "He ran off."

"I know. I'm still scared." She covered her face with her hands. "More than when he shot at us. I—I don't know why."

Why didn't matter, not now. He could no more stop himself than still his heartbeat. He went to her, put his arms around her, and pulled her close. She still trembled, and he felt her tears against his throat. Rubbing her back gently, he tried to soothe her with words. "Sure you're scared. It's okay, baby. You'll feel better. Just take a deep breath, give it a few minutes."

Inane words. Not enough for her. For him either.

Emotions warred inside him. Longing and guilt. Protectiveness and desire.

The scent of her hair, the softness of her breath against his cheek, the warmth of her body overpowered him. In these few days, she'd become the center of his world, the only thing he wanted, needed.

Her breasts pressed against his chest, her arms circled his neck. Do the right thing, he ordered himself. The right thing was to let her go. He knew it, but—

"Oh, hell," he muttered. She needed more than sympathetic words, and dammit, so did he.

His lips hovering an inch from hers, he whispered, "I want to kiss you. You know that, don't you?"

Christy lifted her head and looked into his eyes. "Yes."

She felt his warm breath against her cheek. Being in his arms was so safe, so right. She began to tremble again, not from fear now but from desire. "I want you to kiss me. More than anything. No matter what."

That was all he needed, all they both needed. Within a heartbeat he'd pulled her closer and then his lips covered hers.

He took her mouth with the skill of a man used to kissing, with the tenderness of a man who'd discovered something precious. "Christy," he murmured. "Sweet Christy." His lips left hers and traced her cheekbone, her ear.

Christy sighed and touched his cheek, caressing the rough stubble. He returned to her mouth, and she reveled in the firmness of his lips, the taste of him. Deep and earthy and thrilling. He kissed her harder now. His tongue swept across her lips, probed every corner of her mouth. Hers met it, luring it deeper into her mouth with a primal thrusting rhythm as close to lovemaking as they could get. Maybe he belonged to someone else, but tonight he was hers. Not just his mouth, but more. For these few moments, she knew he belonged only to her, heart and soul.

All the pent-up hunger and longing she hadn't even realized she had for him exploded. She pressed closer, feeling his erection against her belly, his heart pounding against her chest. He ran his hands through her hair, along her cheekbones and across her shoulders.

And then he touched her breast.

As if she'd received an electric shock, she jolted. With a cry, she pressed herself against his hand. *Take more,* her heart cried out. *Take everything.*

Something slapped against the door.

Christy gasped. They broke apart, and J.D. grabbed the gun. "Stay back," he warned and strode across the room.

Christy tried to catch her breath as she watched him part

the blinds a fraction of an inch and look outside. She waited, watched until she saw his shoulders relax.

"Your morning paper," he said. "Look, it's nearly day-break."

Christy realized for the first time that the darkness in the room had subsided. J.D. opened the blinds to a gray pre-dawn world. They stood silently, then looked at each other.

Both of them were tousled, their clothing in disarray. Christy glanced down, saw her breast, barely covered by the thin camisole she'd worn to bed, and hastily straightened her clothes.

"Close call," J.D. murmured, and Christy knew he didn't just mean the prowler. "We almost—"

"I know." She studied her bare feet, then said ruefully, "We can't let this happen again." She'd been crazy to let him kiss her that way. They'd both been insane. Oh, it had been wonderful, but she knew what they'd done was wrong. "We *won't* let it happen," she said more forcefully, swallowing regret and longing.

"Right." He moved toward the door. "I'll get the paper." His voice wasn't quite back to normal.

"No, don't go out," Christy said. "Please."

"All right." He put the gun down again. "Why don't you grab some more shut-eye?"

"Okay," she said. As if she could, with the taste of him still on her tongue, with her cheeks tender from the scrape of his beard. With her arms too empty now.

But she padded back to her bedroom and lay down. As soon as her head hit the pillow, she realized she was exhausted. Too much terror, too much…excitement. Her eyes closed, and within seconds, she was asleep.

The black sedan braked in the parking lot of an all-night café, drawn to its bright lights in an otherwise dark world. He needed a beer. Hell, he needed something a lot stronger than that, the man thought.

He'd been so close, and then the damn mutt had ruined everything. Even tried to take a chunk out of him as he'd raced away. He'd kicked the beast and it had slunk off. Lucky for the goddamned dog he hadn't shot it.

His mind returned to his quarry. "Damn that bastard again," he snarled. Who would've thought he'd gotten hold of a gun? Must've gotten it from the woman. Charmed her into giving him her revolver. Yeah, the bastard was a charmer. Probably was getting it on with the woman. *That's* why he'd holed up with her during the storm. Sooner or later though he'd have to come out.

Trouble was, *he* couldn't wait around. The other night, just before the phones went out, he'd been quick-witted enough to call in to work and say he had a "family emergency" and needed a couple of days' personal time. He never took time off, so when he asked, he got an immediate yes. Paid to be such a committed worker. "A good little soldier," he muttered to himself. Just like his mother had told him when he was small, before she'd taken off for parts unknown.

But his personal time was nearly up. He needed to be back at work soon or they'd start asking questions.

He got out of the car, heard the low hum of the emergency generator, slammed the door, and went into the café. He'd have his beer, maybe two, then he'd drive to the causeway bridge. If it was open, he'd be on his way, get back in plenty of time with no one the wiser. If the bridge was still closed, he'd swipe a boat and sail across to the mainland, take a bus the rest of the way home. He'd wait until morning for that, he decided. A boat heading for the mainland in the middle of the night might arouse suspicion.

And as for his buddy and the broad back there, they hadn't seen the last of him. Next time he came he'd make sure he erased them both. *Erase,* he thought as he settled himself on a stool at the cafe's deserted counter. He liked that. It'd make a good alias. Maybe after he finished with the two of them, he'd leave a note for the cops to find, sign it The Eraser. Yeah, he decided as the pretty waitress sashayed over to take his order. That was cool.

"What can I getcha, Big Boy?" the waitress said, fluttering her lashes.

"Bud Lite." He smiled at the waitress. Little lady didn't have a clue who she was talking to. Maybe someday he'd come back here and tell her. He glanced at her curly auburn hair. Maybe he'd even show her.

Chapter 9

The next morning J.D. watched as Christy picked at her bowl of dry cereal. The couple hours of sleep hadn't been enough for her; she still looked exhausted.

His fault. If he hadn't barged into her life, she'd have been enjoying a lazy summer day at the beach. Sure, her house would have needed some repair work after the storm, but she wouldn't have landed smack in the middle of Hell. "I want to talk to you," he said.

She looked up. "All right."

"The paper says—"

"You went out and got it?" She looked horrified.

"I waited until the sun came up and the guy was gone."

She glanced at the window. "He could have been hiding."

"But he wasn't," J.D. pointed out. "Anyway, the paper said the causeway will be open late today or tomorrow morning. As soon as it does, I want you out of here."

"*You* want *me* out of here. Out of *my* house?" She went still and her eyes narrowed. Her voice was razor-sharp. "Since when do you make the rules?"

"Since I showed up here and got you shot at. Dammit!" His voice rose. "This has nothing to do with one-upmanship or male chauvinism or whatever is going through that red head of yours."

He stood and leaned across the table so his face was inches from hers. "*He*—that guy out there, the one with the rifle—makes the rules. Not me. Not you. I don't want you getting hurt because he's out to get me." His voice cracked, and he dropped back onto his chair. "I couldn't live with it." He didn't even try to hide his pain. The hell with that. Let her see how he felt.

Her eyes were wide, shocked. "All right," she said, her voice calmer now, "you want me to leave. I guess I can spend the rest of my vacation in Houston. What about you?"

"Don't worry. I'll find a place. I'll sleep on the beach or in the park if I have to."

"Oh, that'll be great. And are you going to wear a sign that says 'shoot me'?"

"I said I'll find a place. It's midweek after a storm. The motels can't be too full. Besides," he said with a half smile, "you *are* paying me for the repair work, aren't you?"

"Of course. I'll give you a check…"

"Better make it cash."

She looked puzzled. "Why? Oh…"

"Yeah, no ID."

"I'll cash a check, then," Christy said.

"Good. And then you'll leave," he said firmly.

Christy took a deep breath. "You could come with me."

"And camp in your living room until I get my memory back? Might be years. Might be never. Look," he said, "this is where everything started. Here's where I lost my memory. My best chance of finding it is here, too."

Christy swallowed, looked down at her hands. "When you do, will you let me know?"

"Sure," he answered softly. And if he could, if he was somebody she wouldn't be ashamed to know, he'd come to her. He hoped to God he was free of any entanglements that would keep him from doing that.

"Thanks," she said, "and by the way, don't call me a redhead. My hair's auburn."

"I stand corrected. But you've got a redhead's temper."

She stuck her nose in the air. "I don't have a temper."

"Really? You could have fooled me. What about the glare you just gave me?"

"You pushed the wrong button," she said, fiddling with the ends of her hair. "You reminded me of Keith."

Ah, now he understood. "Sorry."

"It's okay."

It probably wasn't really okay, but at least he'd resolved the main issue. Now that she'd agreed to leave, he wondered if he could get her out of here today. To do that, he'd need to check the bridge, see if it had opened earlier than expected. He could use her car, but no way would he leave her here alone. He'd have to take her with him. He wasn't thrilled with that idea either but he figured they'd have to take a chance on going outside.

He glanced at Christy. Her cheek rested on her hand and she stared into space. She looked miserable. Damn, if she stayed here much longer, she might make herself sick. That decided it. "Now that your car is fixed, how about we drive into town and report the incident last night to the sheriff?"

"Why?" she asked.

"The authorities needed to know what happened."

Christy paused in the midst of shoveling cereal from one side of her bowl to the other. "Um, okay," she said doubtfully. She got up and emptied her half-eaten breakfast into the trash.

He followed.

As she stepped back and he moved forward, their bodies brushed. Immediately, his responded.

"'Scuse me," Christy muttered, reddening.

"Sorry."

As Christy scooted away and busied herself with the dishes, J.D. thought, yeah, he was sorry for a lot of things but not for last night. Those few minutes he'd held her had been the best of his new life, maybe of his old life, too. Not that they'd be repeated, but at least he'd have a memory. No one knew better than he how precious memories were.

By now he knew Christy wanted every dish washed and put in the cabinet. But he waited until she moved well out of his way before taking his place at the sink. He didn't want to risk touching her again. Amnesia or not, he was a healthy male, and that pre-dawn kiss had programmed his body to respond instantly to her. A whiff of the flower-fresh perfume she wore, a brush of her fingertips and he'd be ready to take her to bed.

Damn, he had to stop thinking about how much he wanted her and get her away from here. Away from him.

He folded the dish towel and hung it on a hook under the sink. "Ready to go?"

Christy hesitated. "Maybe we shouldn't go outside."

"It's broad daylight."

"He shot at us yesterday in broad daylight. I—I don't want to go."

"I'll be with you. We'll be careful. It'll be all right."

He led her out of the kitchen and through the living room. "I'll go first," he said and opened the front door.

One glance outside, and he slammed it shut.

"What's wrong?" Christy grabbed his arm. "Is he back?"

"Um, no. Just some trash by the door. Go back in the kitchen. I'll take care of it."

"What is it?" She let go of his hand and before he could stop her, she peered out the window. "Oh, my God." Eyes wide, hand over her mouth, she stared at J.D.

Damn, he hadn't meant for her to see the dead snake parked by the door.

He caught her arm, afraid she'd topple over. "I said I'd take care of it. Go sit down. Put your head between your knees."

"I'm not going to faint. I've seen worse than that in the E.R.," she said, pushing her hair back in a gesture he sensed was defiant. "I'm scared, that's all." She walked over and flipped the light switch as if willing the electricity to be on and the nightmare to end. "That snake didn't drown. It was clubbed. He came back and put it here, didn't he?"

J.D. nodded. "Some time after I got the newspaper."

"Thank heaven for that. He could have taken another shot at you."

"Yeah," J.D. muttered. *And this time he might have gotten lucky.* Keeping his tone as bland as he could, he said, "I'll get rid of the snake. You go…make the beds or something."

She nodded. "Okay."

When he'd finished, he went to find her. She was in the kitchen. She'd found the newspaper he'd brought in earlier and was reading it.

"If we're not going outside, I may as well make myself useful," he told her. "What do you need done in the house?"

"One of the legs on the coffee table is wobbly. Think you could fix it?"

"Sure."

Christy watched him disappear into the living room. Soon he'd disappear from her life. When he found himself, would he call to let her know or just dash off an e-mail? Or, despite his promise just now, would he not give her another thought?

The day stretched before her. She needed to fill her time with something that would keep her mind off the dangerous man outside and the man inside, who was dangerous in a completely different way.

She went to the utility room and got out a package of shelf

paper. Soon she was engrossed in removing dishes from the kitchen cabinets, putting down fresh paper, and setting the dishes back on the shelves. Mindless work like this usually helped her relax. And heaven knew, she needed something to calm her jumpy nerves.

She picked up an old sugar bowl with a chipped handle. Steve had broken it washing the dishes, and her father had glued part of the handle back on. And here was her old plastic cup decorated with a grinning red lobster, a treasure she'd bought at age ten in one of the schlocky souvenir shops along the beach. Christy smiled at the memory, then wondered what J.D. thought about while he was working.

"Hey."

She jumped. Then she turned to find J.D. leaning against the kitchen door, watching her. "You scared me," she accused. "I thought it was… Never mind. What're you doing in here?"

"Waiting for my next job order. Table's fixed."

"Maybe you could, um, wash the windows."

"Consider it done." He grinned at her, and her breath caught.

He looked so—so male standing there. His cheeks were dark with the beginnings of a beard; his teeth were white against the bronze of his face. A face that belonged on the cover of a steamy novel. She wanted to make love with him, to feel his weight pressing her down on the bed. Why had Fate sent him into her life only to steal him away?

Was it really better to have loved and lost than never to have loved at all? Not that this was love exactly. Her friend and fellow nurse Kim would agree and say, "After one kiss? Of course it couldn't be love. It's lust." So she was falling in lust. While lust was an okay thing, Christy knew the kiss wasn't the only reason for her attraction to J.D.

The man himself—his smile, the humor that slipped out

every now and then, the strength and courage in the face of his tragedy—those were what had her nearly melting at his feet.

"You look like you're melting," J.D. said and she jumped. Had she spoken her thoughts aloud? Then she realized he was talking about the heat.

"It is hot," she agreed, swiping a hand at her hair. She got down from the chair she'd been standing on. "I'll get you the window cleaner."

She had to pass close by him to get to the cabinet that held the cleaning supplies. But she was careful to avoid body contact. Only eye contact was allowed. And even that was too much, she thought as she met his dark gaze.

As the day wore on, no matter how cautious they were with one another, the tension between them built and grew higher until she was sure one of them would explode.

Heat, worry and inactivity preyed on her nerves. Once she had no more tasks to give him, J.D. prowled the house. Back and forth to the window or the door, the gun tucked in the waistband of his jeans.

"Do you think he's lurking around?" Christy asked, her mind filled with visions of the hideous snake.

"I hope not, but if he is, I'm ready."

Despite his attempt at reassurance, Christy grew edgier as the hours passed. She felt like a prisoner trapped in these too-close quarters. Every sound from outside accelerated her anxiety. Would the prowler come back and break in? Try to smoke them out some way? When J.D. dropped a book in the living room, she jumped. When she heard a car engine revving down the street, she dropped a can of tomato sauce on her toe. "Ow, dammit," she muttered.

Not only was she frightened that the man would come back, but the sexual tension between her and J.D. was unbearable. Every accidental touch, every covert glance fueled the flames. When would this end?

She needed a break from cleaning so she decided to search for J.D. Maybe they could have a conversation. About what? Movies, she decided. He remembered movies.

At the living-room door she stopped. He was on the floor doing push-ups. Fascinated, she watched him do one after another. Sweat dripped off his shoulders; his biceps bunched as he lifted himself. God, he was in wonderful shape. He wasn't even breathing hard. His lips moved. He was counting.

"Made it to a hundred?" Christy asked.

He stopped. "Eighty-three. I didn't see you standing there."

"You were concentrating. Isn't it too hot for a workout?"

"No hotter than for cleaning windows," he said, wiping his face with a towel. "Besides, exercise is good for reducing all kinds of, um, tension."

She knew about several kinds. "I could use some tension relief myself," she said.

"Why don't you join me?"

"Okay. After all, we told Warner we met in a gym." She kicked off her shoes. "Ready for some sit-ups?"

He gave her a teasing smile. "Sure. How many are you good for?"

Christy calculated. The room was stifling, but God, she needed to expend some of this pent-up energy. "I can manage forty."

He cocked his head. "Nah."

"I'll bet you...a tuna dinner."

J.D. chuckled. "How can I pass that up? Okay, let's go."

Christy sat beside him and they began. They moved in sync as J.D. counted aloud. Christy found it hard to tear her eyes from the masculine form beside her. This was *not* an antidote for sexual tension. Just the opposite, it made her long for a more intimate kind of exercise. Thinking of that, she nearly toppled sideways.

"You okay?" J.D. sat up straight. "Want to stop?"

"No way," she gasped. Growing up with a brother, she'd lived a life of "dare you's." Sexual desire or not, she'd never give up.

Listening to him count, she made it to forty, then collapsed on the floor.

"I'll be darned." J.D. grinned. "I guess I'll have to open the tuna can tonight. You're stronger than you look."

"Have to be," she panted. "I have to maneuver some pretty hefty people in the hospital."

"You look like you could use a drink, with some of that imaginary ice." He stood and stretched out a hand to help her up.

How would it feel if she tripped and landed in his arms?

Bad idea. As soon as she was on her feet, she let go of his hand and stepped back. They had their tepid drink, and she went back to cleaning cabinets.

Late in the afternoon, as Christy rearranged items in the pantry for at least the third time, she heard a sound. A loud hum, deep and steady, it was—

"The air conditioner," she cried as a rush of cool air flowed over her shoulders. "J.D.," she shouted, "the power's back on." She ran to find him.

They almost collided in the living room. "Hallelujah!" he cried, grabbing her in his arms and spinning her in a circle.

For a moment, she hung on, laughing, giddy with relief. Then J.D. set her down, and they both stepped back. One brief hug of celebration was allowed, but extending the embrace would be…madness. Instead Christy concentrated on what was happening around them.

"Let's see if the phone's working, too."

It wasn't, but the light was on in the living room, and sounds from the TV in the kitchen brought the world back.

"Let's check out the news," J.D. suggested.

San Sebastian was too small to have a local station, but a Houston station was broadcasting the six o'clock news. One segment focused on the island. The bridge would be open tomorrow.

"Tomorrow morning—" J.D. began.

"I know, you want me to leave. I'll pack tonight," Christy promised. "Don't nag."

"Why would I? That's a woman's role. Ow," he said as she punched his arm.

"It's dinner time," Christy said as the sports news began. "I wish we had some real food here."

"I can take your car, go pick up some steaks," J.D. offered.

Christy shook her head. She was still frightened at the thought of the outside. "The bet was tuna. There's a can of mushroom soup in the pantry. Know how to make a tuna casserole?"

"Not really."

"So you renege on the bet?" When he nodded, she gave him a mock frown. "Tell you what. I'll make the casserole, and you owe me a steak dinner…sometime." She bit her lip. There she went again, assuming there'd be a "sometime."

While she got ingredients together, J.D. checked the phone again. "Dial tone," he told Christy. "Want to call anyone?"

"My brother. My parents are vacationing in Hawaii." She placed the call, got Steve's answering machine and left a message that she was fine and would be returning home tomorrow. She'd call him from Houston. Then she returned to the kitchen and quickly mixed the tuna and soup.

Watching her put dinner together, J.D. reflected that it was the first time he'd seen her cook. The last time, too. With everything functioning again, her world was back to normal. Tomorrow she'd be out of here, back in Houston, back to everyday life.

And he'd still be…lost. But for now, he only wanted to think of sharing dinner and an evening with Christy.

When they finished their meal, they moved into the living room and turned on the TV there. They sat on the couch…at opposite ends. "What do you want to watch?" Christy asked, offering him the remote.

J.D. flipped through channels. Summer rerun season was in full swing. They debated between an episode from the second season of "Sex and the City" and a newsmagazine show. Christy preferred the comedy, J.D. the news story. "Your house, your choice," J.D. said.

"You're company," Christy argued. "You pick."

Gallantly, J.D. chose "Sex and the City."

"Oh, heck." Christy leaned over and grabbed the remote from his hand. "Stop being so polite. You don't really want to watch a chick show. We'll do 'Dateline.'"

They settled back. A segment on the marketing of pharmaceuticals kept them engrossed and silent. Even the commercials afterward held their attention. "We've been tube-deprived," Christy remarked. "We'll watch anything." Besides, this gave them something to think about other than the predator who might be lurking outside again…and each other.

Stone Phillips introduced the next segment.

Columbus, Georgia, a thriving city of nearly two hundred thousand inhabitants on the western border of the state, is home to the Coca Cola Space Center and to beautiful Calloway Gardens. Bounded on the east and south by Fort Benning, one of the largest army bases in the United States, Columbus is known for providing a warm welcome to the military in its midst. But lately this openness has changed. Distrust and fear now mark the attitude of Columbus citizens to the young soldiers who were once eagerly received here. The reason? A series of brutal killings, which police believe were committed by someone stationed at Fort Benning.

J.D. leaned forward. A series of killings. The phrase grabbed his attention. He concentrated on the scene as the camera panned a field and zoomed in on a muddy spot beneath a tree.

Christy shuddered. "A gravesite," she said.

"Dump site. He buried the body there," J.D. corrected.

Here in this isolated field, the most recent of thirteen bodies was discovered last week, Phillips continued. Like the others, this young victim was a middle-school student. With no success tracking down the killer, police have sought the help of FBI profiler, Horace Means, here with us now. What can you tell us, sir, about this monster who has cut short so many lives?

J.D. frowned. Means would say the killer chose his victims because they were young, nonthreatening…because he was passive…

"The murderer is a passive individual who is intimidated by women, so he chooses young teenagers. They're not yet mature enough to be threats to him. He can—"

"—he can manipulate them," J.D. murmured.

"—bend them to his will," Means said.

"What kind of person is he?" Phillips asked.

"A monster," Christy said.

J.D. started. He'd forgotten she was beside him. No, *monster* was a layman's term, he thought, knowing how the profiler would respond. *He's physically mature but probably inexperienced sexually, possibly a virgin…*

Shaken, J.D. listened as the FBI agent echoed his thoughts. His head began to throb. The scene before him—the field, the police officers, the profiler—everything was eerily familiar. As Means continued, describing the killer's need to prove his manhood by enlisting in the military but probably failing, J.D.'s heart slammed against his chest, adrenaline spurted through his veins. He clutched his pounding head, his eyes fixed on the screen. Sweat poured down his face.

From somewhere far away, he heard a voice. Christy's voice. "J.D., are you all right?"

He didn't answer. Couldn't, because every cell in his body was focused on the television.

Means was right, he thought through the roaring in his ears. He knew because—because *he'd* see the case the same way…because he…

Christy touched his arm. "J.D."

He wasn't J.D.

Dizzy, he turned away from the television set, stared blindly at Christy.

"J.D.," she pleaded, "what's wrong?"

"I remember," he whispered. "I know who I am. My name…is…Jonathan. Jonathan…Talbot." He lurched from the sofa. "I have to call Houston."

Chapter 10

Stunned, Christy watched J.D. stride across the room and grab the phone. He punched in a number, waited. "This is Talbot. Put me through to Chief Nichols."

Nichols. Adam Nichols, Chief of Police in Houston? Was J.D. a cop?

He grimaced. "Here's my number. Have him call me back ASAP."

Christy went to him. "Tell me."

"I'm—" he began.

Noticing his pallor, she interrupted. "Wait, come sit down. You look a little unsteady."

"Yeah." They sat on the couch. "I'm a...no, I *used* to be a profiler for the FBI."

That explained a lot of things. The old bullet wound, the quick reflexes, his ease with a weapon. And his uncanny ability to put information together. "And now?" she asked. She wanted, *needed,* to know everything about this shadow-man who'd been the focus of her life for the past four days.

"I teach in the criminal justice program at the University of Houston," he went on. "Lately I've been working with the Houston police on a case. The Night…Crawler…no, Stalker. The Night Stalker."

"The guy who kills women at the Medical Center."

"Right."

"He's why I bought the gun."

His lips quirked, just a little. "The one you don't feel comfortable using."

Christy nodded. She thought for a moment. "I remember an article in the newspaper a couple of weeks ago. It said the police were forming a task force and they'd hired 'a noted psychologist with FBI experience.'" Dumbstruck, she stared at him. "That's you."

"Apparently it is."

"You're Jonathan Talbot," she said slowly. "*Doctor* Talbot."

"Doctor…I think so." He frowned. "Yes."

"And I accused you of being a criminal. Sorry."

"Don't apologize." He reached over and touched her hand, sending shock waves up her arm. "Based on circumstantial evidence, you had plenty of reasons to think so."

"But, J.D., um, Jonathan, what were you doing in San Sebastian?"

He rubbed his temple, stared into space for a moment. "I came to…question someone, the…ex-husband of one of the Stalker's victims."

"And he hit you?"

"I don't know. When I called to set up the interview, he asked me to park somewhere…I think in the alley behind his house. I remember doing that, getting out of the car…and that's it. *Someone* must've hit me."

"And driven you to the beach. The Night Stalker?" Christy shuddered.

"Good guess. God," he said, kneading his temple, "the task force must be going crazy trying to figure out what happened to me when I didn't show up or call in."

"I imagine." And who else was "going crazy" over his disappearance? So far, he hadn't said anything about a wife or a family.

She turned to him, caught him gazing at her with a dark, intense look. She had to find out where she stood with him. She swallowed, promised herself she'd handle whatever he said, then clenched her hands to keep them from trembling. "What about your family?" she asked, then took a breath. "Your…wife? Won't she be worried?"

"I'm not married," he said. "Not involved."

They gazed into each other's eyes.

The telephone shrilled, and they both started.

"For me, I imagine." Jonathan got up to answer. "Adam, yes, this is Jonathan. Sorry, I've had a little trouble here."

Christy got up and went into her bedroom. She'd give him some privacy.

She stood at the window, staring out. The sun had gone down, and stars dotted the black velvet sky.

She was happy for J.D.—for Jonathan. Of course, she was.

Ah, heck, admit it, Christy. Not completely. Yes, she was thankful he'd recovered his memory. But was she glad that now he could go back to his old life? Her feelings were so muddled, she wasn't sure.

She tried to sort things out. He lived in Houston; so did she. Was this a beginning for them, a chance to spend time together? Or was tonight an ending? Would she soon become just a vague memory, part of a story he'd tell about the time he'd gone after a killer and been hit on the head? An anecdote over dinner or cocktails? A tear trickled down her cheek and she wiped it away.

Footsteps sounded behind her and she turned to find Jonathan in the doorway, his form backlit by the glow from the hall. He's going to tell me goodbye. Trying to smile, she waited.

But he said nothing, just stood across the room, gazing at her, a question in his eyes. Christy couldn't find her voice, couldn't tear her eyes from his.

How many moments passed in silence, she didn't know. How many times the Earth spun around while they stood locked in each other's gazes, she couldn't guess. Her heart beat a deep and steady rhythm in her chest; her blood tingled in her veins. The world shrank, narrowed to only Jonathan and the space between them. Nothing else mattered. Nothing existed beyond this room.

She caught her breath, held it. And waited. Poised, uncertain.

And then, at the same time, both she and Jonathan moved. Closer and closer. Until she was in his arms at last, clutched to his chest, with his heart beating madly against hers.

"I want you," he murmured, his voice hoarse with desire.

"Yes," she whispered, *"yes."*

He bent his head, and his mouth took possession of hers, took it with urgency and thoroughness. He caressed her with his lips and tongue, nipped gently with his teeth, murmured low in his throat with appreciation. She kissed him hungrily, nibbled at the tip of his tongue, invited it deeper. Kissing him now, as a prelude to lovemaking, was like being lifted and spun wildly into a world she'd only imagined. Her legs went weak, and she clung to him. He was the only solid thing in a spinning vortex of desire.

Tearing his lips from hers, he kissed her eyes, her cheeks, her chin. When his tongue dipped into her ear, she cried out from the sheer pleasure of it. He returned to her mouth and drove her higher until she sagged against him, no longer able to hold herself upright.

He lifted her into his arms and carried her to the bed while she kissed him over and over. He set her on the bed and she pulled him down beside her and reached for his shirt. *Hurry,* she thought. But her nurse's fingers, always so nimble, were suddenly inept. She fumbled with the buttons, muttered her frustration.

He caught her hand and kissed it, running his tongue across the palm. "Take it easy." He pressed her hand against his heart. "We've waited for this. Let's go slow."

"Mmm, sounds like a good plan," Christy said. It sounded fabulous. Long, slow lovemaking. Discovering one another, while the night stretched before them and the everyday world was still far away.

Jonathan lifted her hand again, kissed her wrist and spread more kisses up her arm. "Ever since I saw you, I've wanted you. Wanted this."

Christy sighed. "Me, too."

"When I came to after I passed out in your doorway, the first thing I heard was your voice. I thought I'd died and you were an angel."

"I'm not an angel, Jonathan," she said softly. "Just a woman."

"A woman who cared enough to let a stranger in trouble into her home."

Into her heart. Whatever that meant. She refused to face that question. She touched his face. "A woman who wants you."

He smiled. Not that quick grin she'd come to know so well in these past few days, but a slow, tender smile. "Then let's make a memory."

"All right." If he left after tonight, she'd have this. She'd never forget the softness of the pillow beneath her head, the fragrance of the lilac sachet she kept with her linens, mingling with the scent of Jonathan, warm and male. The rich brown of his hair, the shape of his hands, the deep baritone of his voice. All that plus the patch of ebony sky outside her window, the pale light of the new moon, and always in the background, the deep rhythm of the Gulf. No matter what happened after tonight, whenever she heard the tide, whenever she came to the island, she'd remember him.

"You have the sweetest face," he said. He traced the outline of her cheeks, her forehead. Christy's eyes drifted closed as she gave herself up to his touch. He kissed her lashes, the bridge of her nose, then moved slowly, leisurely, down to her chin. "Soft," he said, his voice low and sensuous.

"Now let me," Christy said and took her hands and lips on the same delicious journey. She loved the rough, newly grown beard on his face, the cleft in his chin, his silky lashes.

They undressed each other slowly, button by button. Dreamily, Christy learned the breadth of his shoulders, the texture of his skin, the indentation of his navel. She'd seen him before, but not like this, with every inch of him hers to explore. And explore she did, marveling at the utter maleness of him. Even when he lay pliant in her arms, holding his desire in check and leaving her free to touch and taste to her heart's content, there was a toughness about him, a coiled strength. Somehow she knew he was as much a warrior as a lover. And he was the kind of lover a woman only dreamed of. When he parted her shirt and slipped the bra from her shoulders, his eyes went black, and he looked at her as if he wanted to devour her. She wanted him to.

Her rigid nipples strained toward him, aching for his hands, for his mouth. But he touched only the tip of one, circled it, his finger featherlight, his eyes intent on the turgid bud. Christy moaned.

"Tell me what you want," he murmured.

"More. Everything. You."

"Soon," he said and leaned closer. He took her nipple in

his mouth, sucking deep, until she thought she would surely die from the exquisite torture he inflicted. His other hand roamed downward. Past her stomach, along her hips and thighs. She didn't know she could *want* this much. When he finally found the core of her, she cried out at his touch, heard his answering moan.

"Slow" was forgotten as their legs tangled, their hands flew over one another. Light touches gave way to deep caresses, soft kisses to intense ones. Moans became cries…became…

A groan, then a curse.

"Christy…damn, I'm not…prepared." Jonathan rolled away. "I can't protect you."

Of course he couldn't. He'd come to her with empty pockets. On the brink of completion, she clenched her fists in frustration. They'd waited so long. An eternity. And now…. This was… So incredibly rotten.

Should they take a chance? And complicate an already complicated relationship? Uh-uh. No way.

Suddenly, a thought struck her, and she sat up. "I think I have a solution." Oh, man, she hoped so.

She sprang out of bed, turned to look at him and couldn't help but smile. With the fingers of one hand clenched, and the other arm thrown across his face, he looked utterly miserable. She bent and kissed him. "I'll be right back. Don't lose our place."

She heard him mutter, "Not much chance of that," as she dashed out of her room and down the hall to Steve's. He and Karen had been on the island in June. Hoping he kept a stash of condoms here, she rummaged through his nightstand. A paperback Western, a bottle of aspirin, three pencils, an old fishing magazine. Frantically, she tossed them on the floor. Where the heck did he keep his condoms?

Aha! At the very back of the drawer, not exactly a handy

place to keep it, she discovered an unopened package. "I owe you, big brother," Christy murmured and scurried back down the hall. "Nurse Ratched to the rescue," she said, holding the small box aloft.

"Nurse Ratched, hell. I knew you were an angel."

Christy knelt on the bed beside Jonathan. "I'm going to make sure you believe that." She removed a small packet and laid it beside her. "You've had this memory problem, so just in case you've forgotten where we were, let me remind you."

"Trust me, I haven't forgo— Christy!" he groaned as she bent and took him in her mouth.

The taste of male. The taste of *him* was overpowering.

She drew him in, laving him with her tongue. While she made love to him with her mouth, her hand caressed his thigh, his belly. She lifted her head. "Do you remember?"

"Oh, yes."

"Sure?" She closed her hand around him, worked it slowly up and down his shaft.

"Cross my heart. Woman, you *are* Nurse Ratched. You're driving me insane." He turned and grabbed for the foil packet but she was too quick for him. She snatched it up, tore it open and sheathed him. But slowly, leisurely, until, half laughing, half groaning, he swung around, and pinned her to the bed.

He licked her neck. "Tease," he muttered against her throat. "I'd make you wait, but I…don't think…I can."

"Then don't." She opened her arms, urged his mouth back to hers, and spread her legs in welcome.

He entered her with one powerful thrust. With bodies joined at last, they moved together. Racing, straining toward climax, leaving everything behind but this.

Christy tightened her arms around him. She'd been waiting all her life for this night. That was her last coherent thought before she tumbled into space and shattered.

Afterward, they lay heart to heart. Christy sighed as she drifted back to earth.

"Tired?" Jonathan asked.

Lazily, she traced a finger around his nipple and over his chest. "Happy."

"Satisfied?"

"That, too," she said. "I'm glad I was able to find that box and that you were…available."

"I'm available again," he said.

"Already?"

"The FBI teaches you how to conserve and maintain your energy level."

"For sex?"

"For anything," he said solemnly.

"Care to prove it?" Christy asked.

"Don't mind a bit." He rolled over, straddled her, and proved without a doubt that FBI agents had amazing stamina.

They slept afterward but not for long. They woke hungry, and slipping on their shirts, strolled hand in hand to the kitchen. They raided the pantry, heated up tomato soup and opened a box of crackers.

Seated across from him, Christy tilted her head. She'd spent the last few hours doing the most intimate things with this man, yet he was still a stranger. "How long have you lived in Houston?" she asked.

Jonathan thought for a moment. He frowned and Christy saw a flash of panic in his eyes. "I don't know. Shouldn't I remember that?"

She reached across the table and put her hand on his. "You've only had your memory back a few hours. I'm sure the rest will come." She didn't know if that was true, but it *had* to be. He couldn't just recover part of his life.

"God, this is frustrating."

She kept her voice calm, hoping to reassure them both. "Remember Dr. Mayes said not to force the memories. Think about what you do know."

He nodded, relaxed the fist he'd made. "Okay, I was born in Seattle, grew up there, and went east to college."

"Yale," Christy guessed. "You look like a Yale man."

"Columbia," he said. "You grew up in Texas, went to nursing school in-state."

Had he changed the subject because talking about her was easier? Whatever, she'd go with it. "The accent gives me away," she admitted, "but how do you know the rest?"

"Your family lives nearby. You said your parents bought this place because you could come at Christmas."

"Right. They live in Fort Worth."

"You're close with your family," Jonathan continued. "When you talk about them, your eyes soften. And you chose the house where you spent summers together to think about your future."

"You're right again," she said. "You pick up on everything. I guess that's what makes you a good profiler." She took a sip of sparkling water. "Interesting, isn't it, that you kept right on using those skills even when your memory was gone?"

"I guess I've practiced them so long they've become automatic."

Christy rose to take her bowl to the sink. She handed him the cracker box. "Want more?"

His eyes gleamed. "Crackers? Or something else?"

She laughed. "Whatever you're hungry for."

"That would be you." He tugged her into his lap, and for once Christy forgot about cleaning.

"Here," she whispered, kissing him, "in the kitchen."

He was already ahead of her, fumbling in his shirt pocket for a condom, then pulling up her blouse, baring her breasts, and sliding into her for another wild ride.

Christy collapsed against him. "Wow," she gasped. "All this lacked was whipped cream."

"Have some?" Jonathan asked.

"If I did, it'd be spoiled by now."

"Good, because my FBI training has deserted me. I don't think I'm good for another round, yet."

Christy yawned. "Me, either...yet."

Jonathan woke slowly the next morning. In the pale dawn light, everything seemed strange and unfamiliar. Fear clutched at him. Was he back in the half world of amnesia?

No. He turned his head, and there was Christy beside him. He was in her bed after a night of nonstop lovemaking. Hell, nothing, not even another blow on the head, could make him forget that.

He turned on his side and watched her sleep, her head pillowed on her hand, her mouth as innocent as a child's.

Innocent? No way. That mouth belonged to a witch who could seduce and beguile and kiss a man until his blood sizzled. Who could've guessed, when he'd stumbled into her house, what treasure he'd find?

Hoping to slip out of bed without waking her, he sat up.

"'S it time to get up?" a sleepy voice asked.

He turned and dropped a kiss on her cheek. "Uh-uh. Go back to sleep for a while. I'm going to borrow your father's razor, okay?"

"Yeah, but it'll cost you a kiss," she murmured.

Seemed like a reasonable price to pay. He kissed her, more than once, then grabbed his clothes and left the bedroom.

First things first. He needed a bath but his clothes needed one worse. He dumped them in the washing machine, then went back to the bathroom to shower and shave.

As soon as he was dressed, he called Armand Frazier, head of the Stalker task force. He recalled that he'd come here to question Todd Berlin, ex-husband of the Stalker's first victim, Janice Berlin. But, reluctant to rely on memory, he asked Armand to give him the details of his assignment.

"Berlin had an alibi for the night Janice was killed, but it was shaky," Armand said. "We decided you'd question him. Figured sending a psychologist would keep this low-key, that you could draw him out and see if we need to move him up on the suspect list."

"He's near the top of my list," Jonathan said. "Nichols told you what happened to me, didn't he?"

"Yeah, think it was the Stalker who tried to off you?"

"Good chance. And who had a better opportunity than Berlin? He's been on the island the last few days, for sure. But there's a problem. He doesn't fit the profile."

"Maybe you'll have to revise it," Armand said.

"Yeah. Fill me in on the guy, would you? The details of the case are still fuzzy."

"Berlin managed a construction company in Houston and was doing pretty well. But he was a compulsive gambler, and Janice couldn't take it anymore and wanted out. The word is they fought like dogs over the community property, and the animosity lasted. Meanwhile Todd got remarried, moved to San Sebastian, and started his own company. Made a go of it, too. And allegedly got his gambling habit under control. Last year Janice came on hard times and started blackmailing Todd. Threatened to spill the story of his gambling to the new wife."

"So he murders her and then resorts to overkill to draw suspicion away from himself," Jonathan mused. "Helluva lot of trouble to go to, killing five more women. My memory's still shaky but I don't think that's been done before."

"There's always a first time," Armand reminded him.

When Christy woke again, the sun shone through the window. She sat up, hugged her knees to her chest and smiled, replaying everything that had happened since Jonathan's memory had returned. Recalling his sweet kiss, she touched her lips. Her fingers traced the indentation of his head on the pillow next to hers, then she bent to bury her face in the pillow and breathe in his scent. Where was he? She scooted out of bed, threw on some clothes and went to see.

The aroma of coffee gave her the answer. She padded barefoot down the hall to the kitchen. His back to the door, he was seated at the table with the newspaper spread in front of him. Christy stood for a moment, watching him.

And then he turned to face her.

Christy stared. His face was clean-shaven.

For the first time, she saw him without a beard or a hint of five o'clock shadow. He looked like a stranger.

Chapter 11

"Good morning," Jonathan said. As he got out of his chair and came toward her, his eyes traveled down her body with the familiarity and appreciation of a lover. He pulled her into his arms for a coffee-flavored kiss. "Want some coffee?"

"Mmm-hmm, I'll get it." She went to the counter and poured a cup from the coffeemaker. As she stirred in sweetener, she glanced at Jonathan out of the corner of her eye. His shirt and pants were freshly laundered. Even his sneakers were free of mud.

Slowly, she returned to the table and sat across from him. "You look…different," she said.

He grinned. "Cleaner?"

She managed to smile. "I guess." Not certain she could express what she meant and unwilling to travel farther down that road until she could, she stared into her coffee cup.

Jonathan glanced at the clock they'd reset when the power came on. "I've set up the interrogation I'm supposed to do for ten o'clock." The clock read nine-fifteen. "May I borrow your car?"

"Well, sure…but you don't have your driver's license."

He shrugged. "I'll take a chance. If I get stopped, I'll have them call the Houston police department." He stood. "Want some toast?"

"Thank you." Christy watched him as he strode across the room. No, the difference in him this morning went far deeper than newly washed clothes. She saw it in his demeanor, heard it in his brisk, confident tone. Jonathan Talbot was not J.D.

What did she know about the man who stood across her kitchen putting bread into the toaster? Not much, except he was a fantastic lover. Or had that been J.D.? She'd called him Jonathan, but when they made love, she realized she'd thought of him as J.D.

At dawn, had he completed some sort of transition and become his old self? Because the streak of vulnerability that had drawn her to J.D. had vanished.

She observed him as he walked back to the table. His hair was the same, his eyes the same smokey gray. Well, of course they were. She must be losing her mind. Regaining his memory couldn't change him into a different man…or could it?

He sat down and began spreading jam on his toast. "The causeway bridge is open," he said.

She nodded. He'd be leaving. So would she. She pushed back the plate of toast he'd handed her.

"You could spend the rest of your vacation at your brother's," he continued.

"I don't want to." At Steve's she'd have to deal with all kinds of questions about the storm and why she'd decided to leave San Sebastian. Not to mention advice about the dangers of letting a strange man into her home.

"Go home, then," Jonathan said and reached for her hand. "Don't fight me on this."

"I'll think about it."

He checked the clock again and rose. "Damn, I need to get going. I'll be back in a couple of hours. Think fast."

"Wait!"

He stopped on his way to the door. "What?"

"We talked about this last night. That man you're going to see. He could be the guy who tried to kill you."

"Maybe."

"You're going back there again. You could be walking into another trap." She rushed to him and seized his hand. "Don't go."

He dropped a kiss on her forehead. "Don't worry, I'll be oka—"

"Stop it. Don't patronize me," she snapped. "You may not be okay."

"I'm not patronizing you." He pulled her close, gazed into her eyes. "This is what I do, Christy. But usually I'm armed."

"Take the gun."

"And leave you here with no protection?" He shook his head.

Christy dropped her gaze. "We both know I wouldn't use it."

He hesitated, and she saw him considering the pros and cons. "All right," he said, "I'll take the gun, but *you* stay inside."

She nodded.

"And don't let anyone in."

"You don't have to tell me that." She pulled back.

"You let me in. That was a mistake."

At his words, tears threatened and she turned away. "Was it?"

"No." He caught her against his chest and kissed her. When he let her go, they were both breathless.

He checked the time again, held out a hand. "Keys?"

"I'll get them, and you'd better take some money, too."

She brought him the keys and a twenty-dollar bill along with the gun and ammunition. She watched him check the weapon, drop bullets into the chambers, and shove the gun into his waistband. She'd been right last night; he *was* a warrior, with the cool confidence of a man used to putting himself on the line.

She followed him out to the garage. Warrior or not, he didn't seem like a reckless man to her. Still, she couldn't help saying, "Be careful, please."

"I will."

He got into the car and shut the door. She heard the engine turn over and then he began backing out. She ran to the driver's-side window and tapped on it. When he rolled it down, she said, "If you think I should leave here, I'll go home."

"Good. How long will it take you to get ready?"

"Not long. I pack light."

He nodded. She watched him back out of the driveway and disappear around the corner, then glanced at the yard as she headed back to the door. The flood had left the grass strewn with trash. She'd see about getting someone to clean the yard, maybe replace some of the oleanders.

A glimpse of white in the flower bed by the back door caught her eye, and she bent down. She found pieces of seashells, broken by the wind and tide, but among them she spied a sand dollar. She looked closer. Undamaged by its journey from the Gulf, it lay there, a perfect circle amid the battered bits of shell. How nice to find a survivor.

Christy picked up the sand dollar and carried it inside. Another keepsake.

Jonathan glanced out as he drove along the seawall. The day was clear and bright, and summer's heat had returned. Nevertheless, he decided to roll down the windows. He wanted to feel the sun on his face, to breathe in the salty air, hear the seagulls squawking and the waves booming as they raced toward shore. To rejoice in finding himself again. He'd like to just drive and enjoy the day, to take pleasure in remembering last week or last year, but he didn't have the time.

He needed to plan this morning's interrogation carefully. Presumably, he'd done that last week, but he needed to think his strategy through again.

He thought of what Armand had said about Todd Berlin. Nothing about the guy jibed with what Jonathan knew about serial killers. Most men who murdered multiple victims weren't savvy enough to own businesses. Or determined enough to overcome a gambling addiction…if indeed Todd had kicked his habit. Most relied on murder to give them a sense of competence, because in their daily lives the majority of serial killers were abject failures.

The scenario the task force had come up with for Berlin— that he'd killed multiple women to cover up the murder of his former wife—was unlikely. It made the guy sound like some kind of criminal mastermind. Jonathan frowned, trying to recall what he'd said when they decided he should question Berlin. Whatever his objections, they'd evidently insisted. He couldn't fault them, either. They were all desperate to nail this killer. Pressure from City Council, the media, even the rest of the police force was tremendous.

So today Jonathan's first job was to figure out if Todd really might have pulled off such a scheme. His second was to protect himself.

Armand had given him directions to Berlin's house. Jonathan recalled—and how he relished being able to remember!—that Berlin had told him to park in the alley behind the house when he'd first set up the meeting last week. Didn't want the neighbors to spot Jonathan and recognize a face that had been on the news in connection with the Night Stalker.

The hell with the neighbors. This time Jonathan would park in front.

He found the street and drove along it slowly. Berlin lived in a neighborhood of comfortable, middle-class homes with large, neatly kept lawns. Palm trees grew in most yards. Jonathan's thoughts spiraled back to the day he'd come here for the first time. The wind had howled, and the fronds of those giant palms had blown wildly, like outdoor ceiling fans.

That day he'd driven around to the alley, parked and locked the car. The air had smelled of rain. He remembered looking up at the sky and seeing low, black clouds. Although it was only midafternoon, the light had waned, making it seem later. Behind a fence, a dog had been whining.

Jonathan frowned as he strained to recall what had happened next. The moment he'd started down the alley, the first drops of rain had begun to fall. As if a video played before his eyes, he saw lightning flash. A rumble of thunder followed and the dog began to howl.

Jonathan saw himself stop by a garage marked with the Berlins' house number. As he put his hand on the gate beside it, there was a lull in the wind. Everything went still, even the neighbor's dog. Jonathan remembered having the eerie feeling that the world was holding its breath. Waiting.

What next? Shaking off the fanciful thought, he'd lifted the latch on the gate, then paused. Why?

Because in the quiet, he'd thought he heard a sound behind him. Adrenaline had flooded his body.

He turned, saw a flash of movement. Then an impossible pressure pushed his head forward and down. He'd had only an instant to register pain before stars exploded behind his eyes and everything went black. He remembered nothing more about that afternoon. Everything was blank until he woke on the beach.

Now Jonathan parked Christy's car in front of Berlin's

house. God, the mind was a strange thing. The memory of his earlier visit was so vivid, his head pounded. He sat in the car for a minute, collecting himself, then checked the gun and went to the front door.

A pretty woman, followed by a small boy who looked to be around five years old, answered. "Doctor Talbot?" she said. "Come in."

The child slid behind his mother. "Is the doctor gonna give me a shot?" he asked, peering at Jonathan.

Jonathan smiled at the boy. He was a sucker for kids. "No way," he said.

"You sure?" the boy asked his mother.

"Of course I'm sure, Sean. Doctor Talbot is here to see Daddy."

Sean stepped out and grinned at Jonathan. "Are you gonna give Daddy a shot?"

"No, I'm not."

"Because I could help. I could hold his hand."

"Maybe another time."

"Sean," his mother said, "Doctor Talbot needs to talk business with Daddy. Why don't you put on *Nemo?*"

"Okay." The child scurried off, and Jonathan followed Mrs. Berlin into the living room where her husband sat in an armchair.

With one glance, Jonathan was ninety-nine-percent certain Todd Berlin was off the suspect list. The man had a broken leg.

And badly broken, too. He was in a cast from his ankle nearly to his hip. No way was he the guy who ran from Christy's house the other night. Unless he broke the leg in his flight across the field.

"Excuse my manners, Doctor Talbot," Berlin said. "But as you can see, I'm incapacitated. Take a seat." He frowned at Jonathan. "You're late. I expected you nearly a week ago."

Jonathan tapped the side of his bruised face. "I had an accident myself." He sat across from Berlin. "What happened to your leg?"

"Broke it during the storm. When the wind picked up, it blew out a window in the attic. I slipped on a wet spot at the top of the attic stairs and fell all the way down."

"Ouch," Jonathan said.

"Yeah, they got me to the hospital just before the roads flooded."

That'd be easy enough to check. Berlin hadn't come after *him,* Jonathan concluded, but he could still have killed Janice. Maybe just her or maybe the others, too. But Berlin had evidently anticipated Jonathan's thoughts. He handed over his medical receipts, proving he did indeed break his leg when he said he did.

Jonathan began his questioning. Berlin stuck to the story he'd given the police: that the night of Janice's murder he'd gone to his son's Pee Wee League game, begun feeling ill, and gone home, where he was alone until his wife and Sean arrived around ten-thirty.

"Pretty late bedtime for your son," Jonathan remarked.

"It was a Friday night. After the game, they went out for hamburgers and over to someone's house. Happens all the time." Berlin squirmed in his chair. "Look, I didn't care much for Janice, and I sure as hell didn't like what she was trying to do to me. But I wouldn't kill her."

They talked some more, and Jonathan decided Berlin was highly unlikely to have killed his former wife. Or anyone else. He thanked the man, left, and drove downtown to check on his car.

It had drowned. He'd been thinking of buying a new one anyway. He told the guy at the lot he'd call his insurance company as soon as he got back to Houston.

"You heading back now?" the fellow asked.

"Soon. I'm making a stop on Gulf Bank Road."

"I can tell you a short cut over there."

Jonathan wrote down the directions, something he normally wouldn't do, but he felt uncomfortable relying on memory. Damn, would he always be that way?

He put his frustration aside as he drove away from the lot. He'd be back home this evening, and Christy would be in Houston, too. He wanted to spend time with her, make love with her. Damn, he could hardly wait to hold her again. Whatever had happened to him this week, finding Christy was worth it.

He felt good about his progress on the case. As soon as he got back to his office, he'd look over his latest notes. He had to be getting damn close to fingering the bastard or the guy wouldn't have gone to so much trouble trying to do *him* in.

He whistled softly as he drove into a new housing development. For Sale signs dotted lawns with sprouts of grass poking up. He glanced down a side street and noticed a row of town houses. Impulsively, he turned down the street to get a closer look.

He'd lived in a town house in Washington when he'd been with the Bureau, he recalled. Like that red brick over there. He pulled up and parked across from it. Except for a few details, the resemblance to the one he'd owned was remarkable.

But why did looking at it make his stomach churn? What had happened there?

He shut his eyes as his heart began to pound. Memories flooded his mind. He saw himself on the steps with a woman...with Diane.

Diane Shay. He'd been absorbed in his demanding job with the Bureau and had been leery of commitment. Then he'd told himself he was foolish. He and Diane were in love. He bought a ring, took her to dinner and over chateaubriand, asked her to marry him. She'd said yes. They'd toasted each other with champagne, talked about wedding dates, and afterward…

His heart beat so fast he could hardly catch his breath. *Remember,* he thought…and then, oh, God, no!…he did.

The scene played before his eyes in Technicolor. As he and Diane approached the town house, a man emerged from the shadows. Jonathan recognized him. A year ago he'd been instrumental in apprehending this criminal. Despite Jonathan's testimony against him, the man had been acquitted on a technicality of a brutal rape/murder. The man raised his arm and fired a gun. Even now, Jonathan could feel the impact of the bullet, the pain in his thigh. The bullet wound Christy had found.

He remembered groping for his weapon…too slowly. Then the sound of another shot, Diane grabbing her chest, falling. Lying dead in a pool of blood on his front steps.

With a howl of rage, Jonathan had shot the culprit, who had fallen to the ground dead. Jonathan had managed to crawl inside to the phone and call for help. But it was too late. Too late for Diane, for him, too. As he recuperated from his wound, Jonathan could only wish it had been fatal. Wracked with guilt and aching with loss, as soon as he recovered, he left the Bureau.

And now he'd put another woman in peril. Christy. By staying with her, he'd introduced her to the Stalker, practically served her up to a maniacal killer.

He dropped his head to the steering wheel, shut his eyes, and sat there until a knock on the window roused him. A woman stood beside the car. "Are you okay, sir?" she asked. "Do you need help?"

He shook his head. "Just a headache." When she walked away, he drove out of the subdivision.

Only minutes before, he'd been thinking Christy was the best thing that had happened to him. Now he realized he was the worst thing that had happened to her.

He had to step out of her life. He'd drive back to Houston with her. On the way he'd explain about Diane. And then he'd have her drop him at police headquarters, and say goodbye. He saw no alternative, no matter how it hurt.

He'd been gone more than an hour. Was she all right? Damn, he wished he had a cell phone, but his had either been taken by his assailant or it had drowned along with his car.

As soon as he saw a convenience store, he pulled into a parking space and sprinted inside. Thank God Christy had given him some cash.

He got change and called her, counting the rings until she picked up.

"H-hello." Her voice was thin, not like Christy at all.

"What's wrong?" he snapped.

"Jonathan? I'm glad you called." She sounded close to tears. "I…"

"Did someone try to get in?" he asked.

"No, it's not that," she said. "Someone called."

"And?" he asked impatiently.

"His voice was muffled, but he said… 'I know where you live.'"

"Jesus!" The caller had to be the Night Stalker. "Does your phone have Caller ID?"

"At home. Not here."

"Okay," he said, keeping his voice calm. "I'm not far away. Are the doors and windows locked?"

"Yes."

"Keep them that way," he told her. "I'll be there in ten minutes."

He hung up. Change of plans, he told himself. It was too late to walk away. He'd have to keep Christy safe. And do his damnedest to bring the Stalker in.

He made another phone call and then, breaking every traffic law in creation, sped toward Christy's house.

Chapter 12

Jonathan took the porch steps in one leap and jabbed Christy's bell repeatedly, then paced until she appeared in the doorway. Out of breath, he said, "You should have asked who was here before you opened the door."

Christy's lips thinned. "I peeked out between the blinds. You didn't see because you were tromping around on the porch."

She stood aside and let him in.

He wanted to haul her into his arms and keep her there, safe and sound. Instead, he caught her by the shoulders and asked, "Everything all right?"

"I'm okay," she told him. "I probably overreacted."

"I don't think so." He drew her over to the living-room couch. "Tell me exactly what the caller said."

"Just what I told you. 'I know where you live.'"

"You'd never heard his voice before?"

"I don't think so," Christy said. "It was so muffled, I couldn't tell."

"Let's check your answering machine in Houston and see if he called there, too."

"I hadn't thought of that." Christy went to the phone and dialed. She listened, shaking her head. "Six messages, none from him. Maybe he *doesn't* know. He could just be trying to scare me."

"He knows. All he needed was your license plate number and he got that when he disabled your car."

"But why would he call me? What do I have to do with this?"

"You're the Good Samaritan. You gave me shelter." Jonathan got up to pace the living room. "He must know I'm getting close to him. If he can't get rid of me, he figures the next best move is to distract me, get me riled up over what he could do to you."

"From the way you're stomping around, I'd say it's working," Christy said wryly.

Jonathan shook his head. "Trust me, I'm concentrating on him with every brain cell I have." He flashed a rueful smile. "I think better on my feet."

"What *are* you thinking?"

Jonathan hesitated, something he didn't do often, but he wasn't sure how much to tell Christy. Would she be more cautious if he told her about Diane, or would the story scare her to death? "I—"

The phone rang.

They stared at each other, then both of them jumped up to answer. Jonathan got there first. He held up a hand to shush Christy and picked up the receiver. "Hello."

"Is this the Matthews' residence?" a male voice asked.

Not a voice he'd heard before, Jonathan thought. But the recent past was still unclear so he couldn't be positive. Best thing to do was to keep the guy talking. "Yes, this is the Matthews'. Who's calling?"

Ignoring the question, the caller said, "Let me speak to Christy," then snapped, "Who is this?"

"Jonathan Talbot, and you are—?"

"Christy's brother."

Oops. "Sorry." He handed the phone to Christy. "Your brother," he mouthed.

"From this end, it sounds like you two didn't make friends." She chuckled. "Hi, Steve. Yes, I have a visitor." She turned and lowered her voice, but Jonathan could hear every word, and her annoyance came through loud and clear. "He's a friend. No, Steve, you don't know him. I'll submit his name for your approval on next week's list."

She paused and listened, then sighed. "Apology accepted. Don't be such a worry wart. I'm fine. And by the way, I've decided to spend the rest of my vacation in Houston. Jonathan and I are driving back in a little while. I need to get ready. Give my love to Karen."

When she turned back to him, Jonathan raised a brow. "Steve always that overprotective?"

"He thinks I'm still five years old."

"I notice you didn't tell him what was happening," Jonathan said.

"What could he do, other than fret over it?"

"Insist you come and stay with him," Jonathan replied, "which, by the way, would make sense."

"I told you before, I don't want to. I haven't changed my mind."

Frustrated, Jonathan shook his head. "Of course not. You're far too stubborn."

"I'm not going to answer that," she said coolly. "Look, I'm willing to go back to Houston because…well, because this… situation has ruined San Sebastian for me."

Right on target, Jonathan thought. "I'm sorry," he murmured.

"I wasn't asking for an apology." Christy sat on the arm of a chair. "Here's something I thought of. You may not remember, but the news media said every one of the women who was killed had had morphine in her car."

He *hadn't* remembered that.

"And in case you haven't noticed," Christy continued, "I don't do drugs."

"And your point is?"

"Maybe this guy was their junkie and they owed him money. Or maybe they were stealing drugs for him from the hospitals where they worked and something went wrong with the deal."

Jonathan shook his head. "I remember now. The task force thinks he planted the drugs."

"They could be wrong."

"Or you could be." God, this woman was muleheaded. How would he convince her to accept his protection? Because he'd be damned if he'd let her out of his sight until the Night Stalker was behind bars. Shouldn't be long, because the guy was getting desperate. Soon, like most criminals, he'd make a mistake.

He decided not to tell her about Diane. The story would only terrify her. And this time Jonathan was prepared. This time he'd made arrangements to protect the woman he was...well, responsible for. He couldn't allow himself to think of their relationship as anything else.

He got up. "Let's stop second-guessing this. You need to pack up so we can get out of here and talk about what happens when we get to Houston."

"Okay, I'm almost ready."

"I'll help," he offered, following her into the hall.

"Uh-uh, I'll be quicker if you keep out of my way. Go watch a soap."

Sure, he thought. More melodrama, just what he needed. But he left her alone and sat in the living room.

He shut his eyes. He wondered what in his background had led him to a life bound up with violence. He was a psychologist. Shouldn't he know? But he didn't.

Right now he wished he and Christy were together because they *had* met at the gym, that instead of driving back to Houston, they could go down the hall to Christy's room and make love in the light of day. He wanted to feel her heated skin against cool sheets, hear her cry out with passion, and lie drowsily beside her through the long afternoon.

No such luck.

He heard her footsteps and opened his eyes. "Ready?" At her nod, he picked up her luggage.

Halfway down the walk, Christy stopped. "Be right back." He stowed her bags in the trunk while she ran back into the house.

She returned carrying a plastic baggie. "This morning I found a sand dollar by the back door," she said. "See?" She held it out. "It's all in one piece. Isn't that amazing? It found a way to survive the storm." She grinned at him. "Just like you."

The comparison surprised him. "You think I'm a survivor?"

"Of course you are." She got into the car, fastened her seat belt, and smiled as he slid into the driver's seat. "You didn't just lie on the beach and drown."

He chuckled. "By that definition, everyone's a survivor. They do what they have to, so they can go on."

She put a hand on his arm. "I'm glad you did."

Her sweet touch made his breath catch. He leaned toward her. *Don't,* his brain said. But he could no more pull back than he could stop breathing. He put his arms around her and kissed her, even though he knew he shouldn't drag her deeper into his life, even though he was certain he'd have to leave her soon. He couldn't subject another woman to a lifetime of danger. They broke apart but remained motionless, gazing into one another's eyes. Then Christy smiled. "If you hadn't made it, I'd have missed one heck of a kiss."

He laughed and started the car.

They crossed the causeway bridge and left San Sebastian behind. Houston was a little over an hour away. Christy yawned and leaned back, watching the way Jonathan handled the car. Totally in control, she decided.

Halfway to Houston, Jonathan pulled off the freeway and into a strip center with a little café. "Let's have some lunch," he said.

"Fine with me."

Once they were settled into a booth near the back and had given their orders, he said, "We have to talk about what happens when we get back." He looked grim.

"Okay, talk," she said.

"I have a friend in Houston. Her name is Hannah Neuhaus."

There was the reason for his dark expression, Christy decided. He must have been dreading telling her about another lover.

He paused, and she managed to say, "It's okay. I understand." She was determined to handle this like a sophisticated woman. She wanted to understand, although finding out about another woman hurt. A lot. Jonathan must be embarrassed that he'd remembered Hannah *after* he'd slept with Christy.

Jonathan gave her a puzzled glance. "Understand what?"

"Your girlfriend. Hannah."

"Hannah's not my girlfriend. If Troy, her husband, heard that, he'd have me hog-tied in thirty seconds. He's an FBI agent. So's Hannah."

"Oh." Christy felt her cheeks heat. "I thought…"

"Yeah, well. What I started to say was, Hannah's on maternity leave. Starting tomorrow you'll stay with her during the day. She can use the company and—"

"Whoa, just a minute, Doctor Talbot. What are we talking about here?"

"The phone call you got. That wasn't just a crank call. We're dealing with a homicidal maniac who's killed six women. I want you protected." She opened her mouth to protest, but he held up a hand to silence her. "This is not up for debate." His voice was stern, his expression unyielding. She hadn't seen that kind of look on J.D.'s face.

"Okay, I get the message. You want me protected," Christy said. "But where does your friend come in?"

"Hannah just gave birth to twins. Her husband is away on assignment. While you're still on vacation, you'll spend the days with her. You like babies, right? You give her a little help with the twins, and she keeps you safe. It's the perfect arrangement."

Well, wasn't that just like an arrogant male? Talbot had an idea, thought he could just snap his fingers and presto, it would work out. "Aren't you forgetting something?" she asked.

"What?"

"How do you know Hannah would be interested?"

"She's interested," he said.

"And you know this because…?"

"I called her. From the convenience store. Right after I talked to you."

Astonished, Christy stared at him. "You just called her? Without asking me?"

"This is an emergency," he said implacably. "Manners aren't a priority."

Christy felt a tear threatening and turned away. "This has nothing to do with manners," she said, trying to control her voice. "This has to do with you railroading my life." He responded with a puzzled frown, and she said, "I understand the situation, and I know you're right."

His frown stayed in place. "Then what's the problem?"

"Your attitude's the problem." He sounded like Keith, not at all like J.D. Her thoughts of this morning returned. Who was this man? What was he really like?

"Sorry," Jonathan said, "but as I said before, in this kind of an emergency, neither of us should be worrying about niceties. We're talking about your life here."

Christy sighed. She'd responded to an echo of Keith. Even though she understood the danger she was in and Jonathan's concern for her, she couldn't seem to control her knee-jerk reaction. "I'm not foolish enough to turn down protection. But I don't like to be ordered around."

"Message received," Jonathan said. "Don't worry, this won't have to go on very long. We'll nail this guy soon."

"I hope so," Christy said, "because my vacation is over in a week."

"That'll give me more incentive," he said. "Meantime, you'll like Hannah. She's great. And until we catch the killer, I'll be with you at night."

"So I have a bodyguard 24/7." She hadn't missed his comment that he'd be with her until the killer was caught. And after?

Did she care? How could she possibly answer until she knew Jonathan Talbot better? Spending time with him seemed the best way to do that. So she supposed the arrangement he'd planned was best all the way around. She just wished he'd *asked* her first.

The waitress appeared with their lunch orders, and they ate in silence.

Back in the car afterward, Christy asked, "How do you know you'll catch the Night Stalker soon? Do you think he's the guy you questioned this morning?"

"No, he's off the list." Jonathan explained about Todd Berlin's broken leg, then said, "I don't know if the task force has new information, but my gut tells me this guy's almost at the end of his rope."

"Is that what you go on, your gut?" she asked curiously.

"No, of course not. I study the crime scene—the location, the killer's method, the choice of victim. Even what happens after the killing is important. I put all those things together and come up with a profile."

Christy considered this, then asked, "Can you share your profile of the Night Stalker, or is that classified?"

"Not classified," Jonathan said, "and you need to know for your own protection." Christy shuddered, and he reached across the console and laid a comforting hand on her arm, then removed it. "Here's what we have. This man is angry."

"Man, because serial killers are usually male?" Christy asked. She wished he'd touch her again. The warmth of his hand made her feel more secure.

"That, and what we saw indicated that the killer was much stronger than the victims." He glanced back at Christy. "He may be using these murders as revenge for something that happened during his childhood or adolescence."

"Such as?"

"I can't tell you specifics, but I'd guess he was bullied or beaten over a period of time. Now he wants control…and payback. Killing's the only way he figures he can achieve that."

"Twisted mind," Christy murmured, both horrified and intrigued by the picture Jonathan painted. "Go on."

"We have two possibilities for his occupation—one, that he has a menial job that doesn't require much thought so he has time to focus on those old grievances, or two, that he works in security or even law enforcement."

"Law enforcement? That's creepy. Don't applicants for

police work have to go through some kind of psychological screening?"

"Not really." His expression turned somber as he added, "And that's too bad."

She studied the hard lines of his face. "Do you want to be there when they catch him?"

"You bet I do."

When they approached the Houston city limits, it was mid-afternoon. "I have a task force meeting at police headquarters," Jonathan said. "You'll have to wait for me."

"Jonathan," Christy said sweetly. "Don't tell. Ask."

She was pleased to see his cheeks flush.

"Sorry," he said. "I'd let you drop me and I'd hitch a ride home afterward, but I don't want you to be alone. Will you wait?"

"Sure."

"The, uh, 'clientele' in the waiting room's not classy, but you'll have to put up with it."

Christy chuckled. "Honey, I worked in the E.R. for three years before I moved to orthopedics. I've seen it all."

Perhaps not, she thought when he left her in a dreary, windowless room filled with people whom the term *dregs of humanity* might compliment. The lady across from her alternately prayed and cursed in a strident voice loud enough to make Christy's head ache. A man in an expensive suit sat tapping his foot impatiently. He must be somebody's lawyer, Christy surmised. Two young girls who looked like hookers and probably were sat in a corner eyeing a man sprawled across three seats. The guy hadn't bathed in forever, and the pungent stench he emitted was nauseating. Christy moved as far away from him as possible and still wished she could get through the next hour without breathing.

She glanced at the clock on the wall and wondered how

the task force meeting was going and what new information Jonathan would have when he returned.

Jonathan. She'd learned a lot about him today, she thought, but what she'd discovered generated more questions than answers.

He was serious about his work. It seemed a calling rather than a job. So why didn't he do it full-time? He'd said he'd resigned from the FBI to teach at the university level. What made him change?

What else? she thought. Jonathan was sure of himself, at ease in his body, sure of his professional skills, certain almost to the point of arrogance that his decisions were the right ones. No question she liked his body, too, and she respected his confidence in his work, but arrogance was a big no-no.

Did it matter? Where they went from here was an unanswerable question. They had spent four days in fantasyland, where the past didn't matter. Even now, the two of them were hardly operating in the real world, where everything mattered. Physical attraction aside—

Come on, Christy, she told herself. She couldn't put attraction aside. It was part of the mix and it colored everything else.

The door opened and an officer ushered a girl out. Despite her garish makeup and provocative outfit, she couldn't have been more than fifteen. The two girls in the corner jumped up to greet her, and the three sashayed to the exit, giggling. The heavyset woman broke off a curse and sent up a prayer on their behalf, then went back to cursing. The homeless man, now asleep, snored loudly, and Christy shrank back in her chair and pretended she were somewhere else.

Jonathan was prepared for some good-natured ribbing when he entered the conference room where the Night Stalker task force met. The rest of the members were already seated around the table. The sound of paper shuffling and the odor of cigarettes filled the room.

Detective Luis Ramirez turned in his chair and gave Jonathan a high five. "Hey, pal," he said. "We heard you forgot about this job."

"Yeah, Ramirez," Jonathan replied, "I put you out of my mind." He took a seat beside Luis and glanced at the sheaf of papers at his place.

Marilee Winter from the coroner's office eyed him with concern. "Armand told us someone hit you on the head. Were you badly hurt?"

Jonathan shrugged. "A few stitches."

"What about your memory?"

"Wiped out," Jonathan said, smiling at her, "but I got it back."

"Did you get a look at the guy who smacked you?" Detective Dell Cummings inquired.

"No, he came up behind me. I heard footsteps, but that's all."

"And you don't remember anything?"

"Not until I woke up on the beach."

"How'd you get there?" Ramirez asked.

"I don't kn… Yeah, I do. I was in…a dark place…no air…"

"The trunk of a car," Marilee suggested.

"Yeah, had to be. I must've partially woken up." He rubbed his temple, feeling an echo of the pain, the panic.

"Well, you're damn lucky you have such a hard head," Luis said.

Armand Frazier, who'd been quiet up to now, cleared his throat. "Okay, people, enough about Talbot. Let's get to work." He turned to Jonathan. "What about the guy who lives on San Sebastian? Get anything out of him?"

"Enough to cross him off," Jonathan said and explained Todd Berlin's condition. Then he glanced at the paperwork set before him. "Fill me in on what's happened since I've been away."

Frazier pushed his papers aside. Jonathan knew he didn't need them. Talk about memory, Frazier was a walking encyclopedia. He could tell you every detail about every case he'd worked on in the past twenty years. "No new murders."

Luis crossed himself. "Thank God," he murmured. "Could he have quit?"

"Doubtful," Jonathan said. "He's not likely to quit until he's caught or someone kills him."

Dell Cummings shook his head. "He's too smart to get himself killed."

Jonathan leaned forward. "He hasn't chosen another victim because he's been gone. He followed me to San Sebastian. Once the storm hit, I couldn't get off the island and neither could he."

"So we check our suspects, see who might've been out of pocket for a few days," Armand said. "Agreed?" Murmurs of assent came from around the table, and Armand continued. "Now that Todd Berlin is off the list, we have three good suspects left. Talbot, we'll give you a minute to read over what we've got."

Jonathan scanned the material quickly.

Ramon Torres, former boyfriend of one of the victims, had connections to several others. Currently a parking attendant, he had once worked as a security guard in the medical building where Janice Berlin had been a physician's bookkeeper. On weekends, he worked as a bouncer at a club in a neighborhood generally considered one of the rougher ones in Houston. And, red flag: he'd been fired from several jobs for harassing women and had an arrest for assault on his record.

Second, Jackson Ealy, a hospital janitor. Not the job he'd predicted the killer would have, but Ealy was certainly in the right place, Jonathan mused. Ealy had a history of emotional problems. Like many serial killers, he'd never established a relationship with a woman. At age thirty-five, he still lived at home with his domineering mother. Big red flag.

Finally, Jack O'Neal, a parolee working in an auto parts store several blocks from the medical center. In prison for a series of violent rapes but showed "exemplary behavior" behind bars. Once free, he could have graduated to murder.

"Any of 'em could have done it," Jonathan concluded.

"What insight." Shannon McGinity tossed her blond hair and spoke for the first time. Jonathan knew she didn't like him for personal reasons. She'd made a play for him once, and he'd rebuffed her. Gently, he'd thought, but not gently enough. Now she sent a disgusted look in his direction. "Can't you do any better than that, *Doctor* Talbot?"

He gave her a bland look. "No, sorry."

"When we catch the Night Stalker, we'll do it with solid police work," Shannon went on, "not with some kind of psychobabble."

"Can it, McGinity," Armand said sharply. "We don't have time for snide remarks here. You talk to Ramon Torres. Luis, you take the janitor. Dell, you've got O'Neal. Check their work records, see if anyone was out of town the past week. Moving on, let's talk about the victims—"

"Hold it a minute," Shannon said. "Why question anyone? Why not just check their work sheets?"

Luis grinned. "Nervous about going up against these guys, McGinity?"

Shannon reacted on cue. "Nervous? Why would I be? I'm as good a cop as you. I could go head to head with anyone here—"

Jonathan tried to tune her out. Why this troublemaker was on the task force he didn't know. Yes, he did. Shannon was right—she was a damn good police officer.

She kept talking. "Besides, one thing's for sure. I don't fit the victim profile. I'm not in a medical field. And look at my hair."

"Hair?" Jonathan stared at Shannon. She must be talking about something he wasn't privy to.

Marilee noticed his confusion and leaned forward. "Shannon means her hair isn't the right color. One thing I discovered while you were 'in limbo' is that hair color seems to be important to this guy. Every one of his victims' hair was some shade of red."

Jonathan stared at her. His blood ran cold. Medical workers. Reddish hair. Christy. She was a perfect choice for a victim. And the killer knew where she lived.

Chapter 13

At the sound of the door, Christy opened her eyes. Jonathan strode into the waiting room. For an instant, she thought he looked troubled, but then he erased the worried expression and smiled.

He came to her and put out a hand. "Ready to go?"

Before Christy could answer, the door opened again and several people trooped in. "Hey, Talbot," one of them called, "want to get a bite? We're heading for the Tumbleweed."

Jonathan glanced at Christy. "Sure," she said. She'd enjoy a chance to watch him with his colleagues. Except for their brief conversations with Warner and Ellie Thompson, she hadn't seen Jonathan in a social situation. What would he be like?

He led her to the group and introduced her. Luis Ramirez, a dark-eyed detective with a sexy smile, shook her hand and winked. "*Querida,* forget this chump. Let's slip away and you spend the evening with me."

"He has my car keys. Would sitting next to you at the Tumbleweed be okay?" she asked, laughing.

"Better than nothing. We'll run off together tomorrow."

For a bunch of people who'd spent the last hour discussing a brutal killer, the group seemed lighthearted as they headed toward the door. Christy supposed they weren't much different from medical people. If caregivers obsessed on their patients, they'd soon be no good at treating them. If all these folks did was think about the murderer, they'd have no emotional energy left to figure out how to catch him.

They stepped outside into the twilight. In the west, the sun was setting, washing the sky with pink and coral. The air was warm, but the stifling heat of the afternoon had waned. "Nice evening," Christy murmured to Jonathan as she strolled along the street between him and Luis.

Suddenly a voice called out, "Dr. Talbot."

Jonathan turned. "Ah, hell," he muttered. "The media."

A young woman thrust a microphone at him, and a bearded cameraman hefted a video camera on his shoulder. Jonathan stepped in front of Christy in what she realized was a protective move.

"Dr. Talbot," the news reporter said, "can you tell us what you've determined about the Night Stalker?"

"As soon as we have further information, I'll make a statement."

The reporter started to ask another question, but he sidestepped her and moved on.

"You sure evaded that question," Christy murmured as they continued down the street.

"Tried," Jonathan said.

"Doesn't matter," Luis said. "They'll spin the story however they want. Sensationalism's what counts in local news, right, J.T.?"

For a moment, Christy thought Luis had called Jonathan

J.D., then realized he hadn't. But Jonathan had been close to the truth when he'd come up with those initials. She wondered if she'd ever feel comfortable thinking of him as anything but J.D., then questioned whether their relationship would last long enough for "ever" to matter.

The reporter's appearance seemed to put a damper on the group's good spirits. No one had much to say until they were seated around a long table in the Tumbleweed. Off duty, they ordered beers with their barbecue or burgers, and gradually the banter resumed.

Christy listened with interest, although it was hard to hear over the din. Billed as a down-home Texas restaurant-bar, the Tumbleweed's ambience was rustic, with sawdust-covered floors, cattle brands on the walls and a menu heavy on barbecue and chili. The place drew a boisterous crowd and featured country and western music. Tonight a group called the Lopin' Lizards, with a lead singer who did a fair Willie Nelson imitation, was playing. They were enthusiastic and earsplittingly loud.

Luis leaned across Christy and grinned at Jonathan. He raised his voice. "So, Talbot, you made the most of your time out of mind. How'd you two get together, *querida?*"

"I opened my door and he fell at my feet."

"Romance," Luis said with an exaggerated sigh and raised his glass. "Hey, Talbot, a toast."

"To what?" Jonathan asked.

"To finally getting a life." When Jonathan raised a brow, Luis added mischievously, "And a woman."

Christy watched the flush creep up Jonathan's face. She was both sorry and pleased that her presence embarrassed him.

Luis turned to Christy. "So you just bowled him over, eh? Love at first sight."

"Head injury," Christy corrected him. "That guy really clobbered him."

Dell Cummings—big, broad-shouldered and more serious than Luis—remarked, "Too bad you didn't see him, Talbot."

"Yeah, your one chance to ID the Stalker and you blew it."

Christy glanced sharply at the freckle-faced blonde who'd spoken, surprised at the rancor she directed at Jonathan.

Before Jonathan had a chance to respond, Dell said, "Weren't you listening before, Shannon? He told you the guy hit him from behind. Most people don't have eyes in the back of their heads."

Shannon took a bite of her burger. "Right, but Talbot's not 'most people.' The press thinks he walks on water."

"But what do they know?" Jonathan said mildly. Outwardly, he seemed unfazed by Shannon's hostility, but Christy saw his hand clench below the table. She frowned as she wondered what the source of the obvious bad blood between them might be.

"She's a good cop, but she's a troublemaker," Luis murmured in her ear. "Don't pay her any mind. *He* doesn't."

Good advice, Christy decided, ignored Shannon, and leaned forward to get the attention of Marilee Winters, the other woman in the group. When he'd introduced her, Jonathan had said she worked in the coroner's office. "Are you a pathologist?" Christy asked.

Marilee nodded. "Second in command to the medical examiner."

"I guess you see some pretty interesting…cases."

"Corpses," Marilee corrected. "My work's pretty gory for most people's tastes."

Christy smiled at her. "So's mine. I'm a nurse. Spent three years in the E.R. before I moved on."

Dell glanced her way. "An E.R. nurse? Do you still work in a hospital?"

"Yes, at St. Mary's."

He studied her thoughtfully. "Maybe I saw you there."

"You might have if you ever had a broken bone. I've been in orthopedics for a couple of years."

"Never broke a bone," Dell said, "but you do look familiar."

"She looks like that model, Christie Brinkley," offered Armand Frazier.

Christy chuckled. "Not a chance. The only thing alike about us is the name."

The lighthearted conversation continued, with the group one-upping and teasing one another. Christy liked seeing Jonathan in this setting, liked the easy camaraderie he had with his colleagues. And she was amused by their interest in her. Apparently seeing Jonathan with a woman was a novelty.

She wished he'd dance with her. The vocalist began to sing a Willie Nelson signature ballad, "Blue Eyes Cryin' in the Rain." Christy wanted Jonathan's arms around her, wanted to be held close for a slow dance. But Jonathan was deep in conversation with Dell, so she could only watch the dancers and imagine Jonathan's heart beating against hers, his lips against her hair. *Later,* she promised herself. Later they'd have their private "dance," the most intimate kind two people could have.

Jonathan kept his back turned, his attention trained on Dell. It wasn't easy, with the slow music and the singer crooning a song of love and loss.

Jonathan wasn't interested in Dell's theory on the Night Stalker. He wanted to dance with Christy, inhale the sweet scent she wore, feel the softness of her skin. Sitting so close to her and not touching her was maddening. He wanted to dance with her now, then take her home and make love to her through the night.

He wanted…exactly what he shouldn't. He had no right

to even think of making love to Christy again, not when he knew he was so wrong for her. He'd already screwed up her life. He shouldn't add sex to the mix.

Damn, he could do with a selective memory loss right now. Because he could remember everything about last night. Every touch, every sigh. And the thought of not repeating that incredible lovemaking was pure torture.

After the slow song, the band took a break. "Hey, here comes the news," Marilee said suddenly. All eyes turned to the big-screen TV above the bar.

The news anchor introduced a segment on the Night Stalker. Then the camera focused on the woman who had waylaid Jonathan earlier. With her hair pulled back in a sleek chignon and her navy summer suit, she looked the picture of a confident professional. "A serial killer lurks in Houston. A task force formed by the Houston Police Department meets regularly but has been unable to apprehend the man who has now murdered six women.

"We caught up with noted forensic psychologist, Dr. Jonathan Talbot, who was instrumental in leading Chicago police to the notorious Dr. Death, and who is currently consulting with the HPD."

The brief exchange between her and Jonathan played, and then the camera swung back to the reporter. "It seems the police are no closer to capturing the Night Stalker, the killer who has terrorized the Medical Center area. Houston women, especially those who work in the huge complex of hospitals along Fannin Street, are frightened."

She then interviewed a woman dressed in hospital scrubs who said she was scared to leave the hospital at night. "Women want an end to this," the woman added. "The police should put more detectives on the case."

"Yeah," Dell interjected in a voice tight with frustration, "like we don't already have every cop in the city on the hunt."

"It takes time," Armand said.

Marilee set down her beer. "Exactly what women feel they don't have," she pointed out. "*We* know these cases aren't solved overnight, but *they* don't."

Beer sloshed on the table as Shannon shoved her glass away. "People oughta have more faith in us."

Dell nodded, his face grim. "If they're gonna blame someone, it's always the cops."

"Hey," Armand said, "you can't change human nature. Take it easy."

"Yeah," Luis said. "Chill out, Dell. You got the late shift tomorrow. Go sit by that fishing hole near your house, catch yourself a big ol' catfish." When Dell nodded and visibly relaxed, Luis turned to Shannon. "And you—"

"If you tell me to go take a bubble bath, Ramirez, I'll cream you," Shannon said.

Armand held up a hand. "Children! Calm down. The last thing we need is to fight among ourselves."

Conversation lagged after that, and one by one, people began to leave. Luis said he had a lady friend waiting. Dell had company coming over, and Armand's grandson had a Little League game at eight-thirty.

Only Shannon and Marilee remained when Jonathan and Christy took their leave. As they walked back to police headquarters through the soft twilight, Christy thought about the night they'd spent together and the night to come, and her heart began to pump. With every step her anticipation soared higher. She glanced at the man walking by her side. What would happen between them now?

He kept his eyes straight ahead, and he didn't take her hand. She supposed his mind was on the Night Stalker, so when they got into her car, she took her cue from him and kept her voice even. "My house or yours?"

"He knows where you live, and probably where I live,

too," Jonathan said, then considered for a moment. "Let's go to yours. I want to look it over and see how safe it is."

Abruptly her thoughts, which had been focused on love-making, shifted. Pleasurable excitement gave way to dread. "Do you think he'll come?"

"I don't know, but if he does, we'll be prepared."

She gave him directions to her house and told herself not to be afraid. Jonathan had kept them safe before. But she glanced out her side mirror anyway to see if anyone was following.

"Tell me about Dr. Death," she said, trying to distract herself. "I recognized the alias, but I don't remember the case."

"He was an intern who believed he had a directive from God to murder AIDS patients."

She gazed at Jonathan admiringly. "And you caught him?"

"I constructed his profile. The police caught him."

"Any other especially notorious killers you've identified?"

"The Midnight Angel, a nurse in Portland, Oregon, who put more than twenty people 'out of their misery' before the cops nabbed her. And a young man in Cleveland who began killing off doctors when he wasn't admitted to medical school." ·

"You've worked on a lot of cases connected with medicine."

"Yeah, it's a specialty of sorts. That's why I was called about this one and why I said yes."

They turned off the freeway and drove along a quiet avenue in upscale West University. Not far from the Medical Center, it was a popular neighborhood for physicians and their families, who usually tore down the small bungalows built decades ago and replaced them with megahouses. Keith had coveted such a house. Nothing had pleased him more than moving into this showplace. It was much too big for a woman alone, and Christy had almost decided to put it up for sale. She wondered what Jonathan would think of it.

Now she gazed at his strong profile and wondered about him. What was his life like before now? "What drew you to your career?" she asked. "Was someone important to you a crime victim?"

He shook his head. "No one's asked me that before," he said. "I don't think I've ever asked myself. I should know but I don't. Sounds strange, doesn't it?"

"No," Christy said softly. "I think a lot of people just fall into their careers. But maybe it's one of the things you haven't remembered."

"No, I do remember. I went to law school for a year, didn't like it, and was searching for something else. I read an autobiography of a federal agent, and I started thinking about law *enforcement* and applied to the Bureau."

"Is profiling part of FBI training?"

"All agents have some instruction in it, and some elect to specialize and get more in-depth training. I happened to live next door to a profiler and got interested in his work. The insights he had into the criminal mind were fascinating, so I went for the specialty. And I also returned to college and got a psychology degree. I always tried to emulate my neighbor."

"Sounds like you thought a lot of him."

"I did. He was killed in a raid a few months before I started profiling." He braked for a red light. "I had this…feeling I had to carry on for him." In the traffic light's glow, Christy saw that he looked embarrassed. Just like a man, to feel uncomfortable sharing his deepest feelings. Even male psychologists apparently found that difficult.

She reached across the console and touched his arm. "You're a nice man, Jonathan."

He glanced at her. "As nice as J.D.?"

So he knew she was confused about him and his alter ego. "Just about," she said, "and about as nice-looking, too."

"Aw, aren't you a sweet thang?"

Christy laughed at the exaggerated drawl. "Honey, no matter how hard you try, you'll never sound like a Texan."

She pointed to a cross street. "Turn left here. It's the second house."

Now it was her turn to be uncomfortable. The house was... well, pretentious.

"Big," Jonathan said.

A two-story tan stucco, it was, in Christy's mind, three times bigger than it needed to be. "Yeah, well..."

"Not your style," Jonathan went on. "Your husband's."

"Ex-husband," she reminded him. "I'm thinking of selling. That was one thing I wanted to decide while I was vacationing."

"Sorry I interfered with that," Jonathan said and opened the driver's-side door. He carried her bags in, set them in the entry hall and said, "I'm going to take a look around."

She followed him as he made his inspection. The house had an elaborate alarm system, installed because Keith often "worked late," or so he'd said. And also because he'd insisted on a state-of-the-art media room, which was now empty.

Christy had always felt safe in the house, but suddenly she didn't. Azalea bushes grew near the dining-room windows. They were meant to be decorative, but now they seemed perfect for hiding a killer. The wide glass doors to the back patio and the tall windows in the living room seemed too inviting. And her bedroom had French doors that led out to a balcony...which was much too close to an oak tree that an enterprising burglar, or worse, the Night Stalker, could climb.

Christy waited nervously for Jonathan's opinion. After a thorough tour of the house, he said, "You have a good protection system. We'll just tweak it a little."

"How?"

"I want to put your company on alert, tell them you've had a threatening call and get them to monitor your system closely. And I'll pick up some better locks. Yours are a criminal's dream…"

Christy blanched at his words.

"…that is, *if* he can bypass your alarm system."

"Can he?"

"Doubtful, but you need to hear the worst-case scenario. Even if there were no Night Stalker, you need better locks."

"Okay. Anything else?"

"No." He looked away.

Silence. Stiff, uncomfortable silence. They stood in the kitchen, looking everywhere except at each other. Jonathan stared at the refrigerator as if he'd never seen one before. Suddenly, they seemed to have nothing to say.

"Do you, uh, want some coffee?" Christy asked.

"No, thanks. It's getting late."

"Mmm-hmm." Last night they'd been in bed together. Tonight…

"I'm staying the night," he said. The emotion she'd heard in his voice the other evening was gone. He was just reciting a fact.

She kept her voice cool, too. "I know."

"I'll bunk in your guest room."

Christy felt as if he'd slapped her. She looked past him and said, "The bed isn't made up. I'll get some clean sheets."

"Thank you."

Someone overhearing them would never guess that twenty-four hours ago they'd been locked in a passionate embrace. Feeling as if she were a robot marching stiffly through the house, she went to the linen closet and got out a set of sheets.

She brought them to the guest bedroom. Jonathan was waiting at the door. He reached for the linens. "Thanks."

She held onto them. "I'll make the bed."

"Not necessary."

They stood there, stalemated, both grasping the sheets as if they were the most important things in the world.

Stupid, Christy thought. "Take them." She let go.

Their eyes locked.

She couldn't look away. She had to ask. "Why?" she whispered.

"Because."

She waited.

Jonathan sighed. "Because my life's too complicated. Look what I've gotten you into."

"I'm reminding you, Jonathan, that you didn't do it intentionally."

"No, but sleeping with you wouldn't be right."

"You've done it once. More than once if you want to be precise."

His glance never wavered. "I don't want to be unfair to you."

"Because this won't last?" Christy let out a long breath. "There's no guarantee that anything will last. And truth? I don't know yet if I want this to."

His expression told her nothing. What the heck, she thought. Might as well say it all.

"Jonathan, let me decide what's fair to me. I'm a big girl. I can live with whatever happens." She raised her chin in challenge. "Can *you?*"

Chapter 14

Jonathan stared at her for a long moment. And then he dropped the sheets and pulled her into his arms. "Christy. God, I want you." His mouth covered hers and he kissed her with such urgency and desperation, he took her breath away.

When she could breathe again, Christy tugged at his hand. "Me, too. Come to bed," she whispered. "Quick."

They stumbled across the room, leaving clothes in their wake. His shirt landed on the floor, then his jeans. He struggled with Christy's bra, then tossed it up and over his shoulder toward the nightstand, where it hung on the bedside lampshade. For once, Christy didn't care about the mess. She wanted him naked, mouth to mouth, skin to skin. Sheets forgotten, they made love on the unmade bed.

It was fast, it was wild. It was the most thrilling night of her life. They drove each other harder, higher. He nipped her shoulder. She ran her nails down his back. Groaning, panting, they raced to see who would climax first. Christy did, only seconds before Jonathan joined her.

And then they lay exhausted, side by side. "Like fireworks," she panted. "Like the Fourth of July and New Year's Eve, all rolled into one." Would they ever top this night? she thought, as she fell asleep.

In the morning, reality returned.

Jonathan hurried her through breakfast, barely gave her time for the obligatory table-clearing. When she returned to the bedroom and picked up the discarded sheets, he took them out of her hands and set them on the bed. "Leave them." He glanced at his watch. "Hannah's expecting us."

Christy frowned. "Are you sure this is necessary? I hate to impose—"

"It's taken care of."

Her eyes narrowed. "Jonathan, there's something more. Something you're not telling me."

He looked away, then back. "Marilee came up with one more detail the victims have in common. All of them were redheads."

Christy gasped and touched her hair. "I told you, I'm not—"

"Close enough."

"Should I...dye it?"

He shook his head. "Won't help. He's seen you." When she shivered, he came to her and put his arm around her shoulders. "Let's go."

This time she didn't protest.

She noticed that Jonathan kept his eyes on the rearview mirror as he drove. A couple of times he doubled back and took side streets. She didn't ask him if he thought someone might be following. Clearly, he wasn't taking chances.

Still, Hannah's house wasn't far. A ranch-style brick with a neatly trimmed yard in the pleasant older neighborhood of

Afton Oaks, it looked like a nice place to raise children. Jonathan parked in front.

He glanced at Christy as she scanned the surroundings. "It's safe."

"Oh, I'm sure it is. I was just looking around and thinking this doesn't seem like the home of two federal agents."

"Because there're no bars on the windows? No shotgun shells on the lawn?" Christy flushed, and he lowered his voice as he rang the doorbell. "Most of us try to appear normal."

The door was opened by a woman who indeed appeared normal. In fact, with her pixie face framed by a riot of chestnut curls, she looked more like a kindergarten teacher than an FBI agent.

"Hi, come in," she said. Jonathan introduced Christy, and Hannah shook her hand. Though she looked like a mischievous imp, her grip was strong, reassuring.

"It's nice of you to do this," Christy said.

"No problem." She showed them into a living room crowded with infant paraphernalia. "Sorry about all the junk," she said, "but you've entered baby world."

"Then where are the babies?" Jonathan asked.

"In the bedroom. Infants are like cats. They sleep all day." She grinned at Jonathan. "Want some coffee?"

"No, thanks. I have to leave," Jonathan said. "I'll keep in touch."

"Don't worry, Doc," Hannah told him. "Motherhood hasn't robbed me of my skills."

He hugged her. "I know. I'm just—"

"A father hen…rooster…whatever." She opened the door. "Go." When the door shut behind him, Hannah turned back to Christy with a wide smile. "How about the coffee?"

"I'd love some."

"Great. Come on and we'll sit and talk. I'm so looking forward to being with a person who says something besides 'wah wah wah.'"

In the kitchen, she got down two cups, and filled them. "Don't get me wrong. I adore my babies, but their communication leaves something to be desired. I find myself having three-way conversations with me taking all three parts." She glanced over her shoulder. "Sugar, cream?"

"Sugar."

Hannah brought the cups to the table. "So tell me, how'd you get mixed up in this serial-killer business?"

After Christy explained, Hannah said, "Jonathan's great. He's a decent guy and a good agent. He'll keep you safe."

Christy stirred her coffee. "You said he's an agent, but he's not anymore, is he?"

"Nope, he's a college professor. Good at that, too, from what I hear."

"Why did he leave the FBI?" Christy asked.

From Hannah's expression, she realized she'd put Hannah in an uncomfortable position. "Sorry," she said hastily, "I didn't mean to pry." Lord, what must the woman think of her, coming in here and five minutes later grilling her about Jonathan?

"The story's not exactly classified," Hannah said, "but you should hear it from him."

Christy nodded and wondered what the "story" could possibly be. "I'm not usually so nosy, but Jonathan and I met under such bizarre circumstances, and even though we were together 24/7, cut off from everything, I didn't really get to know him. I mean, I got to know J.D.—that's what he called himself. But he's a different person now."

"Do you think he could change that much?" Hannah asked. "Seems to me, he's who he is on the inside, no matter what he remembers."

"I'd like to think that. I…liked J.D. a lot."

"Liked?"

"More than liked, but I…don't know. I'm a cautious person."

Hannah took a last sip from her cup. "Oh, sure. You let that beat-up stranger into your house."

"He tells me I should never have done that."

"He's right." Hannah pushed her cup away. "But it's too late to obsess over that now. You'll just have to let things play out."

A tiny cry sounded from another room, and she stood up, her face softening, eyes glowing. "Hey, there's Alex. Wanna see my boys?"

"I'd love to." Christy picked up the cups and rinsed them. "Can you tell their cries apart?"

"Absolutely."

They walked through the house and into a bedroom decorated in a Peter Pan motif. Along one light-blue wall stood two cribs, each with a name stenciled on it: Alex and Zachary.

"Nice names," Christy remarked.

Hannah leaned over to pick up a howling, red-faced infant. "Thanks. We planned on two babies and when they came in a package, we decided they'd be our *A* to *Z*." She winked. "To remind us we've completed our family."

Soothing the baby, she changed him, then sat down in a white bentwood rocker, unbuttoned her blouse, and put the infant to her breast. Christy listened to the baby's little grunts as he fed and Hannah's answering murmurs. How she ached to suckle an infant.

She tiptoed over to the other crib and watched Zachary sleep. So adorable. So sweet.

The baby stirred. His tiny hands moved, one foot poked out from under the receiving blanket, and he whimpered softly.

"Want to hold him till it's his turn?" Hannah asked.

"I'd love to." She bent and picked up the wiggly bundle. "Oh, you're so precious," she cooed. "And wet. May I change him?"

"Be my guest."

Christy carried him to the changing table and carefully replaced the soaked diaper with a dry one. She couldn't resist tickling his tummy and when he responded with a gurgle, she knew she'd lost her heart.

She sat in the twin to Hannah's rocker and gazed into Zachary's blue eyes. Her hand brushed over his hair, his angel-soft skin. If only she and Jonathan—

What was she thinking?

She and Jonathan were about as far from discussing a baby as Earth was from Mars. She didn't even *know* him.

In his own way, he was as controlling as Keith. And, like Keith, he was far too attractive for his own good. Keith had made the most of his good looks, even after marriage.

Was it her fate to fall in love with handsome, domineering men? But she wasn't in love, she told herself, and even if she were, it took two to tango. Or tangle. Well, they'd certainly done that. And very well, too.

She'd told Jonathan she could take it when their affair was over. She wondered if she'd lied.

Demanding her attention, Zachary kicked his feet. Christy grabbed one chubby little foot and kissed the sole. "You are so cute," she told him and was rewarded with a wide, toothless smile. "I'm in love," she told Hannah.

"Are you into guy-swapping?" Hannah asked, "because you can hold Alex while Zack gets his breakfast."

They traded babies and Christy lost her heart all over again.

The morning was a baby-lover's heaven. She helped Hannah bathe the boys, watched them play, even changed a dirty diaper. "Sure you don't mind?" Hannah asked.

"Are you kidding? I'm a nurse."

When the phone rang at noon and she heard Hannah saying, "Jonathan, we're fine," she was surprised that the time had gone so fast.

Hannah handed her the phone. "Let him hear your voice or he won't pay the ransom."

Christy took the phone. "Hi."

"Are you okay?" Jonathan asked.

"Yes, of course, I'm all right. Matter of fact, I'm having a wonderful time. See you later."

Jonathan hung up the phone, leaned back in his chair, and stretched. So far, the day had been busy. After he'd dropped Christy off at Hannah's, he'd stopped by his house, grabbed his mail, and—hallelujah!—changed clothes. The ones he'd worn for nearly a week were practically part of his skin. He considered burning them, then tossed them in the washer. He sorted through his mail, checked his answering machine and called his insurance company, then made arrangements for a rental car. He didn't want to use Christy's any longer than he had to. On the way downtown, he stopped to pick up a new cell phone. Thank God it was July and he wasn't teaching at the university during the summer semester. One less thing to deal with.

Once in his office at headquarters, he read the updates on the Stalker files. No new evidence had turned up, and nothing new had surfaced on their three suspects. He hoped the questioning this morning would be productive. They'd better come up with something soon, or people would be clamoring for every task force member's head. Worse, the police would be pressured to arrest someone, anyone, and there was always the danger that an innocent person would be charged while the killer slipped away.

He heard a rap on the door of the office he used at the HPD. "Come in," he called.

Armand stuck his head in. "Task force meeting in five."

"On my way."

Members of the task force came into the conference room and took their seats. Today there was no bantering; this was too serious. Folders lay before each place. A whiteboard with markers sat in the corner.

Armand tossed down the morning edition of the *Houston Chronicle.* "Anyone read the op-ed page?"

"I did," Marilee said. "We didn't come off well."

"That's putting it mildly. Listen up, everyone." The editorial blasted the HPD in general and the task force in particular. If these people couldn't produce, the chief should appoint a new task force. If not, the paper intimated, a group of citizens was ready to hire its own.

"Lynch-mob mentality," Armand said, "but we need to get somewhere on this case." His voice rose, and he pounded the table with a beefy fist. "I want answers. Ramirez, what do you have?"

"Nothing, sir. Jackson Ealy was at work at the hospital all last week. Plenty of witnesses saw him."

Armand wrote that on the board. "McGinity?"

Shannon tossed a worksheet on the table. "Here's a copy of Torres's hours. They check out." She turned to Dell. "What about O'Neal?"

"He reported to his parole officer on schedule. He signed in and out of work. He's a punctual guy, never a minute late. Sorry."

"So where does that leave us?" Frazier asked.

"Could any of these guys have had time to get down to San Sebastian, clobber Talbot, and get back in time for work?" Marilee asked. "It's only an hour away."

"Yeah, in good weather," Jonathan said, "but he wouldn't have been able to leave the island once the storm kicked up."

"He could've used a boat," Dell suggested.

"Good idea," Jonathan said. "But he couldn't have crossed to the mainland in a boat the night the storm blew in. And all these guys were at work early the next morning."

"Maybe he's a superhero," Dell said.

Shannon scowled at him, then at Jonathan. "You're barking up the wrong tree, all of you," she said, "adding Talbot's head-bashing into the mix."

"Why is that?" Luis asked.

"It was probably a random act of violence."

"I don't think so," Jonathan said. "If it was random, he wouldn't have come after me again."

"So it was somebody who doesn't like you," Shannon said.

"You, for instance?" Luis asked and got a glare in reply.

"You heard Talbot say he was hit by a man."

Shannon's sarcasm did not go over well. "Maybe he got you confused, Miss Femininity," Luis suggested.

Shannon's face went crimson and her fists clenched.

"Okay, knock it off," Armand snapped. "Talbot, what's your take on this?"

Jonathan stood up to pace. "Our janitor, Jackson Ealy, fits the standard profile—"

"If all we have to look for is someone who fits a 'standard,' what do we need a profiler for?" Shannon, still fuming, muttered.

"Let me finish," Jonathan said. "I've studied O'Neal's prison records and the reports of psychologists who interviewed him before his trial. I think he's the least likely of the three to go in for serial murder. In an impulsive moment, yes, but not like this. Torres is the most likely. He's angry, and from reports of people who knew about his relationship with one of the victims, he's a control freak." He ranked the three names on the board, paused.

Still standing, he said, "Torres has a clean work record. He doesn't draw attention to himself there. But after hours, his anger spurts out and he becomes a predator."

Marilee nodded. "He hunts for victims who fit a pattern that's meaningful for him—red-haired women who work in health care. They remind him of someone. We just don't know who."

"That still doesn't explain how Torres got back and forth between San Sebastian and Houston during a tropical storm," Armand said. "*If* he did."

"Let's think this through," Luis suggested. "Torres hits Talbot, drives back across the bridge before it's impassable and gets to work early Monday. Two days later he goes back again by that boat Dell came up with, does his dirty work, and gets back to work with no one the wiser. He could manage it."

"Ramirez, check out his hours again," Armand said. "Talk to his supervisor at work. Meanwhile, Talbot, do you have any other ideas?"

"We should check out other security companies that serve hospitals and businesses in and around the Medical Center. I like Torres as our guy, but at this point we can't rule out other possibilities."

"Okay, people, get on it," Armand said and called out assignments. "We'll meet tomorrow."

As task force members filed out, Jonathan pulled Shannon aside. "I want to apologize for Luis," he told her quietly. Although she stiffened, he continued. "Luis is stressed, like all of us. But that 'femininity' remark was uncalled for."

Shannon's shoulders relaxed, and she looked at Jonathan almost hopefully. "Think so?"

"Definitely."

She gave him a tentative smile. "Thanks. I guess I'm touchy about my femininity. I get a lot of digs about being a cop."

"Don't believe 'em."

They separated, and Jonathan walked back to his office.

Shannon wasn't unfeminine at all. In fact, she was pretty. But she wasn't his type. He went back to his office and picked up the phone to check again on Christy.

Hannah laughed at his anxious question and said, "She's *still* fine. Right now she's in the babies' room, singing Zachary to sleep. Want me to get her?"

"No, don't disturb her." In his mind, he saw Christy with an infant in her arms. He imagined her tender smile, her soft voice, and a sweet warmth blossomed in his heart. He cleared his throat. "How about if I pick up some dinner for the three of us?"

"That'd be heaven."

"What's your choice?"

"Chinese, but let me check with Christy." In a moment, she came back. "Moo goo gai pan for both of us."

The sound of the doorbell made Christy's heart leap. It had to be Jonathan. "I'll get it," she called and wondered if doorbells would be forever associated with him in her mind.

As certain as she was that Jonathan stood on the other side of the door, she peered through the peephole first. Yes, it was him, his arms full of white boxes. With a smile, she opened the door. "Hi."

He frowned. "Did you look out first?"

Control again. "Is this *Self-Protection for Dummies*?" she snapped. "Of course I did."

He came inside. "You should have let Hannah get it."

"She's feeding the baby. I can't substitute for that. Sorry."

His gaze dropped to her breasts, and his eyes darkened. Annoyed as she was, Christy couldn't still the flutter in her heart, the throbbing in her belly. Damn, even when she was angry with him, he turned her on. If he wanted to make love to her here on the living-room carpet, surrounded by Chinese takeout and baby toys, she'd probably say yes.

They went into the kitchen. Hannah was seated at the kitchen table patting Alex's back after his feeding. "Hi, Doc," she said.

"Hi, Mom."

"We're almost done here." As if to agree, Alex burped. "You can put dinner in the microwave. You know how to do that, don't you?"

"I know how to *cook*."

Christy rolled her eyes. She wasn't sure about that.

Jonathan put the boxes in the oven and came back to look at Zachary, who was propped in a baby bouncer. "Hey, big guy. Wanna get outa there?" He bent down and picked up the baby, then lifted him high in the air. Zachary kicked and gurgled, and Jonathan laughed.

He sat down by the table and held Zachary on his lap. The baby grabbed Jonathan's finger. As his tiny hand closed over it, Christy saw Jonathan's gentle smile. Her heart turned over.

"He misses his dad," Hannah remarked.

"What's going on with Troy?" Jonathan asked.

They discussed the case Hannah's husband was on while Hannah nursed the baby. Over dinner, they talked about the Night Stalker. Jonathan's frustration was evident to Christy.

Apparently Hannah noticed it, too. "Let's change the subject," she said. "Anyone know any good jokes?"

The atmosphere calmed as their conversation lightened. After clearing the table and cleaning up, Jonathan and Christy left.

"Are you okay with the arrangement?" he asked Christy as they got into the car.

"Love it. Thanks." She glanced out the window and noticed he was headed away from her house. "Running an errand?" she asked.

"Heading for my house. I don't want to get into a pattern."

"Good idea." Besides, she was eager to see how Jonathan lived.

He took the Loop that encircled the central area of town, got off and headed north. Soon they were in the Heights, a much older section. A mixture of small shabby cottages with siding in need of paint and stately two-story brick homes, the neighborhood was eclectic and interesting. Jonathan pulled into the driveway of a Craftsman bungalow that had been freshly painted. A big oak tree dominated the small front yard. He parked in the garage and they went in.

The living room was spartan, with wooden floors and a minimum of furniture. "Nice," Christy said. Cozier than her ostentatious home for sure. And neat enough to meet her own high standards.

He gave her a tour. The front bedroom had been turned into an office, with all the high-tech gadgets a former FBI man would be used to. On the bookshelf, Christy spotted a photograph of a smiling Jonathan, holding a plaque and shaking hands with Bill Clinton. The president had signed the picture, "To Jonathan Talbot, a true patriot, with best regards."

"Gosh," she said, "I'm impressed. What did you do to get that?"

He shrugged. "Helped catch a guy who'd written threatening letters to the president."

The plaque hung on the wall. Christy read the inscription and wondered if Jonathan missed his old profession and, again, speculated on why he had left.

"Fax came in," Jonathan said and pulled a sheet of paper off the machine. He glanced at it and his face darkened. Christy looked over his shoulder.

Written in block letters, the message read, "I know where you live, too." In the lower corner of the page was a drawing of a revolver.

"Of course he does," Jonathan muttered. "And how long before he tracks you down at Hannah's?"

Chapter 15

Two nights later, Christy and Jonathan relaxed on the couch in their room at the Marriott across from the elegant Galleria Shopping Center. At Jonathan's insistence, they'd stayed at different places each night. Now they were registered as Mr. and Mrs. J. D. Russell, the name Jonathan had used in San Sebastian. Christy wondered what had gone through Jonathan's mind when he'd signed the register. Did he focus on the Mr. and Mrs. or was it just part of his plan to keep the Night Stalker from finding them?

Again, she and Jonathan were spending time together, locked away from the world. Now, with Jonathan's memories returning at an accelerating pace, they'd talked endlessly. She learned about his childhood: his dogs and Blacky, a pet crow, his success in Little League, his passion for reading. She'd told him about her early life, too. They'd compared childhood heroes from favorite books: Jo in *Little Women* for her, Frank Hardy for Jonathan. They'd shared dreams that had come true and those that hadn't.

But all this would end soon. In three days Christy's vacation would be over. Although Jonathan urged her to ask for more time off, she refused. She had to risk returning to work, even though the thought of a killer lurking in the cavernous hospital with its maze of corridors, its closets and cubbyholes, made her shudder.

But she didn't want to think about that. She'd play Scarlett and think about it tomorrow…or the next day. For now, she just wanted to be with Jonathan.

He'd kicked off his shoes, and he lay with his head in her lap as they watched *The Philadelphia Story* on the classic movie channel.

Christy stroked his hair. The area Dr. Mayes had stitched was growing back. Tomorrow the stitches would come out. "Tired?" she asked.

"A little. The task force has a huge database to work with now. A lot of security companies with dozens of employees operate in the Medical Center area. I'm doing a spread sheet to see who matches the characteristics of the Stalker."

Christy bent to kiss his temple. "Don't think about it tonight. Watch the movie." She turned her attention to the TV. "I love Katharine Hepburn. She was such a gutsy lady."

He smiled up at her. "Like you."

Christy stared at him in surprise. "I'm not gutsy."

"You're tougher than you think," he said and turned back to the television. "I like her slinky dresses."

"I have a slinky negligée."

That got his attention. "With you?"

"As a matter of fact."

With deft fingers, he unbuttoned her blouse and opened the front snap of her bra. "On second thought, I like you better without it." Lazily, he traced a finger around her nipple and watched as it pebbled.

Christy saw his eyes go dark, his pupils widen with desire. But his touch stayed featherlight on her breast.

"Come closer," he whispered. He raised his other arm and drew her down toward him. He flicked his tongue over her nipple, then drew it into his mouth. The movie—the dialogue, the music, even the room where they sat—faded. All Christy's senses focused on her breast. For a moment, all she could do was be still and absorb the sensations—the rhythmic movements of his tongue, the warm pressure of his hand on her shoulder, the longing he stirred inside her.

She wanted to give him those same feelings. Tearing her attention from what he was doing to her, Christy covered the hard mound in his jeans. She pressed and it grew harder, released and it went harder still. She stroked, teasing him, then unfastened the snap at his waist and slowly undid his zipper.

He moaned, then said, "The pants. Gotta…get 'em off."

"Let me." She slipped out of his grasp, knelt by the couch and began to ease the jeans off. He reached to help her, but she pushed his hands away. "I said, let me. I want to make you crazy."

"Trust me, you are," he gasped.

"Good. Now lie back and relax."

"Relax? Not…possible." But he stilled his hands and let her have her way.

For now, she was in total control. And it was heaven. To watch his chest, see the effort he made to slow his breathing. To hear him groan with passion, to make him *want*. Want only her.

"Lift up." He did and she slid his pants down over his buttocks and then down his legs inch by inch. She paused to run her fingernails over his thighs and was rewarded with a groan. "I love your thighs. The muscles are so strong," she murmured, then dropped a kiss on one knee. A reflexive jerk made her chuckle, and then she continued kissing his legs until she had his jeans off. She pulled off his socks and took a foot in her hand. "Such sexy feet," she murmured. She kissed his toes and laughed when they wriggled.

"Christy..." He started to sit up, but she pushed him back. "Not done yet. We have a long way to go to get you naked."

"Good grief."

He started to tug at the waistband of his briefs, but she grabbed his hand. "Uh-uh. That's last. Shirt next."

Her breath was almost gone but she refused to rush. She unbuttoned his shirt, urged him up so she could slip it off, then pleasured them both by kissing his nipples, laving and sucking them as he had done hers.

He couldn't stay still any longer. His body began to writhe...and she loved it, but she put her hand on his chest. "Shh, wait."

"You're driving me...insane."

"Told you so," she whispered and silenced his mouth with hers. Then she murmured, "Now," and slipped off his briefs.

She sat back for a moment and gazed at him in all his masculine glory. "You're beautiful, you know," she told him. "Sexy and beautiful."

"Men aren't beautiful."

"You are. Just looking at you makes me...hungry." She took him in her mouth, savored the male taste of him, his rock-hard desire. But now she couldn't wait either.

Pulling her clothes off, she sheathed him, then mounted him and guided him inside her, as deep as he could go.

Now neither of them could go slow. Their movements quickened, their sighs became moans until finally, with cries of ecstasy, they flew over the edge and into oblivion.

Wrapped together, they surfaced slowly. Jonathan kissed the tip of Christy's nose. "Condom sales are soaring."

She laughed. "And all because of us. Helping the economy

is good." She sat up and pushed her hair back from her face. "I need a shower. Care to join me?"

In moments they were under the spray together and soaping one another, laughing as Christy drew a happy face on Jonathan's chest with soap bubbles. Afterward, they dried each other and then, wrapped in towels, strolled back into the bedroom.

"Hungry?" Jonathan asked.

"A little. Thirsty, too. Shall we call room service or get dressed and go downstairs?"

"Neither. We'll raid the in-room bar. I think I saw a couple of bottles of wine." He opened the refrigerator door, and they chose a chablis, some crackers and a pâté. Jonathan turned to her. "Where's that slinky negligée?"

"I'll get it. I'll be Katharine, you be Cary."

Jonathan figured he was going to enjoy this. He leaned back in his chair, stretched out his legs and waited.

A few minutes later, Christy's hand appeared on the bathroom door frame, then she peeped around the edge of the door. "Here I come," she said and stepped into the bedroom.

His eyes widened. She wore a long silk negligée in pale bronze, not sheer but transparent enough to show the outlines of dusky nipples, the dark triangle below her belly. The gown clung to her, outlining her sweet curves, accentuating her long slim legs. She'd brushed her hair into a long, straight fall. As she walked slowly toward him in high-heeled slippers, she looked like a confection good enough to eat, delicious enough to devour.

"Like it?" she asked huskily.

Unable to find his voice, he nodded. Like it? With every step she took, he grew harder. He rose and went to her, took her in his arms and kissed her.

"Nice," she murmured. "I guess that means you like me, you really, really like me."

"Wrong movie star, but I do," he chuckled, still holding her close. "So, Kate, will you have a drink?"

"Delighted."

She put her arm around his waist and, punctuating each step with a kiss, they moved to the table. He pulled out her chair and seated her, left for a moment to turn the radio to a Golden Oldies station, then returned and poured the wine with a flourish.

With the music soft in the background, they held hands across the table, fed each other bits of pâté. They gazed into one another's eyes as they sipped the wine. "Well, Cary, no clever repartee?" Christy asked.

"Uh-uh, I can't think of anything to say." He leaned his cheek on his hand. "I just want to look at you." He traced her lips, brushed his finger over her chin. "You have such a delectable mouth, such a sweet chin."

She caught his hand, kissed the fingers one by one, then touched his chin. "You have a cleft in your chin. Sexy."

"Nah. A hole in my chin's not sexy."

"Mmm, but it is." She leaned over the table and dipped her tongue inside it. "Pour me some more wine. Not too much, I'm already floating."

"Maybe we should go to bed."

Christy chuckled. He could tell she was already feeling the wine. "Maybe we should dance."

"Why not?" He got up and put out a hand. She took it, and he pulled her close, spun her in a circle, and dipped her back over his arm.

"It'd be better on a hard surface. You know, like a floor." She giggled, definitely feeling the wine now, he decided. "Can I have some more to drink?"

"I don't think so."

"Spoilsport."

He kissed the pout off her lips and led her across the room

in intricate steps that seemed to come naturally though he was sure he'd never danced quite this way before. She put both arms around his neck and gazed into his eyes. She was so sexy. His hands traveled down to her waist, brushing her breasts. The silky fabric was sexy, too, but no more so than her skin.

"Kiss me while we're dancing, Jonathan," she murmured. "That's so 'old romantic movie,' don't you think?"

He couldn't think, not with her body pressed against him, her mouth teasing his. He kissed her longer, deeper, tasting the wine on her tongue.

He waltzed her to the bed, bent her back…and let her go. She plopped on the bed, laughing, and he followed her down. Had it only been an hour or so since they'd last made love? How could he be so ravenous so soon?

He parted her negligée, hungry for her skin. Ah, there she was. Satin smooth, soap-scented, and warm. Growing warmer under his kisses.

She took his face in her hands. "I've never been danced to bed before. You're so creative."

Though he was intent on other things, a laugh burst out. "Stop teasing me and let me have you."

"But old movies fade out with a kiss. Those people never had sex."

He undid the sash at her waist. "This is a remake."

"Oh, in that case…" She unbuttoned his shirt, planted kisses across his chest. Quickly they disposed of the rest of their clothes and soon were lost in the rhythm of love.

Jonathan lay on his side and watched Christy sleep. How long would this union last? Only until he made sure her life was no longer in danger. To do that, he had to catch the Night Stalker.

The killer was smart. He was careful to leave no trace of

himself at the murder scenes. They needed a break. They needed him to make a mistake.

How could he let Christy go back to work? He knew the killer would go after her eventually. And what better place than in the hospital? So many strangers prowling the halls, so much confusion. People weren't alert. They were focused on their own pain, not on a pretty nurse being accosted by a man. The thought made him ill.

Nothing could happen to Christy. She was too…special. Special in a way he hadn't ever experienced before. She made him laugh, she made him want…

…what he couldn't have. *Shouldn't* have.

He leaned over and kissed her cheek, listened to her sigh, then gathered her close against his heart and fell asleep.

Across town a man clenched his fists as he relived his past.

A little boy again, he sat at the breakfast table dreaming, as his hand automatically guided the spoon from the cereal bowl to his mouth. Lost in a fantasy far out in space, he jumped as footsteps came up beside him. Blinking, he looked up and stared into the angry eyes of his Aunt Meg.

"You."

She never called him by his name, just "you" or something worse. He was in for it, he supposed, and tried not to cringe as Meg loomed over him in her faded robe, her dyed red hair tangled around her face. "Yes'm."

"Why're you dawdling over your breakfast? Put those dishes in the sink."

"Momma always said to eat a good meal so I could be strong," he protested.

"Yeah, well, your momma's long gone. Dumped you on me." Her mouth twisted in rage and disgust as she glared at the teaspoon-sized red stain on the breakfast table. "Spilled ketchup makin' your lunch, didn't you, you mangy little creep." Her voice was raspy from too much booze and too many cigarettes. "Can't keep your fat face outa trouble five minutes. Clean up the mess. I gotta get to work at the hospital. I got rooms to clean an' bedpans to empty. I don't have time to come along behind you, taking care of *your* sloppiness."

Obediently, he got up and started for the kitchen, but Meg grabbed his arm, her fingernails digging into his soft flesh. "Where do you think you're goin'?"

"T-to get a rag."

She gave him a shove. "Use your shirt."

"B-but it's my only clean one and—and it's picture-taking day at school."

"Picture-takin' day, huh?" Her lips curled into a sneer. "Then you'll look just right, you dirty little pig."

Scared of what she'd do if he argued, he wiped the table, then backed toward the door.

"Not so fast. You didn't get your punishment." She grabbed him by the collar and reached for the paddle she always kept handy.

The board slammed against his back, his legs, his bottom again and again. He tried to wriggle away, but she held him fast, so he endured the pain. For now.

But someday, he thought…someday he'd be big. Bigger than she was. Stronger, too. Then he'd fix her, punish her back. He could feel his fists connecting with her, feel the strength behind his blows…

He blinked, and a face swam into view. Not Meg's. Another woman's, a stranger's. Fists clenched, he stared down at her, trying to make sense of the scene.

A moonless night. The smell of fetid water from a drainage ditch mingled with the odor of disinfectant from the woman's hands. No one nearby. A dog howling somewhere in the distance.

He stared at his hand—not a boy's now but a man's—then frowned again at the red-haired woman. He'd brought her here to punish her.

She was different from the others, stronger, too. She'd fought him. But she was no match for him. In minutes, he'd overpowered her. Had her sniffling, begging for mercy. Now he was done.

He bent over and pushed her lifeless body into the ditch.

Chapter 16

The ring of the telephone roused Jonathan from sleep. Dawn was just breaking, tinting the hotel room a soft gray. He groped for the phone, managed a sleepy "Hello."

Luis's voice brought him to full alert. "Get over here. We found another body."

Jonathan reached for a pencil. "Where?" He scribbled the directions and hung up, then turned to Christy and gently shook her shoulder until she stirred.

"'S'matter?" she mumbled.

"Get dressed. We need to go."

She sat up, her eyes wide, frightened. "What's wrong?"

He stroked her arm. "Nothing here. But they've found another body."

"Oh, God, no."

"I have to go over there."

"Of course." She swung her legs off the bed. "Get dressed.

I'll call Hannah. She's bound to be up for the boys' early feeding."

Within minutes they were dressed and out of their room. While Christy checked out, Jonathan brought the car around to the front of the hotel. Fortunately, they weren't far from Hannah's. He dropped Christy off and was on his way.

Half an hour later he turned onto a narrow lane, and his heart began pumping. Houses. Not many, but a couple of ramshackle huts stood just in from the corner. This could be the break they needed. Houses meant people. Witnesses.

He parked at the far end of the street near a drainage ditch. No more houses here. As he got out of his car, he inhaled the odor of refuse…and death.

The crime scene unit had, of course, already arrived, and he spotted Luis in the group milling around. Jonathan held up a badge and nodded to the sergeant in charge and the man stood back respectfully and let him pass.

Luis hurried over. "Hey, *compadre,*" he said. "Looks like things are going our way for once."

"Yeah, I noticed the houses."

"Homicide cops are fanning out over the area. Keep your fingers crossed." He nodded toward the group clustered around a still form. "Come take a look."

The woman had been beaten. Not with a blunt instrument but with fists. Jonathan had seen enough bodies to know the difference. Someone had hit her repeatedly. Her neck was broken, and her red hair lay tangled about her shoulders.

Bile rose in his throat. Christy could be lying there. He turned away, then forced himself to look again. The only way he could keep this from happening to Christy was to learn everything he could from this murder scene. "Who is she?" he asked.

"Wanda Mulroney," Luis answered. "She's a nurse."

Although he'd expected it, the word *nurse* hit him like a

punch in the gut. Whatever happened to the Night Stalker in the past was connected with medicine, he knew that. But why in God's name had the woman who'd rescued *him* from the storm turned out to be a nurse? *Focus,* he ordered himself and shut down the useless questions.

"When did it happen?" he asked.

One of the investigators answered. "Sometime during the night. She was on the three-to-eleven shift at St. Mary's."

St. Mary's. Christy's hospital. Jonathan bit the inside of his cheek and forced himself to stay calm.

The investigator continued. "When she didn't show up at home by twelve-thirty, her husband called the police, and they started searching. They found her car parked about two blocks from St. Mary's and, since this spot is pretty close to the hospital, it didn't take long to find her."

Too long for her. The murderer had had maybe forty-five minutes to pick her up, get her here, and kill her. How frightened was she? Could she have escaped? What if she'd had a weapon?

Tonight, as soon as he finished, he'd take Christy out to the firing range for the lesson he'd promised. Now the impulsive offer to help her improve her skill with a weapon was more than a friendly promise. It was vital.

"Our guy's getting edgy. He's starting to make mistakes," Luis remarked. "He's usually driven his victims a long way before killing them." He pointed to the body. "And look at her hands."

Jonathan bent to study them. Defensive wounds, and two broken fingernails. She'd fought back. And that meant…

"DNA," he said, looking up at Luis.

"You got it. Looks like this time we really do have a break."

Christy and Hannah were watching *Oprah* when the phone rang. Hannah picked it up. "It's Jonathan," she said, handing Christy the phone.

Almost five. He should be here soon. "Hi," she said.

"Hi," he answered, and Christy felt the quick jolt of excitement his deep voice always brought. "I called to say I may run late."

"That's okay. What did you find out?" He said nothing but she heard him expel a long breath. "Jonathan?"

"She was a nurse. At St. Mary's."

Christy swallowed. "What's... I mean, what was her name?" Again, he didn't answer, and she said, "You may as well tell me. I'll hear it on the five o'clock news."

"Wanda Mulroney."

Knees suddenly weak, Christy sank onto a chair. "Wanda," she whispered. "I—I know her. She works...worked in pediatrics..." She was crying now.

"I'm sorry," Jonathan said. He paused, then asked, "Do you know if she was a drug user?"

"Absolutely not."

"They found morphine in her glove compartment."

Christy's tears stopped and anger replaced them. "If they did, someone planted it. Wanda was a good person. She went to church, she took care of her family and she loved the kids on the pediatric floor. She'd never, *never* do drugs."

"I believe you. What I need to figure out is why the drugs were planted." His voice gentled. "Hang in there. I'll see you as soon as I can." He hung up.

Christy sat with the receiver in her lap.

Hannah came to her and put a hand on her shoulder. "Bad news?"

"Yeah. The woman they found this morning, she worked at my hospital. Wanda was her name. She has two kids. I saw her right before my vacation. She said her son, Jeremy, just learned to ride a two-wheeler. She was so proud." Christy rubbed a hand across her wet cheek. "Sorry, I'm..."

"You go ahead and cry, sweetie. It's okay. She was your friend."

Christy sniffled and reached for a napkin. "Not a close one, but—but I *knew* her." She blew her nose and looked up at Hannah. "I guess you've lost people you worked with."

Hannah got a glass of ice water, handed it to Christy and sat beside her. "Several. It's always tough. The ones left behind just have to be there for each other." She patted Christy's hand.

"Thanks for being here for me." Christy took a sip of water. "That guy, the Night Stalker, he's a madman. I—I worry about Jonathan."

"You're falling in love with him."

Christy sniffled again. "I'm not sure I want to be, but I think so." She sighed. "Heck, I don't know what I think or what I feel."

"Love ain't easy."

"No kidding," Christy sighed. She took another drink. "I know so little about Jonathan. I keep asking myself how I could be falling for a man I've known less than two weeks. Less than one if you count the real Jonathan Talbot."

"Trust your heart," Hannah said. "I know that sounds corny, but what does it tell you?"

"It keeps saying, 'I'm confused.'"

Hannah laughed. "You knew the minute you saw him standing in the rain that he was a good man. Wasn't that your heart talking?"

"Yes," Christy sighed. "but I don't believe in love at first sight."

"I do." Hannah said. "With Troy and me, it was like that old song. We saw each other across a crowded room, and we *knew*."

"I have to know someone really well to trust him."

"From what you've told me, you trusted Jonathan almost

from the start. If not, you'd have kicked him out no matter what condition he was in." She got up and began clearing the table.

"After this case is over and both of you are back to normal, you'll have time to get to know him better."

"The message I'm getting from him is that there won't be an 'after' for us," Christy said. She felt tears coming again and blinked them away.

Hannah rested her chin on her hands. "You two need to talk."

"You're right," Christy said, determined to do just that as soon as possible.

"We need to talk," Jonathan said. He pulled into Christy's driveway and shut off the engine. He'd picked her up late, nearly eight-thirty. Christy had already eaten, and Hannah had wrapped up a sandwich for him to take with him. He'd insisted they spend the night at Christy's so he could check her house again.

"All right," Christy said, glad *he'd* made the suggestion about talking. "Let's do it."

Inside, they sat at the breakfast table. Jonathan took a bite, put the sandwich down, and said, "I want you to take some more time off."

Wrong button again. "Giving more orders, Dr. Talbot?" she asked.

"Dammit, yes."

"Remember, Jonathan… Ask, don't tell. And you might consider mentioning *why* you think I need more time away from work." Before he could answer, she said, "Know what? I'm going stir-crazy. First we were holed up in San Sebastian. Now you're out and about but I'm cooped up in—"

"I thought you liked Hannah." He sounded puzzled.

"I do. I love her and I love being around the kids, but for

heaven's sake, Jonathan, can't you see I need my life to be normal again?"

He pushed the sandwich away. "Christy, this situation is anything but normal. I apologize for ordering you around like Keith did, but dammit, I'm scared. The woman this morning, Wanda Mulroney, had red hair, she was a nurse, she was picked up two blocks from St. Mary's Hospital. We found her car." His voice broke. "I don't want you to be next." Abruptly, he got up and stalked to the window.

Christy stared at his back, at his shoulders so taut with tension. She went to him and touched his arm. "Do you think *I* want to be?"

Without looking at her, he shook his head. "We're close to catching him. I can feel it. But if you're at the hospital, I can't protect you." He turned and pulled her against him, buried his face in her hair. "Hang on a little longer, can't you?"

She felt his heart throbbing against hers, felt the arms that held her tremble. "I'll think about it. I still have tomorrow off."

"Think hard."

"I promise I will." She took his hand. "Come and eat your sandwich."

"Not hungry."

"Sit down and relax, then." She tugged him into the great room. He sat in an armchair, and Christy stood behind him and began massaging his neck. When she felt the tension ease, she said softly, "Jonathan, why did you leave the FBI?"

He didn't answer for so long, she thought perhaps he'd fallen asleep and hadn't heard her. "Jonathan?"

He turned and reached for her hand. "I wasn't going to tell you."

"Why?"

"Sit down," he said.

All sorts of questions ran through her mind as she sat

across from him. Had he been kicked out for some terrible infraction? Had he leaked classified information? Of course, he hadn't. No way in the world could this man have done anything wrong.

"I didn't want to frighten you," he began.

"Well, you're scaring me now." She clasped her hands and waited. "What happened to you?"

"Not to me. To my fiancée."

Fiancée. Of all the things he could have started with, that surprised her most. And hurt her, too. Which didn't make any sense at all. Did she suppose Jonathan hadn't had a life before she met him?

"Her name was Diane Shay."

"Was she an agent?" Christy asked.

"No, an attorney. She was on the staff of Senator Carl Reynard. We were planning to be married…" He paused again, then said, "We were coming back to my town house from dinner one evening when a guy I'd profiled and testified against jumped out of the bushes and shot her."

Christy's eyes widened. Her lips felt frozen, but she managed to ask, "Did he k…?"

"She died instantly."

His voice was flat. If she hadn't been looking at him, she'd have imagined he was reciting a dry fact. But she *was* looking, and the pain she saw was so stark, so deep, she knew it cut him to the heart. Sometimes, she thought, it was better not to remember.

"I got away with a bullet wound in the thigh, the one you found that first night."

"And the man?"

"I shot him."

Jonathan shut his eyes, but Christy knew he still saw the scene. Saw Diane. Felt…

"You think it was your fault," she said.

"It *was* my fault." He covered his face with his hands. Christy hurt for him. She longed to take him in her arms and hold him close, soothe him until the pain disappeared. But unaccountably, she was angry, too. "*She* chose to become engaged to an FBI agent. She must've known what she was getting into."

He looked up and Christy saw a flash of anger in his eyes. "She might have realized something could happen to me. But not to her."

"And so you quit."

"And took a job teaching at the University of Houston. I promised myself I'd never put someone I loved in jeopardy again."

Momentarily, Christy wondered if he realized he'd said *loved,* then decided he meant it as a general rule, not something that applied to her personally. "I'm so sorry for your loss, Jonathan," she said softly, taking his hands. "I understand why you feel especially responsible for me, I really do. But I can't stay locked away forever. I'm sure Diane would have said the same thing."

He laughed harshly. "Yeah, she would." His fingers tightened on hers. "Give me a week, Christy. Please."

Now that she understood, she couldn't refuse him. "All right. I'll call in tomorrow."

His hands relaxed, and he sat back. "Thanks."

A thought crossed Christy's mind. "You said you quit, but you haven't. You're still profiling. Why?"

"That's a good question." He stared into space for a moment. "When I came down here, I started getting calls immediately from local police forces wanting help with cases. I turned them down flat, didn't even want to hear about the cases.

"Then, when I'd been here almost a year, a young girl in Brenham went missing. It's a small town, a quiet place where you wouldn't expect this to happen. The sheriff's department in Washington County called and asked me to consult on the case. I said no."

"What changed your mind?" Christy asked.

"The girl's mother called."

Christy smiled. "And you said you'd help."

"I told her the same thing I told the sheriff. No. Then she asked me how I'd feel if my child disappeared and an expert who could help refused."

Christy pictured Jonathan sitting at his desk, listening to the woman's voice. She could imagine the war going on inside him.

Jonathan shut his eyes, and she knew he was reliving that day, too. "I can hear her voice," he said. "She told me she didn't know why I'd given up profiling, but it was selfish to have a gift and refuse to use it to help others.

"'You'll go the rest of your life knowing you might have saved my daughter, that your knowledge might have made a difference between life and death for a fifteen-year-old who had so much to live for. You'll know it,' she said, 'and so will I.'

"And then she hung up. Thirty seconds later I called her back and said I'd help."

"Did they find her daughter?"

"Yeah," he said, his lips curving slightly, "and she was okay."

Christy's eyes were moist when he finished the story. "And then what?" she asked.

"I realized I have a calling, and I can't deny it. I don't want to go back to the Bureau. I had enough. But if there's another kid who's missing or a woman who's been brutalized, I can't turn my back."

He leaned forward earnestly. "Do you understand?"

"I do." And she truly did.

Jonathan looked drained. "Ready for bed?" Christy asked. "As soon as I check the house."

Christy tagged along while he surveyed her home. And the garage. And the yard. Clearly, he was taking no chances. When he finished, Christy insisted that he eat the rest of his dinner. "Your contribution to the starving children in third-world countries," she reminded him. "And I'm going to sit here and make sure you eat every bite."

"The return of Nurse Ratched," he grumbled, but he sat.

As he was finishing his sandwich, the phone rang. They looked at each other. "Go ahead," Jonathan said, and Christy picked it up.

"H-hello."

"Christy, it's Hannah. I'm glad I got you." Her voice was high and shaky.

"What's wrong?" *Not Troy, not one of the boys, please God.*

"My—my mom just called. My dad had a heart attack. He's—he's in pretty bad shape. The twins and I are flying to Minneapolis in the morning. I'm sorry, but I'll have to leave you alone."

Frowning, Jonathan got up from the table. "It's Hannah," Christy mouthed and motioned for him to pick up the extension in the great room. Meanwhile, she needed to reassure her friend. "Don't worry about me. I'll be fine. Just concentrate on your dad."

Jonathan's voice interrupted. "Hannah, what's the matter?"

Hannah repeated what she'd told Christy, and Jonathan said, "Of course you have to leave. Take care of your folks. I'll see that Christy's okay."

"What time is your flight?" Christy asked.

"The earliest I could get was at one o'clock. I have to be at Bush Intercontinental at eleven."

"Jonathan, why don't you take me to Hannah's when you drive in to the HPD. I'll help her get ready, and she can drop me back at home on her way to the airport. It's only a minute out of the way."

"That'd be great. I could use the support." Hannah's voice was shaky again.

"Okay, then. And in the meantime, know that we'll keep your dad in our prayers. Go get some sleep and I'll see you tomorrow."

Christy hung up and met Jonathan as he hurried back into the kitchen. She put up a hand to stop the words she was certain he was going to say. "I really *will* be fine here."

"I'll look for somewhere else for you. Luis has a friend—"

"Did you hear me, Doctor Worrywart? I'll be okay. I have a super alarm system, a peep hole in the front door, and dead bolts on it and the back door. Not to mention a gun. I won't let anyone in, even the mailman. And rest assured, I will *not* play Nancy Drew and go out to catch the killer myself by luring him into a dark alley."

"I guess that sums it up," Jonathan said, but he didn't look convinced.

"How about I distract you by tearing off your clothes and making you crazy again?"

"That'd work."

"For me, too." Christy took hold of his tie and led him upstairs.

Chapter 17

Early the next morning Jonathan let Christy out of the car and watched her sprint up the walk to Hannah's door. He leaned out of the window. "Wait," he called.

Christy turned and loped back to the car.

Jonathan grabbed her hand. "When you get home, keep the gun loaded and handy. And check in with me every hour, would you?"

She looked annoyed, but she nodded. His hand was on the window ledge, and she covered it with hers. "Please don't worry, Jonathan. You have a killer to catch."

"How can I not worry?" he said. "You're important to me."

"Important." Her voice quivered. "What does that mean?"

"That I…care about you."

"So do I…care about you." She took a step back. "You're on the front lines. Be careful. Please."

"Sure."

He waited while Christy rang the doorbell. When Hannah

opened the door, the two women embraced. Over Christy's shoulder Hannah waved at Jonathan before she and Christy went inside.

He sent up a prayer for his friend's dad and then drove away, heading for downtown Houston. The early-morning sun gleamed off the roof of the car in front of him, momentarily blinding him. He put down his visor and turned onto the freeway ramp, then merged with traffic. Was the Night Stalker in one of the cars streaming toward the center of the city? Was he at work now, planning his next move?

Jonathan asked himself if Christy was safer at home than she would be at the hospital. Hard to tell. He wished he hadn't been so late the other night and that he'd had time to take her to the firing range. If she had to use the gun, would she?

When he got to headquarters, he suppressed the urge to call her at Hannah's and began running the data on security workers, asking the computer to target those with the characteristics that fit the profile. The computer spat out thirty names. Damn, there were too many.

After an hour, his phone rang. Armand wanted to talk to him along with Luis and Dell. Jonathan strode down the hall and tapped on Armand's door, then let himself in. The room smelled of stale cigarettes. A half-full cup of coffee and an empty donut box sat on the desk. The trash can overflowed with papers. "Looks like you've been here all night," Jonathan said. Armand's night hadn't been as pleasurable as his, for sure. Jonathan's lips curved. Christy had been quite inventive in her efforts to distract him.

Luis and Dell filed in, and the three of them sat across from Armand.

Jonathan glanced at his watch. Was Christy on her way home yet? No, too early.

Armand cleared his throat. "Talbot. You with me?"

"Sorry. I was distracted. I'm worried about my...uh..." What should he call her? "...my friend."

Armand looked puzzled.

"Lady friend," Luis offered helpfully. "You know, the chick who went to dinner with us."

Dell snickered, and Armand shot him a disapproving look. "Let's get down to business," he said. "What do you have on the security personnel?"

"I'll have to narrow them down some more," Jonathan said.

"Is this productive?" Armand's voice betrayed frustration. "Isn't Torres our man?"

"The more I think about it, the less I believe so." Surreptitiously, he glanced at his watch again. "Yeah, Torres was once a security guard and he knew one of the victims, but what's his link to the others? Except for working near Janice Berlin, he has no connection. Remember, all these women apparently got into the killer's car without protest. Only Wanda Mulroney struggled. How are they all connected to the killer? We don't know."

"We can question the families again," Armand said.

"Yes," Jonathan said and noted Armand's grim expression. "My gut tells me Torres isn't the man, and the Night Stalker is walking around somewhere, laughing at us."

"Then find him," Armand said harshly. "Give us the last laugh."

"Happy-face rattle," Hannah called out.

Christy peered into the suitcase. "Check."

"Bunny jammies."

"Check."

"That's it, thank heaven," Hannah sighed and sat back on her heels. "Traveling with two babies is not for the faint-hearted. Thanks so much for coming over this morning."

"I wanted to be with you."

"The help was nice but having someone to talk to was what I really appreciate. I'm so scared about my dad…"

"I know, but they've made great strides in cardiac care in the past few years. People recover and lead normal lives."

"I'm glad you're a nurse. Other people deal in platitudes but you tell it like it is."

Christy smiled.

"I'm sorry I won't be here for you," Hannah added.

"Jonathan thinks they'll catch the guy soon." Christy hesitated, knowing Hannah's thoughts were elsewhere, but the words flowed out. "He told me about Diane."

"Oh." Hannah's eyes fastened on hers. "I'm glad he did. Now you understand him better."

Christy fiddled with the tiny T-shirt she'd been holding. "I understand there isn't a future for us. He's so guilt-ridden over her, he can't take a chance on falling in love again."

"And you? Sounds like you've decided how you feel."

Christy sighed. "Ironic isn't it? I realize I'm in love with him just when he tells me he'll never get involved with another woman. Sounds like a soap opera, doesn't it?"

"So what are you going to do? Just roll over and take it?"

Christy couldn't help but smile. "Spoken like a tough FBI agent." She frowned. "I don't know," she admitted. "Fighting a phantom is impossible."

"Nothing's impossible."

"Even living with a man who's in danger every day?"

Hannah's hands stilled. "You're asking how I cope with Troy's job. And how he copes with mine." She glanced at her wedding ring. "It isn't easy for either of us, but I fell in love with a man who puts his life on the line, and that's part of who he is. Same with him for me. Besides," she added, picking up a pair of baby's pajamas, "Jonathan's not doing that anymore."

"Except sometimes. And from the way he talks, that will continue."

"Then you have to make a decision."

Christy sighed. "If he gives me the chance. I—"

The phone interrupted them. Face pale, Hannah jumped up and rushed to answer. "Hello?" Her shoulders relaxed and she let out a sigh. "Oh, it's you, Talbot. Yes, of course she's here." She held out the phone.

Christy took it. "Hi, I'm fine. I should be home in about an hour. I'll call as soon as I get there. How are things going with you?"

His voice ripe with frustration, he answered, "Slowly."

"Keep plugging," she said and hung up.

Hannah glanced at her over the top of the suitcase. "My intuition says don't give up on the guy just yet. If I were you, I'd follow my own advice—keep plugging."

An hour later, Jonathan rubbed his eyes. All the names on his list of security guards were beginning to look alike. In the offices on either side of his, he knew Luis and Dell were scrolling through notes, scheduling family members and friends of the Night Stalker's victims for further questioning. Would their efforts pay off? Damned if he could guess.

All he did know was that this was the most baffling case he'd ever worked on. The killer was one smart bastard.

He rose and stretched, then trudged into Dell's office. Luis was there, too, leaning against the bookcase, drinking a soda. "Either of you come up with anything?" Jonathan asked.

"Nada," Luis said, and Dell nodded.

"It bothers me that none of these women put up a fight. Victims number three and four were hefty gals—yet their autopsies show they did nothing to defend themselves."

"The guy was so intimidating, they didn't dare resist," Dell suggested.

"Or," Luis added, "he was such a pip-squeak they didn't think they had to. Which puts our skinny janitor, Jackson Ealy, back on the list."

The sound of Jonathan's cell phone interrupted their conversation. He glanced at the screen and saw Christy's home number. Relieved, he pressed Talk. "Hi."

"Hi. Nurse Ratched reporting in. I'm home now."

"Good. Keep everything locked up and call me later."

When he hung up, Luis asked, "The chick?"

"Yeah." Jonathan put his cell phone back in his pocket. "I'm worried about her. She's home alone."

"Why worry?" Luis asked, then said, "Ah, she's a redhead."

"Not that she admits it, but yes."

"Mmm-hmm. A red-haired nurse," Dell said.

"Exactly."

"But would she get into a car…at night…with a stranger?" Luis asked.

"God, I hope not."

Libby Hammond, a rookie cop, stuck her head in the door. "Dr. Talbot, you have a meeting in ten minutes with Armand, Chief Nichols and the mayor."

Just what he needed to fill up his day. "Thanks," Jonathan said, then stopped her. "Wait a minute. We need a female perspective here. Why would a woman get into a car with a stranger? Dell says because something about the man intimidates her. What about a man, other than size, would do that?"

"Fame. Looks. A combination of both," Libby suggested promptly. "Trust me, if Johnny Depp offered me a ride, I'd get into his car so fast it'd make your head spin."

"We'll assume Johnny is not a serial killer. What else?"

"Authority. He has an ID that shows he's a judge or a senator, maybe an astronaut. Or he's a marine with a chestful of medals. Gosh, I'd even go for a package delivery guy in those cute little brown shorts."

Jonathan nodded. "Authority. That fits with what I've said all along. Real or not, he projects it. I'm betting when the Night Stalker goes after his prey, he's wearing a uniform."

The meeting with the mayor took longer than expected, but held no surprises. The pressure was on. The mayor was getting flack; therefore he had to pass it on to the chief, who lobbed it to Armand and so on down the line. As the profiler, Jonathan had gotten a hefty share of it.

On top of his own frustration and his concern for Christy, this precipitated a foul mood. He stopped at a vending machine, bought lunch, a soda and a bag of chips and headed back to his office, then changed his mind.

He needed to get out. Another look at the crime scene wouldn't hurt. He scribbled a note, put it on Dell's desk, then left the building.

Christy wandered aimlessly through her house. Too big. *Way* too big. Yet she was as much a prisoner here as she'd been in San Sebastian. The terror outside was as real, no, even more real than the one she'd faced last week.

She opened the door to a pristine bathroom. Pretty guest towels and a basket with an array of scented soaps sat invitingly on the counter. Nothing in here had ever been used. By the time she and Keith had moved into "his" dream home, they weren't entertaining guests.

As soon as this Stalker situation was over—if that ever happened—she'd put the house up for sale and move into smaller quarters, something more like Jonathan's bungalow. For all she cared, whoever bought this palace could take everything in it, down to the last cake of jasmine soap.

She shut the bathroom door, plodded into the kitchen, and made herself a cup of instant coffee. She pressed the TV remote. The midmorning soap operas were on. Quickly, she turned the TV off. She had more than enough melodrama in her own life.

Maybe she'd bake Jonathan a cake. From scratch. That would keep her busy and would cheer him up after a day in the trenches. Pleased with the idea, she flipped through her recipe file and selected one for pineapple upside down cake. Seemed appropriate. He'd turned her life upside down.

"Flour, sugar... Heck." The flour canister was almost empty. Christy went to the window and peered out. The street was deserted. Surely, in broad daylight she could make it to the supermarket and back without any trouble.

She hurried upstairs to get her purse and slipped the gun inside it. Halfway down, her conscience reared its head. "You promised," it said sternly. She gave in. She'd always been one who followed the rules, and in this case the rules made sense.

Downstairs, she set her purse on the coffee table. She'd find something else to do after she put the ingredients for the cake away. She hadn't yet looked at the morning paper. If she read every single article, no skipping, she should be busy all day.

She was headed back to the kitchen when the doorbell rang.

Startled, she jumped. On the way to the door, she replayed Jonathan's warning: "Don't let anyone inside." She wouldn't. She'd had one bout with temptation, and that was plenty.

She tiptoed to the door and looked out the peephole. A man stood on the porch. He was turned away, facing the street, and all she could see was his shadow, looming across the walkway.

Judging from the shadow, he was big. A giant. What did he want? He lifted an arm to lean against one of the columns on the porch, and she saw his muscles ripple. Dear God, he could batter the door down if he chose.

Trembling, she tried to decide what to do. Call Jonathan. Call 911. Better yet, call both.

The man turned. Christy let out a sigh of relief and leaned against the door to collect herself. It was Dell Cummings. She opened the door.

"Hi," he said. "You okay? You look a little pale."

"You just startled me. I wasn't expecting anyone." She stood aside. "Come in."

He did. As he passed her, she smelled sweat. He must have been out at the crime scene again.

"Um, can I help you?" she asked.

"Jonathan sent me. He's worried about you, but he's tied up right now. He asked me to come by and pick you up. Thought you'd be safer down at headquarters."

"All right," Christy said. "I'll just get my purse." She started for the living room, then turned. "It was nice of you to come."

He smiled. "No problem. We'll make a quick stop and then head downtown. I'm glad to help out."

Jonathan drove toward the site of the last murder. Just jogging from police headquarters to the garage had left him damp with sweat. Another hot summer day that made you long for evening. Tonight was a full moon. That always brought out the crazies. The mayor had promised to appear personally on the evening news shows on all three major Houston channels, warning women, especially those in the Medical Center, to take extra care tonight.

Within thirty minutes Jonathan reached the spot where Wanda Mulroney had spent her last moments. Technicians were still on site, searching for clues. A half dozen homicide detectives in blue police uniforms were there as well. Yellow crime-scene tape marked an area about ten yards square. Jonathan hailed Manny Parker, the guy in charge, and headed in his direction. "What's up?"

Parker shrugged. "Not much. You can see by the way the

grass is trampled along here that he dragged her over near the tree. First time he's done that."

Jonathan nodded. "You gotta wonder why none of the others put up a struggle."

"I'd say he drugged them, but there was no evidence of anything in the autopsies."

"Mind if I wander around?" Jonathan asked.

"Be my guest."

Jonathan walked the perimeter, his eyes on the ground.

He wasn't sure what he expected to find. Their man was too smart to leave a half-smoked cigarette or even a tissue behind. Near the tree, he stopped and studied the ground. Something caught his eye. At first he thought it was a bottle cap, but he bent to look closer.

A light blue button lay beneath a leaf, half-buried in the dirt.

He jogged back to Manny. "I've spotted something. Come take a look."

Together they stared at Jonathan's find. Then Manny straightened. "Hey, you-all," he called. "Get over here." When the others gathered around, he said, "Anybody lose a button?"

Looking puzzled, people checked their shirts. One by one, they shook their heads. "Dockens," Manny ordered, "see that button down there? Get it into an evidence bag."

The young man lifted the button with tweezers and dropped it into a bag. "Now take a closer look," Manny said. "That damn button is a perfect match for the ones on every shirt you cops are wearing."

The group stared at him, their faces stunned.

Jonathan's eyes fixed on the small button in Dockens' bag. A sick feeling spread from his stomach to his throat. He'd been correct in his assessment this morning. The man they were after wore a uniform when he killed. Unless an investigator who was here the other night had lost a button, the Night Stalker was a cop.

No wonder all the murder victims had gone with him. He'd probably stopped them for "speeding," opened their glove compartments and slipped drugs inside. He "discovered" the drugs, then told the women they'd have to come down to the precinct. Trusting in "the law," they'd gotten into his car. And taken the last ride of their lives.

Icy fear ripped through him. *Christy.* Would she get into a car with a stranger? Yeah, she would if the stranger was a cop. He grabbed his cell phone and dialed her number. The phone rang three times before it was picked up.

But it wasn't Christy. It was her answering machine.

Chapter 18

Jonathan raced to his car as if the devil were at his heels. As he ran, he redialed Christy's number. The machine again. "Christy," he shouted into the phone, "pick up."

Rage mingled with his fear. Where in hell was she? He jumped into the car, jammed the key into the ignition and gunned the motor. The car careened down the road, hit a pothole and bounced. Dammit, he'd told her to stay inside. Where could she have gone?

Think. She could be in the bathroom or up on a ladder cleaning specks of dust from the chandelier. Yeah, knowing Christy, that's exactly what she was doing.

But hell, she knew he was worried about her. By the second call, she'd had time to climb down and get to the phone. He tried again. Still the damned machine. He tried her cell, got her voice mail. Cursing, he swerved around the corner and onto the next street.

Could she have gone to the hospital? Maybe someone

couldn't come in to work and Christy had agreed to substitute. Long shot, because she hadn't called to tell him, but he phoned St. Mary's just in case. She wasn't there, hadn't called, was still on vacation for all they knew.

Was she at a neighbor's? He realized suddenly that he didn't know the names of any of her friends and had no idea who to call. But again, she should have called to let him know if she'd gone somewhere. He played his messages at home, at the university and at police headquarters. Nothing from Christy.

He checked the dashboard clock. Still fifteen minutes to Christy's. Ten if he got really lucky. He wished he'd commandeered a police vehicle this morning rather than using his rental car. He could use a siren right about now.

He thanked God they'd happened on that button at the crime scene. If not, he'd have called a task force member who might be closer to her house to check on Christy. Not now.

Because one of them, one of the people he'd been working with on a daily basis, could be the Night Stalker. He'd never have thought it possible, but now it made perfect sense.

The Night Stalker knew too much about what was going on. He knew Jonathan was getting closer. He'd already tried to kill Jonathan without success. Next best thing was to do away with Jonathan's woman.

So who—

His cell phone rang. *Thank you, God.* He punched Talk. "Yes."

"Dr. Talbot, this is Mindy at the University of Houston."

He'd been fully expecting the call to be from Christy and when the graduate assistant's tentative voice came on instead, he was shocked into silence.

"Um, are you there?"

"Yes, what is it? I'm in a hurry." He cut in front of a slow-moving SUV and ignored the angry honk that ensued.

"I wouldn't be bothering you except—"

"Just get to it." If Mindy were any more timid, she'd be a mouse. He had no time to bolster her self-esteem.

"You got this fax a few minutes ago and it's, like, weird."

Sure, bother him with some student's bizarre thoughts on the criminal justice system. "Read it."

"It says…well, it's written by hand and, like, the writing's sort of jumbled."

And this woman had aspirations of becoming a trial attorney. He clenched his teeth. "Just read it the best you can."

"I showed it to Nancy McKay, and we both think it says something like, well, like 'Gotcha.'"

"Gotcha?" He braked at a red light.

"Or maybe 'got her.' Yeah, I think that's what it says. Nancy thought it might make sense to you. Does it?"

Perfect sense. Too perfect. Jonathan felt his blood freeze at the implication.

"Um, shall I save it for you?"

"Do that, and tell me what number it came from." When she read it, he knew immediately it wasn't a fax from police headquarters. They all came from the same exchange. So the Stalker had gone outside to send it. Well, no one said he was stupid. Jonathan doubted that trying to track the fax would be useful. Where it came from wasn't important. *Who* sent it was what mattered.

"I'm sorry to—"

"No, you did the right thing, Mindy, and if another fax comes in, call me immediately."

"Yes, sir."

He hit the brake as traffic slowed to a standstill in front of him. What in hell was this?

He leaned out of his window, then leaned on the horn. All he got for that was an obscene gesture from the driver of the car in front of him.

As he waited, growing edgier by the second, he asked

himself if anyone on the task force could be a serial killer? Or could the culprit be someone they were close to, someone they talked with? Drawing any of them out about the latest findings on the case wouldn't be hard.

The car ahead of him inched forward enough so Jonathan could turn into a gas station. He drove across the open area and over a curb into the supermarket lot next door. He ignored the clattering of the car's chassis and kept going. Through the lot, onto the next street, and around several corners. He was out of the pileup, but he'd lost time. And time was what mattered.

Christy smiled at Dell Cummings as he politely held the car door open for her and reminded her to fasten her seat belt. When he got into the car, she asked, "What's going on that worried Jonathan?"

He started the car. "We have a good lead on the killer. Jonathan didn't want you alone. He might be working late tonight."

"Is it one of the guys on your list?"

Looking surprised, Dell glanced at her. "How do you know about the list?"

"Jonathan and I have talked about the case quite a bit. After all, I got myself in the middle of it when I let him into my house during the storm."

"Why did you do that?"

"Let him in, you mean? He was hurt, and besides, I had a gun."

Dell laughed. He had the loud laugh of a big man. "Do you know how to use it?"

"To be honest, not well. And I finally admitted to Jonathan I probably couldn't pull the trigger on anyone."

He grinned. "Know how to heal but not kill, huh?"

"I guess you could say that."

"Maybe you know how to kill in small steps."

"That sounds creepy." Christy frowned at him. "What do you mean?"

"Nothing special." He turned onto the Southwest Freeway but headed away from downtown.

"I thought we were going to police headquarters," Christy said.

"I got somewhere else to go first." He turned and glared at her. "You tryin' to tell me what to do?"

"No, sorry." Dell seemed edgy. Understandable, with all the pressure the task force was under. She certainly didn't want to upset him. "I, um, just thought you said Jonathan was worried."

Dell shrugged. "He's out at the crime scene. I'm sure he wouldn't mind if we stopped. You're safe with me." He chuckled. "*I* know how to use my gun."

He turned onto the Loop. After a few minutes he said, "You okay? Air conditioning's not on too high for you, is it?"

"I'm fine." Dell seemed a strange mixture of politeness and temper. But he was Jonathan's colleague and since she was spending time with him, she might learn more about Jonathan. "Do you think Jonathan's all right?"

Dell edged into the right lane. "Worried about him?"

Christy nodded.

"You don't have to be. He's not in any danger. Just out there at the crime scene, digging around."

"Do you think he'll find anything?"

Dell shook his head. "Talbot thinks so, but to tell the truth, I doubt it. Our killer's a real smart boy."

He took the Memorial exit. Here they left the heavy traffic and drove past Memorial Park, an unspoiled tract that was a mecca for bikers, picnickers, joggers and lovers of the outdoors. Shaded by oaks, it was quiet and peaceful, despite its proximity to an area dense with offices and shopping centers.

On this midweek afternoon the jogging trail was crowded with perspiring joggers and walkers. People here, a good distance from the Medical Center, seemed unconcerned that a brutal killer was on the prowl in Houston. Maybe by tomorrow, Christy hoped, the Night Stalker would be in police custody and *no one* in the city would have to worry.

Dell slowed and eyed the jogging trail and the trees clustered behind it. "Could he be in there somewhere?" Christy asked.

"Nah. Too crowded."

Christy let out a breath. She'd hate to think of the man lurking nearby. "He usually…um, works at night, doesn't he?"

"Usually," Dell replied. "But there are exceptions to every rule."

At his response, Christy shivered. She was glad she'd decided not to run over to the grocery store. Then she might have missed Dell, and Jonathan would be worried about her. Not to mention annoyed. Fortunately, she'd stayed home, and now she supposed she was as safe as she could be anywhere, riding with a cop.

Jonathan swerved into Christy's driveway and slammed on the brakes. He got out and raced to the front door, glancing through the garage windows as he passed. Her car was there. Would she have walked somewhere or was she inside, unable to call for help? Injured…or worse?

He punched the doorbell and pounded on the door, waited for a full minute, but no one answered. He had to go in. To hell with her state-of-the-art alarm system, he decided, as he ran back to the car and opened the trunk. He grabbed the tire jack and raced to the back door. One hard slam and he'd broken a pane. He slipped his arm through, and ignoring the ribbon of blood that appeared on his wrist, and the sound of the alarm, unlocked the dead bolt, then gave the knob a twist and pushed the door open.

"Christy," he yelled. "Christy, where are you?"

No answer.

A hand mixer and ingredients for some kind of pastry sat on the kitchen counter, so someone or something must have interrupted her in the midst of a baking project. Unusual for Christy not to have put everything away before leaving.

His sense of panic rising, he sped from room to room. Nothing was amiss. He saw no sign of forced entry.

In the great room, he stopped and took a breath. With all the effort he possessed, he forced himself to revert to agent mode. Observant. Objective. Focused.

The woman he was searching for wasn't Christy, he told himself. This was a woman he'd never met, never held, never wanted with every fiber of his being.

Okay, what evidence did he have? A pristine house, a button torn from a police officer's uniform, a fax with the message "got her" scrawled on it.

The condition of the house told him there had been no struggle, so if she'd gone with someone, it was a person she knew and trusted. His idea earlier that the killer might be a buddy of someone assigned to the Stalker case was wrong. He had to believe Christy wouldn't willingly leave the house in the company of someone she'd never met, cop or not. At least not without calling to let him know.

That left the unthinkable. The killer *was* someone on the task force. He, of all people, knew Jonathan was getting closer to nailing him. Jonathan had given his fax number at the University of Houston to every member of the task force. Now the killer was using it to taunt him. The button confirmed he was a police officer.

But who was it?

Neither of the women. Marilee was a slight woman, nearly fifty, and a good three inches shorter than Christy. If she were the killer, she'd have to be prepared for a struggle and know it was unlikely she could subdue Christy. Marilee had access to chloroform and could overcome Christy that way, but she'd never be able to get her out of the house afterward.

Shannon was a trained police officer, tall and strong, but no way could she be mistaken for the man who'd run from the bushes in front of Christy's house on San Sebastian. And, of course, Marilee couldn't either.

That left the men.

Jonathan grabbed his cell phone and called headquarters. First thing he wanted to know was who was in and who was out.

Only Armand was there now. But that didn't rule him out. He could have been away just long enough to come here, get Christy and…hurt her. "Has Armand been there all morning?" he asked.

"Yes, sir. Never left his office," Tina Becker, Armand's assistant, said.

Okay, Luis and Dell were out in the field. Had to be one of them. But God, they'd both worked alongside him, commiserated over their failure to take down this maniac. All the while one of them was laughing up his sleeve.

"Put Lieutenant Frazier on," he said.

Armand came on the line. "Yeah, Talbot. What's up?"

"I know who he is."

Total silence for a moment, then he said, "The killer? For crissakes, who?"

"Luis or Dell."

"What the hell?" Armand said. "Are you crazy?"

"Was one of them off work while I was on the island?"

"Yes, but why would you think—"

"Don't ask questions," Jonathan growled. "Which one?"

"If you're wrong—"

"Then fire me. Dammit, you're wasting time. *The guy's got Christy.*"

There was silence, then Armand said softly, "Dell took time off. Personal business. Something to do with his aunt."

Before Jonathan could manage a word, Armand said, "Damn, the chief's on the other line. I'll get back to you."

Jonathan hung up. He pictured Dell, with his big smile and his boisterous laugh. The bastard had sat right across from Christy. He'd asked her questions, found out she was a nurse.

Jonathan raced outside, got into his car and slammed the door. Dell had a head start on him. Which direction should he go?

Where would Dell take her? He'd always killed his victims outside, but always at night. What would he do, where would he go in broad daylight?

With the entire sprawling city of Houston to search through, how in hell was Jonathan going to find her before it was too late?

Chapter 19

As Dell drove out of the park and headed toward the downtown area, Christy asked a few questions about Jonathan's role on the task force. Dell answered in monosyllables, then lapsed into silence. If she'd expected to discover anything more about Jonathan, she realized she was going to be disappointed. Maybe Dell would rather talk about himself. "Are you from around here?" she asked.

"East Texas. Tyler."

"Do your parents still live there?"

He looked surprised that she'd ask. "They never did. I stayed with my Aunt Meg. She worked in a hospital. Like you."

"Was she a nurse?"

"She pretended like she was, but…nah, she just cleaned rooms." His voice was sad, and Christy decided she'd better leave that subject alone.

Dell flipped on the radio and found a country music station. "Don't you have to keep the radio off so the dispatcher can reach you?" Christy asked curiously.

"This isn't a police car, in case you didn't notice," Dell said.

"Isn't it an unmarked police car?" Christy asked.

"Nope, a rental."

"Like Jonathan's. Is your car in the shop, too?"

"No."

He said nothing else and Christy wondered why he needed to rent a vehicle when his was apparently running. She decided Dell was a little weird. Well, soon they'd part ways.

Dell made a left turn. Christy glanced out as he drove north through the Sixth Ward, a neighborhood that was once rundown but was now undergoing gentrification. "Where are we going?" she asked.

"I told you, I gotta run an errand."

Why hadn't she picked up her cell phone? She could see it on the kitchen counter where she'd left it. Darn, she'd promised Jonathan she'd check in with him every hour. She hated for him to be worried about her. "Can I borrow your phone?" she asked.

"My phone? No way. It's for police business."

His tone was angry, almost a snarl, and she shrank back.

"Sorry." God, she'd hate to cross this guy. She wished she'd insisted he drop her off at headquarters before running his errand, but it was too late now. She tried to concentrate on Garth Brooks crooning a country ballad instead of on Dell's surly expression.

It was hard not to notice Dell though. He took up a lot of space. Broad shoulders, thick arms, big hands. His sleeves were rolled up, and she saw he had a tattoo above his right wrist. A dragon.

He had a jagged scar on his left cheek. Looked like a knife wound that hadn't healed well. Another man might have gotten a plastic surgeon to work on it, but she suspected Dell considered it a badge of honor.

He checked his watch, frowned and muttered, "One-thirty. Got a meeting at four. Gotta get this business done."

Christy hoped he'd finish whatever business he had soon. She didn't want to spend any more time than she had to with Dell. He was beginning to give her the creeps.

Jonathan sat in his car. "Okay," he muttered, "you're a serial killer. You've got the woman who fits all your criteria and best of all, she's the lover of the man who's after you. Where do you take her?"

There was a small park a few blocks away. Not there. Too likely to be spotted. West University had plenty of stay-at-home moms as well as nannies for mothers who worked. Someone might bring a toddler to the park and catch the Night Stalker in action.

Memorial Park? Lots of trees, but an even greater chance of someone wandering by. Couples had been known to slip into the forested area for an afternoon quickie. Not a place a killer would choose.

So where—

His phone rang. The readout showed it was Armand calling back. "Yeah."

"I'm putting out an APB on Dell's cruiser—"

"Hold on. Get Tina in on this, see if she's talked to him. She might have an idea where he is."

Armand called out to his assistant, then she came on the line, too. "I spoke to him about an hour and a half ago," she said. "He said he was out tracking a lead, so I just reminded him of the task force meeting at four."

Damn. She'd put him under time pressure.

Armand spoke. "So we put out the bulletin."

"No, dammit. That's the last thing we do. If he knows we're on his tail, he's likely to freak and…"

"So we let him drive around, maybe right past a patrol car, and no one's looking for him? I don't like that plan."

Jonathan clenched his fists, forced himself to keep his temper in check. "He's already under pressure with a meeting coming up. We can't take a chance of spooking him any further. Announcing we're after him would sure as hell do that." He took a breath. "Look, give me two hours to see if I can track him down—"

"One hour. No more."

"Okay." He checked the dashboard clock as he pulled away from the curb and started down Christy's street.

"Tina," Armand said, "look up the number of his patrol car. If Talbot doesn't find him, we go with the APB."

"You don't need to look for his cruiser, sir," she said. "He's not driving it."

Jonathan's heart jumped. "Are you sure?"

"Absolutely. I saw him in the garage this morning. He was driving a rental car."

"What make?"

"Dark blue Volvo. It was from Alamo Rentals. I noticed the sticker on the back window."

"Tina, you may have just saved someone's life. Get on the phone to Alamo and get that license number."

She hung up, and Armand said, "Where do you figure he is? When we get the license, I can contact units in the area and put them on his tail."

That he could go along with. "Good idea. I figure in broad daylight and with limited time, he's headed for his comfort zone, the place he feels most secure."

"You're the profiler. You should know," Armand said. "Got any idea where that would be?"

"Somewhere close to home," Jonathan said. "Somewhere quiet where he can chill out."

Chill out. Someone had said that…where? When?

And then he knew. "Get Luis on the phone," he told Armand. "Find out where Dell goes fishing."

Dell's car slowed, came to a standstill. Ahead of them was a line of cars. Other vehicles drove up behind them. In the lanes on either side were more cars. Drivers honked, leaned out windows, cursed and shouted questions.

After sitting for a good ten minutes, they'd moved no more than one car length. Dell flipped through radio stations until they heard, "Traffic on the eights. A gas main has broken at Yale and Eighteenth, and firefighters are on the scene. Several streets have been blocked off."

"Hemmed in." Dell added an obscenity. "Quarter to two," he muttered, checking his watch again. "Running out of time." He brought his fist down on the steering wheel.

"Maybe we should try to get out of this and go back downtown," Christy suggested.

She blanched when he turned, his face a mask of anger. "Who's in charge here, you or me?" he snarled.

"Y-you," Christy whispered. She slid toward the door. She'd get out, find a ride downtown, walk if necessary. Her fingers were closing on the door handle when Dell gunned the motor, shot over the esplanade, and roared off in the direction they'd come from. Christy gripped the seat as he swerved around a corner and into a side street that was also clogged with cars trying to get away from the tie-up behind them. Face red, he muttered under his breath until they made it down the street and turned north again.

Once going in the direction he intended, Dell slowed his speed a bit. Soon he turned off the main street and into an undeveloped area. The road was bordered with ramshackle houses and a few stores selling hub caps and tools. Behind the houses to her right, Christy noticed woods. "What kind of errand do you have out here?" she asked quietly. She didn't want to set him off again.

He smiled at her. "You'll know soon enough."

There was something sly in his tone this time that made her even more uncomfortable than his angry response of a while ago. She should ask him to drop her off somewhere and she could call a cab. But where? There were even fewer stores and houses now.

Dell braked and turned onto a gravel path. "Wh-where are we?" Christy asked. She was really frightened now.

"Where we're going," he said, grinning. "It's almost time."

"Time for what?" As she spoke, she furtively unfastened her seat belt. If he gave her another bizarre answer, she would jump out of the car and take her chances in the woods. Leaning forward so he couldn't see her hand if he turned in her direction, she reached for the door handle.

As her hand closed over the handle, she heard a click. He'd locked the door from the driver's side. She could still get out though. Furtively, she felt for the switch to her door, found it and pushed. Nothing happened.

She pushed again. And got the same result. He'd disconnected the passenger-side switch.

But the door could be unlocked manually. She tried, pushing the lock desperately. It didn't work. He'd dismantled it, too. She was locked in.

Christy's breath backed up in her lungs. For long seconds, she couldn't move as the car headed farther into the woods. Finally, she managed to swivel around to face Dell and saw that his grin had widened and his eyes now glittered with a strange light. To Christy he looked larger and more menacing than he had a few minutes ago. He looked like a monster. "Wh-what are you doing?" she whispered through frozen lips.

"You know, Meg," he said and stopped the car beside a creek. *Meg.* Had he mentioned that name before? With her heart pounding in her ears, she couldn't think. Christy scrambled toward the door, holding her purse in front of her as a shield. She had to answer Dell, get him to see he had her confused with someone else. Would he listen? Or was he beyond reason now? She had to try.

Swallowing her fear, she met his eyes. "You know me, Dell," she said in a soothing voice. "I'm not Meg. My name's Christy."

"Don't play games with me, Auntie. I know who you are."

His aunt. The woman he'd mentioned earlier. Who'd raised him and who'd pretended to be a nurse. Should she play along with him, Christy asked herself, as terror turned her bones to jelly. Or should she be logical and hope he'd return to reality?

Logic, she decided. "I don't know what you mean," she said. *"I'm not Meg."*

"But you are," he said, "and it's time for your punishment."

"I'm *not*," she cried, her voice cracking. *Stay strong. Stay calm,* she ordered herself. *It's your only chance.* Gritting her teeth, she stared into Dell's eyes.

"Oh, yes," he said, and his voice became a childish singsong. "You have red hair…and green eyes…and you work in a hopsital…hos…pi…tal." He leaned toward her and grasped a lock of her hair. "You went away but you came back. I thought you'd be different this time, but you talked nasty to me."

"I'm sorry," she said softly. "I—I didn't mean to hurt your feelings."

"You should have stayed away, Auntie," the little-boy voice retorted.

Coming from the mouth of this burly man, the voice sounded more than frightening. It sounded mad. Dell Cummings was a madman. How could she get away?

"Yeah, you should never have come around," Dell continued, "'cause now you're gonna get your punishment." He reached for her, grabbing her arm and tugging her toward the console.

Her mind cried out for Jonathan as she struggled against Dell's brutal strength. What would Jonathan tell her to do? *Play for time.* With all her strength, she pulled back. "You're the Night Stalker," she accused. "You're the one who attacked Jonathan."

For a moment, his eyes cleared as if he fully comprehended, but then he said in his childish singsong, "Jonathan? Yeah, I did." He giggled then, a hideous sound. "I wanted to play a trick, make everybody think that man on the island did it." His brows furrowed. "The trick didn't work. Because you sent Jonathan after me. You told him it was me, didn't you, Auntie?"

"No, I—"

"I've killed you before, but you always come back," he said plaintively. "Why?"

"You killed somebody else. She wasn't Meg. I'm not, either…"

"Shut up." His voice deepened, became a man's. "Enough talking. Get out of the car."

"You—you've locked me in."

"Oh, yeah. I'll come around for you," he said with a nasty chuckle. "I'm a gentleman."

He got out of the car, locking it behind him and swaggered toward the passenger side. This was it, Christy thought. Why hadn't she put her cell in her purse? Then she could've used these few seconds to call Jonathan. She hadn't even told him she loved him. Now she'd never have a chance…

Her purse. She'd forgotten what she did have in it. The gun.

Dell had a gun, too, of course, but he hadn't taken it out. He was too confident.

She opened the purse and pulled out the revolver, keeping

it low so Dell wouldn't see. Jonathan's warning last week played in her head. "Don't aim a gun at someone unless you're going to use it."

In a split second she made her decision.

Dell unlocked the door. "Get out," he growled and stepped back.

Christy got out.

Eyes glittering like a cat with a mouse, Dell stood and watched her. And let out a howl of rage and pain as she shot him in the shoulder.

She'd meant to aim at his chest, but she'd done the best she could. As he lurched back against the car, Christy raced toward the road.

"You bitch. Now you've made me angry," Dell thundered. She heard footsteps and glanced back to see him lumbering after her. Too frightened to stop and aim again, she kept running. But even injured, he was faster than she.

She heard him behind her, felt his breath on her neck. He caught her by her arm and swung her around. With a brutal chop to her wrist, he knocked the gun from her hand.

She screamed with pain, but she scrambled after the gun. His reach was longer, and he grabbed it, then jerked Christy to her feet. "I never shot any of the others," he snarled, "but I told you, there's always an exception. You're it."

She couldn't do much now, not against a gun. She shut her eyes, held her breath, and waited.

Suddenly she heard the squeal of tires, and her eyes flew open. A car pulled up behind them. Jonathan's car.

He jumped out. "Drop it, Cummings," he said, his voice deadly. He, too, had a gun.

Dell stared at him for an endless moment, then he tossed the weapon on the ground, turned and ran into the woods. Behind him, drops of blood formed a trail.

Jonathan raced after him.

Cars roared into the clearing, their tires spitting gravel. Armand jumped out of one, and two patrol officers leaped from the other. "One of you stay with her," Jonathan yelled as he disappeared into the woods.

Suddenly Christy realized the danger Jonathan was in. He thought Dell had thrown down his weapon, but it was *hers*. "Jonathan," she shouted, "be careful. He has another gun."

She didn't think he'd heard her. She had to warn him.

She ran toward the trees, but the young officer who'd stayed behind caught up and grabbed her arm. "You can't go in there, Miss. It's too dangerous."

She tugged at her arm, but he held her in place. Tears of frustration clogged her throat. "Let me go," she choked.

"Can't. You'll get hurt in there."

"Then you go. They have to know he has another gun." The cop hesitated. "I'll be okay. Please, go."

He nodded and rushed off. Christy sank down under a tree. She heard shouts from the woods and tried to make out Jonathan's voice but couldn't.

She leaned back against the tree trunk, shut her eyes and prayed as hard as she could. *Please don't let him shoot Jonathan. Don't let anyone get hurt.*

A shot rang out. Christy jolted upright, and then she heard a second shot.

Time passed in slow motion. Every moment without knowing what happened in the woods was unbearable.

Finally she heard voices. She wanted to shut her eyes again, afraid of what she'd see. She forced herself to keep them open.

And then, Jonathan strode out of the woods, his face grim. *Thank God.* Behind him came the two cops with Dell handcuffed between them. Armand followed.

Jonathan dropped down beside her. "Christy. Sweetheart."

He opened his arms, and she came into them and burrowed into his chest. Only then, with the danger past, did she begin to tremble.

"It's okay, sweetheart. You're safe now." He kissed her forehead, her hair.

Tears slid down her cheeks. "I was so scared."

"I know. So was I."

"I was afraid for you, too," she said. "You didn't know he still had his gun when he ran."

"Yes, I did. I heard you and realized why he ran. He intended to lead me into the woods, then turn around and shoot."

Christy shivered. Jonathan held her for a moment, stroking her back. Then he pulled away and looked into her eyes. Gently, he wiped a streak of mud from her cheek, then reached into his pants pocket and handed her a handkerchief.

As she lifted a hand to wipe her eyes, he gasped. "You're bleeding."

"What? No, *Dell* was bleeding. I guess when he grabbed me, he got some on my shirt."

"You shot him," Jonathan said, his tone disbelieving.

Christy managed to smile. "I know. I don't believe it myself."

He traced her lips with a gentle finger. "You're so brave."

"So are you. You looked fierce, standing there pointing the gun."

"FBI training. Comes in handy."

Christy said nothing more. She was mesmerized by the look in Jonathan's eyes. Her lips parted, his covered them, and he kissed her with care and tenderness.

His hands tightened on her shoulders. "I was almost too late."

"But you weren't. How did you know where to find us?"

He gestured toward the creek. "Dell's fishing hole. This is it."

She stared at the peaceful-looking stream and shivered.

Dell would have— No, the thought was too horrible to contemplate. She pulled Jonathan closer. "Hold me. Please."

The sound of a throat clearing intruded and they turned to see Armand standing beside them. "We'll take Cummings in," he said, then gestured to Christy. "She can give her statement later."

"Tomorrow," Jonathan said.

"Okay."

The group moved away. Armand got into his car, and the two officers put Dell in theirs.

As they drove off, another car pulled in. "Crime-scene investigators," Jonathan said and went over to talk to them.

When he returned, he held out a hand to Christy. She took it, but when his fingers closed over her wrist, she gasped with pain.

"What is it?" Jonathan asked.

"My—my wrist. It must've gotten sprained when he knocked the gun out of my hand."

"Okay, we're going to the hospital." He bent and lifted her into his arms.

Christy smiled at his gallantry. "Jonathan, it's my wrist that's hurting, not my leg."

"Nevertheless, I'm not letting you out of my arms." Holding her securely against his chest, he strode to his car and settled her into the front seat.

He got in and reached across the console to fold her hand in his. He didn't let go once as they drove. When they pulled out of the wooded area and onto the road, he asked gently, "Do you want to talk about it?"

She nodded and, managing to keep her voice steady, recounted the events of the past few hours. "How did you figure it out?" she asked.

He told her about the button and how it had led him to the conclusion that the killer was a police officer, then that the officer was Dell and finally where he had taken her.

"Lucky a broken gas main had traffic stalled," Christy said, "or you might not have made it."

She felt Jonathan's grip tighten on hers and added, "There's an old nursery rhyme that starts, 'For the want of a nail a shoe was lost,' and goes all the way to a kingdom being lost. That's what happened today, isn't it? A button led you to a killer."

"It's always the small things," Jonathan agreed.

They were quiet the rest of the way into the center of the city. Although Jonathan wanted to take her to St. Mary's to be checked over, Christy insisted on a smaller hospital. She supposed the gossip mill would be going full force later, but she didn't want to fuel it today.

As she suspected, her wrist was only sprained. The emergency room physician taped it, suggested an over-the-counter pain medication and sent her on her way.

When they got to her house, Jonathan said, "I have to go down to headquarters. You'll need to go, too, to make a statement, but that can wait until tomorrow. Take it easy, and I'll be back as soon as I can." He kissed her, holding her tightly. "Will you be okay by yourself?"

She wasn't sure, but she knew he had to go. "I'll be fine," she said. "If I need company, I'll call my neighbor."

She locked the door after he left and dragged herself upstairs where she took a long, warm bath and lay down on the bed. She didn't think she'd be able to sleep, but she was so drained from her ordeal, she couldn't stay awake. Only the sound of the doorbell several hours later roused her. She sat up, disoriented, surprised to see that the sun had set.

She padded barefoot downstairs and went to the door. Automatically she peered out of the peephole, but to open the door without fear seemed unfamiliar. And wonderful.

Jonathan stood on the other side, his arms loaded with takeout boxes. "Dinner," he said.

Over Chinese delicacies from a nearby restaurant, he told her more about Dell. "He confessed to the killings and to abducting you. Told us everything about his past. He was an only child. He didn't know his father, and his mother walked out when he was five. His aunt raised him."

"Meg."

"Yes, she was abusive, both verbally and physically."

Christy sipped her tea. "She worked in a hospital, and she had red hair."

"Courtesy of a bottle, apparently. Dell ran away when he was sixteen, moved to Houston and applied to the police academy when he was old enough. He did well as a cop. He was able to suppress all the horror of his childhood until last fall when Aunt Meg suddenly turned up."

Christy shuddered. "That opened all the old wounds, I guess. I wonder why she came."

"She'd been ill and couldn't work, so she needed money. She figured she'd get it from Dell."

"That was a mistake," Christy said.

"Yeah, he'd always hated her and promised himself he'd punish her. After she visited him, he began acting out his childhood fantasies."

"Did—did he kill Meg, too?"

Jonathan shook his head. "He picked substitutes."

"Health-care workers with reddish hair."

Jonathan reached for her hand. "I'm sorry you were one of them."

"I'm glad there won't be any more. And that you figured out who it was and where he took me."

"He's no different than most killers. They get over-confident. Dell sure did. He sent me a fax telling me he had you *before* he got to your house." His hand tightened on hers and his voice thickened. "I keep seeing him with that gun pointed at you. It's my fault that—"

"Shh. It's no one's fault, just chance. And it's over." She tightened her hold on his hand. "Come to bed, Jonathan. We both need to be close."

Chapter 20

The next morning Jonathan drove Christy to police headquarters. The feelings were still so strong, the thought of her brush with death so vivid, that just walking into the building and seeing uniformed cops made Christy feel ill, but Jonathan held her hand and she managed to get through the morning. She gave her statement and felt relieved, knowing Dell was off the streets.

Afterward Jonathan drove her home and followed her inside. Christy tossed her purse on the counter. "Tomorrow I go back to work," she said. "It's hard to believe life's going to be normal again."

Jonathan put his hand on her arm. "Let's sit down. I want to talk to you."

His expression was somber, and Christy felt a premonition. Something bad was about to happen.

She sat on the couch in the great room, and he took a seat across from her. This was the first time since they'd begun making love that he hadn't sat within touching distance. He's going to end it, she thought.

"What happened yesterday was my fault," Jonathan began.

"No," Christy said, "it wasn't. Everything that happened, from Dell's murdering red-haired women to your working with the HPD, to Dell seeing me and deciding I was another incarnation of Aunt Meg, was chance. Just one toss of the dice after another. You didn't mean for anything to happen to me. I know that. You know that." She leaned forward, her eyes fastened to his, "Jonathan, let it go."

He rose and paced to the window. "I can't."

Christy went after him and put her hand on his shoulder. "I'm not Diane."

He swung around, his face bleak. "No, you're not, but if it had taken me one more minute to get to you, or if I'd been wrong about where Dell took you, you'd have been..." He swallowed. "You'd have been as dead as she is."

"But I'm not," Christy said. "Look at me, Jonathan. I'm not." She spread her hands. "Another roll of the dice, but this was a lucky one."

"I can't take another chance. Something like this could happen again."

"Or maybe it won't. Maybe another case won't come up."

"It will." He took her hand, led her back to the couch. "Look, I've quit the bureau, but I know myself. If someone needs my skills, I won't say no. It's what I do. It's who I am. I owe it to society—"

"What do you owe yourself?" She'd fought a killer yesterday, Christy told herself. Dammit, she'd fight for what she wanted.

"That's not the issue," he said implacably.

"All right, then. What do you owe me?"

"Safety," he said promptly.

She took a breath. "Dammit, Jonathan, I'm in love with you."

His eyes filled with pain. "Christy—"

"I can live with what you do," she interrupted, rushing to say everything she had to before he could walk away. "I want to."

"How do you know that?" he asked sadly. "You've only known me a couple of weeks. You told me you and Keith were together two years before you decided to marry him."

"And obviously two years didn't tell me a thing," she answered wryly. She shut her eyes, not sure she could bear looking at him while she said her last piece. "I know more about you after two weeks than I did about Keith in all the time we were together. You have integrity—"

He laughed mirthlessly. "If I do, then I have to do the right thing."

"And you think the 'right thing' is leaving?"

"Yes."

As angry now as she was hurt, she said, "Okay, then. Leave." She left the room and headed for the stairs.

"Christy—"

"Excuse me if I don't show you out," she said. "You'll have to find your own way."

She continued up the steps, and a minute later she heard the door shut. She went into her room, lay down on the bed, and stared at the ceiling. Although tears welled up behind her eyes, she refused to cry.

After a while she got up and went to the dresser to brush her hair. Her gaze lit on the sand dollar she'd brought back from San Sebastian. She picked it up and turned it over gently in her hand. Like the sea creature, she was a survivor and would remain one. She'd made it through the last two weeks and she'd make it through the next…and the next.

And she'd develop her own case of amnesia: forget Jonathan Talbot and everything about him.

* * *

Jonathan hadn't slept well in a week. Doing the right thing wasn't easy.

He rubbed his eyes as he opened his car door in the police garage. He missed Christy. Not just her warm body curled against his, but her smile, her voice, her companionship and conversation. He saw her face in the supermarket, on the street, and most of all, in his dreams. The reason, pure and simple, was that he'd fallen in love with her. But a future together was impossible.

He made his way from the garage to the meeting room where the Night Stalker task force was convening this afternoon for the last time. Everyone was already there, with one notable exception. Dell's chair was empty.

Armand began. "We're winding up today. I want to begin by thanking you all for your hard work. This was a tough one, and I know we're all saddened by the fact that the killer was…" He cleared his throat. "…one of us." He glanced around the table. "Anyone have anything to say about that?" No one responded. "Talbot, you have a report for us."

"Right here." Jonathan reached in his briefcase and passed out copies for everyone. There was silence as the others read the five-page summary.

When he'd finished reading, Armand pushed the papers to the side and said, "You all know that the grand jury made the case a priority. Dell was indicted earlier this week, and the court has appointed defense counsel. They'll probably plead insanity."

"And get him off," Shannon grumbled.

"But he'll be confined to a mental institution," Marilee said. "Not much better than prison."

"Our psychologist examined him yesterday," Armand said, handing out a stack of papers, "and she concluded that he can stand trial. In fact, she said he would probably have gone on leading a normal life if his aunt hadn't shown up and revived all those childhood traumas. He'd been pretty successful at repressing them, performing above-average as a cop, but Auntie appeared, and boom! He was off on a murder spree." He shook his head. "God, what a mess. Okay, anyone have any questions before we write 'finish' on this one?"

No one did. As everyone filed out, Marilee fell into step with Jonathan. "How's Christy getting along?"

"I'm…not sure. I haven't talked to her."

"Really? I thought you two were—" Jonathan's grim face must have warned her to go no further. "Sorry, didn't mean to pry." She headed for the stairs. "It's been great working with you. Hope we don't have to do it again soon."

"Me, too," he said. He hoped they'd *never* have to do this again, but that wasn't likely.

He continued down the hall, intending to clean out the desk he'd been using when Luis, who'd been walking ahead of him, slowed. "Yo, *compadre,* something go wrong between you and your lady?" He grinned. "*I* don't mind sticking my nose in."

"She's not my lady," Jonathan said stonily.

"Sure looked like it when I saw you together. Man, the way she looked at you was rich."

"And also temporary."

"Well, I'm sorry to hear that," Luis said. He put out his hand. "It's been great working with you, Doc, as always."

"Thanks, same here."

"Don't be a stranger," Luis said, "and if you ever feel like spilling your guts, I'm a good listener."

"Thank you," Jonathan said. He cleaned the last batch of papers out of the office he'd been using and left police headquarters, relieved to put the Night Stalker case behind him. Now maybe he could get on with his life, such as it was.

At home later, he checked his answering machine. "Hi, there." A woman's voice.

For a second, he thought it was Christy's but then he recognized Hannah. "I'm back," she said. "Decided Dad needs quiet around the house while he's recuperating from his bypass, so the boys and I came home. Come by and have dinner tomorrow night, okay? You bring the beer."

Jonathan smiled. Sounded like a good idea.

The next evening over burgers, while the twins played in their bouncy chairs, Hannah filled him in on her dad. Then she brought up the Night Stalker. "He made CNN," she said, "so I heard a little, but I figure you can fill me in on the details."

When he had, she said, "Wow, that's really bizarre. How's Christy managing after all that horror?"

Jonathan said nothing for a moment, then sighed. "I don't know. We aren't seeing each other anymore." He met Hannah's eyes. "You already know that, don't you?"

"Yeah, I talked to Christy this morning."

"How is she?"

Hannah shook her head. "If you want to know, call her yourself." She held his gaze. "Are you going to tell me your version of what happened, or do I have to subject you to some FBI torture?"

He told her.

When he finished, Hannah said, "You know something, Talbot, you're an idiot. You find the perfect woman and you just turn tail and leave her? I don't believe it."

"I have to think of her safety."

Hannah uttered an unladylike expletive. "Look at Troy and me. He's in Venezuela right now going after drug dealers, the world's worst scum. Any one of them could kill him, but I have to let him go because that's who he is. When I'm working undercover, he has to do the same."

"God, how do you live with it?"

"One day at a time. If, God forbid, something happens to

one of us, the other will go on. We'll both know we've had something special...for however long it lasted." Her eyes rested on Alex, who had fallen asleep in his bouncy chair. "I'd better put you to bed, Mr. A." She went to him and picked him up. "Be right back."

While she was in the other room, Jonathan went over to Zachary. The baby welcomed him with kicking feet and waving arms. "Hey, fella," Jonathan murmured, bent and stretched out his finger. The baby grasped it and broke into a wide smile.

Suddenly he had a vision of himself and Christy leaning over a baby's crib. Their baby, his eyes the green of Christy's, his hair as dark as Jonathan's. He could almost hear Christy's voice: "You see what we could have."

Hannah returned and stood watching him, her hands on her hips. "All this could be yours, Doc."

Jonathan shook his head, and she sighed. "You've wallowed in guilt too long, Jonathan. Give yourself a chance. Give Christy a chance."

"I don't know."

"Well, at least, think about it."

At home later, he did. Slouched in his armchair, he gazed around him. The house was so damn empty compared to Hannah's. And it would always be this way. He pictured himself growing older, always alone. No happy shouts of children, no loving companionship. That was what he'd chosen.

He'd made the wrong choice.

The next evening Christy was at home alone. She'd had the early shift, left the hospital at three o'clock and spent the afternoon in busy work, running errands, checking e-mail, filing her nails. By evening she needed something more to do, something to keep at bay the bitter loneliness she'd felt since Jonathan had left.

She'd had the gardener help her move furniture out of the great room and into the dining room last week so she could wax the hardwood floors. But her wrist had still hurt and she'd postponed the waxing. Now her wrist was better and she had the time. What better way to discharge some of the anger she'd been carrying around than by tackling those floors? She got to work.

The day had been gray and cloudy, a perfect match for her mood. As she worked, she heard the sound of rain, a steady downpour that continued into the evening as she waxed and polished. She had nearly finished the floor when the doorbell rang. Who could that be?

She wiped her sweaty face and pushed her hair back behind her ears, then went to the front door. She turned the light on, then peered out the peep hole and nearly lost her breath.

Jonathan stood on her front porch, raindrops glistening in his hair.

Déjà vu, she thought. But this time she wouldn't let him in so easily. She unlocked the door and yanked it halfway open, startling him. "What do you want?"

"May I come in?" he asked.

"I let you in once," she replied. "I'm not sure I want to do it again."

"Please."

She stood still, one hand across the doorway, blocking the entrance. "What are you doing here? Did you forget something?"

He shook his head. "I left something."

Christy frowned. She hadn't noticed anything of his lying around. "What?"

"My heart."

Her breath caught, her own heart began to pound. "Wh-what do you mean?"

He touched her hand, gently, tentatively. "I love you. Leaving you was the biggest mistake I ever made. Can we start over?"

"Jonathan," she breathed, staring into the deep gray eyes so filled with love. "I—I want to."

He lifted her hand and kissed her fingers. "Are you going to let me in?"

She stood aside. She'd never thought she'd see him again, and here he was, saying everything she'd longed to hear. "Come into the kitchen," she said, glancing over her shoulder as she led him into the living room. "Be careful in here. It's slippe—"

His feet flew out from under him, and he landed on the floor on his backside. "Not again," he muttered.

She whirled around and bent over him. "Are you all right?"

"I'm okay. Except for my dignity."

Christy couldn't help herself. A laugh bubbled out. She put out a hand to Jonathan, but instead of rising, he pulled her down into his lap. His arms tightened around her, and she felt his heart pounding in rhythm with hers.

"I've been a jerk," he said, "caught up in guilt I can't do anything about. I missed you. I don't want to waste whatever time we can have together."

"Neither do I."

"I love you," Jonathan murmured. "You'll hear me say it every day from now on if you'll marry me."

"I love you, too," she sighed and nestled against him. "I want a family, Jonathan. Soon."

"Right away."

"You won't forget?"

"How could I," he laughed, "when I have you to help me remember."

And then he kissed her, again and again.

* * * * *

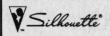

INTIMATE MOMENTS™

presents a provocative new miniseries by
award-winning author

INGRID WEAVER

PAYBACK

Three rebels were brought back from the brink and
recruited into the shadowy Payback Organization.
In return for this extraordinary second chance, they
must each repay one favor in the future. But if they
renege on their promise, everything that matters
will be ripped away…including love!

Available in March 2005:

The Angel and the Outlaw
(IM #1352)

Hayley Tavistock will do anything to avenge the
murder of her brother—including forming an
uneasy alliance with gruff ex-con Cooper Webb.
With the walls closing in around them, can love
defy the odds?

Watch for Book #2 in June 2005…

Loving the Lone Wolf
(IM #1370)

Available at your favorite retail outlet.

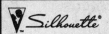

INTIMATE MOMENTS™

Explosive action,
explosive passion
from

CINDY DEES!

Charlie Squad

**No mission is too dangerous for these
modern-day warriors when lives—
and love—are on the line.**

She was his enemy's daughter. But Julia Ferrare had
called *him*—soldier Jim "Dutch" Dutcher—for help
in escaping from her father. She was beautiful,
fragile, kind...and most likely setting him up for
a con. Ten years ago, she'd stolen his family, his
memories, his heart. He'd be a fool to trust her
again. But sometimes even a hardened soldier
could be a fool...for love.

Her Secret Agent Man
by Cindy Dees

Silhouette Intimate Moments #1353

On sale March 2005!

Only from Silhouette Books!

If you enjoyed what you just read,
then we've got an offer you can't resist!

Take 2 bestselling love stories FREE!

Plus get a FREE surprise gift!

Clip this page and mail it to Silhouette Reader Service™

IN U.S.A.	**IN CANADA**
3010 Walden Ave.	P.O. Box 609
P.O. Box 1867	Fort Erie, Ontario
Buffalo, N.Y. 14240-1867	L2A 5X3

YES! Please send me 2 free Silhouette Intimate Moments® novels and my free surprise gift. After receiving them, if I don't wish to receive anymore, I can return the shipping statement marked cancel. If I don't cancel, I will receive 6 brand-new novels every month, before they're available in stores! In the U.S.A., bill me at the bargain price of $4.24 plus 25¢ shipping and handling per book and applicable sales tax, if any*. In Canada, bill me at the bargain price of $4.99 plus 25¢ shipping and handling per book and applicable taxes**. That's the complete price and a savings of at least 10% off the cover prices—what a great deal! I understand that accepting the 2 free books and gift places me under no obligation ever to buy any books. I can always return a shipment and cancel at any time. Even if I never buy another book from Silhouette, the 2 free books and gift are mine to keep forever.

245 SDN DZ9A
345 SDN DZ9C

Name	(PLEASE PRINT)	
Address	Apt.#	
City	State/Prov.	Zip/Postal Code

Not valid to current Silhouette Intimate Moments® subscribers.

Want to try two free books from another series?
Call 1-800-873-8635 or visit www.morefreebooks.com.

* Terms and prices subject to change without notice. Sales tax applicable in N.Y.
** Canadian residents will be charged applicable provincial taxes and GST.
All orders subject to approval. Offer limited to one per household].
® are registered trademarks owned and used by the trademark owner and or its licensee.

INMOM04R   ©2004 Harlequin Enterprises Limited

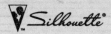

SPECIAL EDITION™

Introducing a brand-new miniseries by
Silhouette Special Edition favorite author
Marie Ferrarella

The Cameo

One special necklace,
three charm-filled romances!

BECAUSE A HUSBAND IS FOREVER

by Marie Ferrarella

Available March 2005
Silhouette Special Edition #1671

Dakota Delany had always wanted a marriage like
the one her parents had, but after she found her
fiancé cheating, she gave up on love. When her
radio talk show came up with the idea of having her
spend two weeks with hunky bodyguard Ian Russell,
she protested—until she discovered she wanted Ian
to continue guarding her body forever!

Available at your favorite retail outlet.

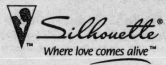
Silhouette®
Where love comes alive™

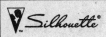

INTIMATE MOMENTS™

Don't miss the eerie
Intimate Moments debut
by

MARGARET CARTER

Embracing Darkness

Linnet Carroll's life was perfectly ordinary
and admittedly rather boring—until
she crossed paths with Max Tremayne.
The seductive and mysterious Max
claimed to be a 500-year-old vampire…
and Linnet believed him. Romance ignited
as they joined together to hunt down
the renegade vampire responsible for
the deaths of Max's brother and Linnet's
niece. But even if they succeeded, would
fate ever give this mismatched couple a
future together?

***Available March 2005
at your favorite retail outlet.***

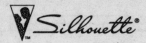

COMING NEXT MONTH